ILLUSIONS

D0913807

ILLUSIONS

PAMELA LEIGH STARR

Genesis Press, Inc.

Indigo

An imprint of Genesis Press, Inc.
Publishing Company

Genesis Press, Inc.
P.O. Box 101
Columbus, MS 39703

All rights reserved. Except for use in any review, the reproduction or utilization of this work in whole or in part in any form by any electronic, mechanical, or other means, not known or hereafter invented, including xerography, photocopying and recording, or in any information storage or retrieval system, is forbidden without written permission of the publisher, Genesis Press, Inc. For information write Genesis Press, Inc., P.O. Box 101, Columbus, MS 39703.

All characters in this book have no existence outside the imagination of the author and have no relation whatsoever to anyone bearing the same name or names. They are not even distantly inspired by any individual known or unknown to the author and all incidents are pure invention.

Copyright© 2001, 2007 by Pamela Leigh Starr. All rights reserved.

ISBN-13: 978-1-58571-229-8
ISBN-10: 1-58571-229-9
Manufactured in the United States of America

First Edition 2001
Second Edition 2007

Visit us at www.genesis-press.com or call at 1-888-Indigo-1

DEDICATION

To B.J., my thirteen-year-old son who has lived with diabetes
for the last four years of his life.
His self-control and dedication
in doing all that he can to control
this disease is beyond amazing.
B.J., you're my hero.
Love,
Mom

CHAPTER 1

Asa rubbed her palms across the black skirt she wore. She sat in the chair that had been offered by her soon-to-be employer. She hoped. Asa needed this job. She knew that she was a bit overqualified, but she'd had enough of job hunting and sponging off her cousin. The month-long search felt so much longer.

The man before her wasn't what she had expected. Especially after Brent's outrageous description. This man seemed approachable and more than pleasant. Still, the nervousness stayed alive inside her, bouncing across her stomach like a rubber ball let loose in a marble house.

Asa kept her feelings hidden. She'd had enough lessons in hiding any outward emotion from her previous employer. Besides, if even half of what Brent said about this man were true, he was only half the tyrant Mr. Stewart had been.

"Let's get right down to it, Ms. Taylor."

His friendly smile had faded. *Good things never last long*, she thought to herself.

"Not just anyone can fill this job. We need a secretary. But what we want is more than a secretary," he was saying. "We need someone familiar with computer software technology. Someone who can pull knowledge of the industry from their experience or know how and where to find needed information."

Asa nodded, listening intently, a confident expression on her face. This job appeared to be no different from what she'd been doing before. Hopefully, she would be able to perform her duties without the constant ridicule and verbal abuse she had been subjected to in the last two years.

"Of all the applicants I've seen today, you are the last and the most qualified."

Asa nodded again, continuing to stare at his smooth, brown, handsome face. She studied his light brown eyes intently, absently noticing the close-cut hair style and natural waves accenting a clean cut image. Maybe this time her boss wouldn't be a persecutor of women who could do nothing but sit and give orders.

"Can you handle that?"

Handle what? Asa thought not allowing the question to appear on her face, hoping he hadn't added anything more to the list of duties he had previously stated.

"If Maria hadn't suddenly decided to go into labor an entire month early you would have had some training. Someone to guide you, to show you how we do things here at Execute."

"No problem, Mr. Darby," Asa told him, knowing the duties he'd described, before his handsomeness distracted her, were precisely what she was used to dealing with. And why had she been staring? This strange fascination with the man sitting before her was something completely new.

"Darby? You thought I was Zain Darby?" He laughed pleasantly. "The name's Lance Handle, and even though I admire my partner, neither I nor anyone else in this world can claim to be Zain Darby but Zain himself."

"Sorry about the mistake," Asa cringed inside. *Who is this Zain Darby?* she wondered.

"An understandable mistake. He was scheduled to interview you today but had to fly out on business."

"Then it was unfortunate for you, Mr. Handle." Had she just tried to flirt with the man?

"No problem." He smiled at her again. "Any questions?"

"Yes, there is one thing." Only the most important requirement she hadn't discussed. Asa was not going to accept any job if her employer could not be flexible about this issue.

"Go on."

"If you noticed, my file states that I'm a diabetic."

"Yes, but that won't interfere with your ability to do the work, will it?"

Asa's back went up at that. She disliked the idea of anyone treating her any differently because of a disease she developed as a young child. "Of course not. But you need to understand that keeping my health requires checking my blood sugar at various times and eating on a regular schedule." Juvenile diabetes, unlike adult-onset diabetes required a strict eating schedule to help balance the amount of sugar in her body to the amount of insulin she took twice a day. A sugar level that was too high or too low had its consequences. Keeping a fine balance between the two, and maintaining a normal sugar level as her pancreas had done before her auto-immune system turned on itself was a skill she had learned long ago.

"Is that all?" Mr. Handle asked.

"Pretty much, except for the slight chance that I might one day pass out due to low-blood sugar." Asa hated bringing up this possibility and stated it as casually as she could. She knew, in all fairness, that her employer needed to be informed.

"In that event you'd need to have something with sugar. Some juice or milk, right?"

"That's right?" Had she died and gone to job heaven?

"No problem. A friend of mine developed juvenile diabetes when we were kids. I understand your concern. You have nothing to worry about."

She *had* died and gone to heaven. Asa handed a neatly typed sheet to the handsome man in front of her. "Here's a copy of my eating schedule."

Lance Handle scanned it, then placed it into a folder in front of him.

This seemed too good to be true. Asa would be working for a pleasant, gorgeous man who understood her disease. A tremendous burden lifted from her shoulders. What a relief.

"Sorry to rush you out, Miss Taylor, but I have a wedding rehearsal to attend."

"Someone close to you getting married?" Asa felt safe in asking the question despite having knowing him for no more than twenty minutes. Lance Handle's open, friendly manner brought out her curious side.

"Yes. Me."

Asa was disappointed with that bit of news. "Congratulations," she remembered to say.

"Thank you. You'll meet Mr. Darby on Monday. Be here seven-thirty sharp. He starts early and has little tolerance for lateness. I myself will be on my honeymoon."

Mr. Lance Handle, the heaven-sent answer to her prayers, was not going to be here when she reported to work Monday morning. Asa watched as Mr. Handle closed the file folder and turned to place it inside a metal cabinet behind him. There was a knock on the door. "Come in."

Both of them turned to find a delivery man at the door, package in hand. Neither one noticed two pieces of paper slide out of the folder and softly land in the trash can beside the desk.

CHAPTER 2

"I'm calling that more than luck," Brent told Asa, meeting her on the first floor of the office building on Carondelet Street. They walked out the building and a few blocks down until they reached Canal Street, continuing to the ferry docking area at the foot of Canal Street.

"What can I say?"

"Thank you, God. That's what. If 'Zain the Pain' had been your interviewer you might not be so happy about this position."

"'Zain the Pain'? Brent, you're regressing to our child-hood days. Adults don't give other adults foolish names. Besides, this can't be any worse than working for the late Mr. Lloyd Stewart of Stewart Software."

"I wouldn't know." Brent pressed his lips into a grim line. He was still furious with her. Asa had never, in the two years she had lived next to Brent in Algiers Point, told him of all her problems with her boss.

"You can't still be that mad at me. It's been over a month since Mr. Stewart died."

They stopped before the steps leading to the ferry. Agitated, Brent leaned his tall, lanky frame against a colored post that directed people to various New Orleans attractions. The Riverwalk and Convention Center to the right, the Aquarium and French Quarter to the left. Brent was so tall his head nearly touched the bottom sign.

"True, but I think you know what really got to me."

Asa hated seeing Brent work himself up like this, but it was about time he got it all out in the open. Beads of perspiration appeared on his forehead. His eyebrows rose, even the fat curls on top of his head moved in aggravation as he turned his head first one way then the other.

"I would have never known if it weren't for Evelyn."

Evelyn, her fellow sufferer and mother figure, had had more than a mouthful to say about their late boss at the funeral. That was it. Poor Brent felt betrayed. Her self-appointed protector, her only family member in New Orleans, was hurt because she hadn't confided in him.

"Brent, you can't protect me forever."

"I could have been a listening ear."

"True, but would you have stopped at that?"

He looked down at his watch, then back at her. "Probably not. Let's go before the ferry leaves. It's getting late and you have to eat by seven."

Asa shook her head as he moved ahead of her. Brent turned back a second later to see what was taking her so long.

"What?" he asked her.

"You just can't help it, huh?"

"Somebody's got to take care of you. It might as well be someone who's done it for most of your life already."

Aboard the ferry Asa stood at the rail studying the view of New Orleans, the churning muddy waters of the Mississippi, and her favorite and only cousin. All Brent said was true. He had taken care of her for as long as she could remember. He was only twenty-five, two years older than she, but had developed a protectiveness toward her from the beginning.

Brent's mother and her own were sisters, both raised in New Orleans. But Ann Marie, Asa's mother had followed her husband all over the world as he built a military career. After she was born Asa traveled with them until she was ready for school. Then her mother did what she thought was the best thing for her. She'd shipped her off to live with her Aunt Irene, Brent's mother.

Auntie Reenie and her Uncle Boyd became her role models. Because of them she'd had a pretty normal childhood. Because of Brent she'd had a constant playmate and protector.

It was Brent who'd come to her tea parties, listened to her recite a poem about Harriet Tubman, and watched her practice an African dance she'd made up after seeing a performance at school. He'd helped her with her homework and introduced her to the wonderful world of books. And it was Brent who found her passed out in the backyard just before she was diagnosed with juvenile diabetes.

Auntie Reenie, Uncle Boyd and Brent had filled her world with a familial love that helped her adjust to the regimen of diet, shots, and blood glucose testing. Asa doubted she would have adjusted so well in the topsy-turvy world of her parents.

This all explained and put into perspective Brent's overly-protective tendencies. Lately his concern for her made her feel guilty. In the last two years Asa hadn't seen him go on one date. She knew there were women out there who went crazy for curly-haired, fair-skinned black men.

"What are you thinking about? Not worrying about 'Zain the Pain', are you?"

"Not at all. I'll tell you what I was wondering about. You. When was the last time you went out on a date?"

Brent pointed his chin upward, effectively hiding his expression. "Right before Christmas," he finally answered, looking down at her.

"When I went to meet my parents for that holiday ski trip? That was three months ago!"

"That sounds about right."

"Well, what happened?"

"What do you mean, what happened? I went on a date, had a good time, and took her home."

"What did she look like? What was her name? And didn't you ask her out again?"

"I had other things on my mind."

"Me."

"Asa, don't start that again."

"I knew living next to you was a mistake. You're putting your life on hold because of me."

"Not at all. My work is important, renovating the house I just bought across the street from us is important. Women are on the bottom of my list right now." The ferry had already landed by the time he finished listing his reasons. "Let's go." Brent moved out, hoping to change the subject.

Asa let the discussion go as they walked the three blocks to the double they shared in Algiers Point, a distinctive part of New Orleans on the Mississippi River's west bank. Its charm and historic flavor brought out a deep appreciation in both of them. She and Brent were in love with this part of the city.

As they reached home, entering through their own separate doors, Asa made up her mind to make sure Brent began to direct his romantic and protective instincts elsewhere.

❋

Zain Darby drove slowly down the ferry exit ramp leading to the CBD, the Central Business District. Not because he wanted to. He had no choice. Two bicyclists, walking side by side, talked and laughed as they slowly exited the ferry. *Can't you people read?* he wanted to yell. Bicycles were to *wait* for all vehicles to disembark.

They were making their own rules. Somewhat as he'd done so many times to get where he was now.

He'd started out as a small businessman selling, then designing, computer games. Then using what he'd learned along the way he'd built a strong solvent company that developed anti-virus software programs for larger industries. His latest trip to Atlanta was another success in providing anti-virus software and technical services for a large company.

Zain had driven straight from the airport to the community home where his grandmother resided on the west bank. He had driven through the surprisingly light traffic of Kenner, and Metairie, and crossed the Cresent City Connection in no time. Unfortunately, it had taken hours to assure his grandmother that there were no pygmy dancers under her bed.

He'd tried to catch Lance at the office before he left for the wedding rehearsal and dinner. Zain had promised Lance's fiancée, Katrina, that there would be no business discussion at wedding functions. But it looked as if these bicyclists might interfere with that plan.

Frustrated, Zain started to lean his hands on the horn, but stopped when he spotted the familiar face of Brent Thomas, one of his young programming geniuses, whose height made him stand out in the crowd. Beside him was a woman. That in itself was strange. While his other employees joked and boasted about women, Brent Thomas never had much to say. But there he was having what looked like an intimate conversation with a beautiful woman. Zain didn't know Thomas had it in him.

Zain studied the woman, intrigued by the mere fact that she was with Thomas. He had to take an interest, Zain told himself. This woman could end up being a distraction to Thomas, therefore an interference to Execute.

The woman was tall. She had to nearly reach Thomas's chin. The man had to be at least six feet three inches. She had a graceful look, but projected a prim and proper image with that long black skirt and button-to-the-neck blouse.

Not his type. But then Zain looked at her face. It was round and cute with cheeks that were pronounced. Her hair was in a tight bun on top of her head, more proof that she was too uptight for him. "Have at it, Thomas," Zain whispered to himself, wishing his employee luck. "Just don't let her interfere with your work."

Zain's eyes remained on the couple. He watched as Thomas looked at his watch, left, then waited for the woman to catch up. Now that view, her walk, made up for everything else.

A horn blew behind him. Zain looked forward, ready to lay it on the bike riders, but the street was clear. He drove to the office, parked and promptly forgot Thomas and his love interest.

Six o'clock, he noticed as he stepped out of the elevator onto the fifth floor. He went straight to Lance's office. Gone. Zain was disappointed but not surprised. Lance had gone wacko this last year. There was a time when neither would leave the office before nine or ten o'clock at night. Of course that was in the beginning, but Zain still found himself doing it more times than not. His partner's idea of normal working hours had started at the same time Lance met Katrina at a Zulu Mardi Gras Ball. His partner had been stolen from him. Katrina had snapped him up. Zain had known it would happen sooner or later with all Lance's talk of a wife and family. He'd hoped for later. Not that Katrina wasn't a good match for his friend.

Katrina. She was going to have a fit when he showed up with these papers tonight. *But hey, he wasn't bringing them to the actual wedding. This is only the rehearsal,* Zain reminded himself. It was either that or follow them to their honeymoon. Lance, Zain was sure, would prefer to get it over with tonight.

Zain spent an hour catching up on work he would have done if he had been in the office today. Before he knew it, seven o'clock arrived. Zain had half an hour to get to the church. He cleared his desk, almost missing a hastily written note from Lance.

> *Hired a secretary/assistant. Very Experienced.*
> *Starts Monday. Asa Taylor. Read file ASAP.*

At least that was out of the way. Zain hated the interview process, and wasn't welcoming the chore of having to train someone again. Maria had been a perfect addition to Execute from the very beginning. But from the moment she first got married Zain had known that eventually Maria would start a family and he would lose a perfect secretary. Her knowledge of the business and efficiency helped his office run smoothly. And her sassy mouth kept him in line. Zain doubted there was another Maria out there. But if Lance hired this Asa Taylor, she had to at least know her job.

Zain left the office, papers secured in the briefcase he carried.

CHAPTER 3

"Wake up. You can't be late your first day on the job." Brent banged on Asa's bedroom door. "A-one, a-two, a-three," Asa counted in her head.

"Asa, say something."

"I'm alive and well." She walked to the door, opening it a crack. "I did not pass out in my sleep. My sugar was fine last night, and I had my bedtime snack like a good girl. Stop worrying about me, Brent."

"Right. I'm still working on that, remember?"

"I'll be on your side as soon as I'm dressed."

"Don't take too long."

"Won't," Asa gave the customary answer to Brent's precautionary statement as he turned to go.

"Hey," Brent turned back around, "good morning."

"Morning, cousin."

Change was never easy, Asa knew, but getting Brent to ease up was going to be a mountainous task. She went through her normal morning routine and in no time was dressed in her standard office wear. A plaid navy skirt this time, not quite as long as her others. A navy blue blouse with white trim gave it a touch of the sailor look and made her feel proper, yet businesslike. Exactly the image she wanted to portray.

Asa applied her makeup, as always sucking her teeth at her rounded cheeks. Brent claimed they made her look like a pixie. Who wanted to be a pixie?

"Well, shiver me timbers, what do we have here?" Brent bellowed as Asa walked into the kitchen through the only connecting door of the double they shared.

"Thanks for building up my confidence."

"Hey, I like the look, a pixie sailor. If 'Zain the Pain' is too difficult to work for, you could always join the Navy, be their mascot."

Asa smiled at that. "You can't talk about clothes, Mr. Casual."

"I'm wearing a tie."

"And jeans."

"It's acceptable attire for a genius. Zain is a pain, but he knows genius when he sees it and excuses our strange little habits."

Brent sat across from her, not saying another word as she pricked her finger, applying a drop of blood onto the strip inserted into the glucose monitor. "Eighty-five," she said, knowing he was dying to ask her the sugar reading.

"Good."

Asa had to hand it to him. He didn't remind her that although it was a good reading it was close to a low blood sugar, and that it was a good thing she woke up in time for breakfast. Or that this reading was better than the slightly higher-than-normal reading of one hundred forty-five at dinnertime yesterday. He was putting forth a concerted effort to stop mothering her.

Asa's reflection on Brent's dateless status Friday had triggered an entire weekend spent arguing about his social life. It had ended last night with Brent agreeing to ween himself from constantly checking on her and worrying about every single detail of her life. He was doing great, Asa noticed, as he plopped a plate of toasted whole wheat bagels in the middle of the table. He hadn't measured the right amount of cream cheese and low sugar jelly for her. Neither did he remind her of the amount of carbohydrates in each food item.

Asa went back into her side of the house, drew up her insulin, and took her shot before returning to a nice breakfast with her cousin, who looked as if he was ready to burst with the reminders and information he normally gave every morning.

"That was delicious. My turn for breakfast tomorrow." Asa cleared the table and rinsed the dirty dishes. "Let me grab my stuff and we can catch the ferry."

"Umm—" Brent hesitated, then went on. "I've got some seedless grapes in the fridge if you want some for your morning snack."

"Thanks, I'd like that." Poor Brent, let out a huge sigh of relief. "It's been that bad this morning?"

"Old habits die hard. Especially those involving someone you care about."

"You are going to make someone a wonderful husband."

"If you had your way it would happen overnight." He handed her a small ziploc bag full of grapes.

"I'll bet this contains sixteen grapes all the same size, equaling exactly fifteen carbs."

"Right."

"How many packs do you have in there like this?"

Brent closed the refrigerator door behind him. "Go on, get your stuff. You don't want to be late."

Asa let it go. "Meet you on the porch." Going back into the kitchen, she grabbed her lunch and afternoon snack, prepared last night, and stored them in her fancy insulated bag with her initials embroidered outside, ACT. She dropped her pumps and emergency pack of juice and crackers in case of a low blood sugar into her matching briefcase. Another emergency pack, glucose tablets, her quick take monitor, insulin and now her bag of grapes were stored in the purse that completed the matching set.

Asa closed the connecting door and headed to the front of the house. She was locking her door just as Brent did the same to his. Their living separate but together had been an ideal situation after she had gotten her degree. But now Asa felt that she should probably be moving out. Working and living so close to her cousin was going to make worse his obsession with keeping her healthy. But she would miss this house with its intricate carvings on the matching wooden doors, the decorative overhang and long narrow shutters— simply the look and feel of Algiers Point.

"Let's get moving. It's later than I thought," Brent told her.

They walked quickly on sneaker-clad feet, running the last block to catch the ferry just before the attendant closed the gate barring any more passengers. This morning they remained on the passenger level. Brent pulled out a few sheets of newspaper from his briefcase for them to sit on. The ferry's seats tended to be covered with years of ground-in dirt. Despite that, Asa loved riding the ferry every day to work. It beat the hassle of driving through traffic and paying for parking. Besides, it added a little regular exercise to their normal routine.

Even when Asa had worked for Stewart Software she had ridden the ferry with Brent, then taken the bus, leaving her Beetle parked in the driveway on the opposite side of her cousin's Jeep. Now, as always, Brent studied some papers from his briefcase as Asa studied the view.

Entering the city each day Asa enjoyed the sights of New Orleans: the twin bridges spanning the Mississippi; the Riverwalk running alongside its eastern bank; the collection of steamboats docked and ready to begin their daily run; Jax Brewery, an actual brewery turned shopping center; St. Louis Cathedral; and the Aquarium. These daily sights gave her a deep appreciation and love for the city.

Before long they were off the ferry and entering the building that housed Execute Computer Services. Asa made a pit stop in the first floor bathroom to change her shoes and freshen up. Brent was waiting for her when she came out.

Asa sighed inwardly and tried to control her irritation. "You could have gone up, Brent. I can make my way to the fifth floor."

"Hey, it's your first day," he said in way of explanation.

She looked up at him with a you've-got-to-be-kidding expression dominating her face.

"You look like a mad pixie sailor. The Navy won't have anything to do with you now," he teased.

Asa laughed at that, punching him on the shoulder. The elevator door opened in time for Brent to throw himself into the empty car moaning in misery over the lick she'd given him. Asa shook her head and laughed as she walked in behind him.

"Okay, Brent, you can stop it now."

"That hurt. You've been working out behind my back?"

"No more than you."

Brent winced, holding his shoulder. He looked ridiculous.

"What do you want me to do? Kiss it and make it better?"

"Sure, why not?"

Asa was doing just that when someone else entered the elevator. So early in the morning the first floor was quiet, which was why Asa had gone along with Brent's foolishness.

The person who had entered was a man; she could tell by his heavy tread. Asa stepped away from her cousin to peer over at him. He was nearly as tall as Brent. But where her cousin was lanky and thin, this man was solid and firm, masculine, powerful, a god among men, Asa thought, the images of Zeus and other gods of Greek mythology entering her mind.

"Good morning," Brent eeked out. Not in any fear or nervousness, Asa detected, but from keeping the rush of explosive laughter from escaping. Sometimes when Brent laughed, his entire body let loose. The sight of arms waving and feet stomping as he laughed loud and long was more than embarrassing.

"Thomas," the man addressed Brent, using his last name, then nodded in their direction.

Asa assumed the nod included her and gave the god of all men one right back. Asa then turned to Brent and shared a secret smile with him over his predicament. Whoever this man was, Brent did not want to let loose in front of him.

Whoever this man was, he had been staring at them for quite a while, not even bothering to press a button to a floor. Brent reached over to do the honors. The god then focused solely on her. Asa was sure that imprints of his eyes were branded all over her before they reached the fifth floor. When the elevators doors opened, he took in her length one more time then exited with unhurried strides.

Asa leaned a hand against the close door button. They both let loose their pent-up hilarity, not finishing until all the bubbles of silliness faded completely.

"Who...Oh Brent...Who was that?"

"Asa, you don't want me to tell you."

"You'd better. What if I meet him in the hallway or the elevators again. He was so serious, so overpowering. So..."

"Zain Darby."

Asa stood perfectly still. "That was my new boss?"

"'Zain the Pain.'"

"I can't work for him."

"You know you can, and I know you will," Brent told her, completely serious.

Asa gave him a skeptical look.

"You're more than qualified for the job. It's either work for Zain Darby or go back to being dependent on your ole cousin here."

"You know how I feel about that."

"Have I told you why they call him 'Zain the Pain'?" Brent asked, changing the subject.

Asa shook her head.

"Take a ride down to the first floor with me."

Shifting into foolish mode again, Brent bent to whisper a series of ridiculous stories that supposedly had prompted the name from Zain Darby's employees.

"I don't believe a word, Brent Thomas," Asa told her cousin just before the elevator doors opened on their floor once again. "How am I supposed to work now with that trash floating in my head?"

"That's the idea." Brent stepped out with her. "If things get rocky, remember one of my little 'stories.'" Brent kissed her on the cheek before turning to the offices on the left. Asa turned right, remembering from the interview exactly where to go.

She stopped as she rounded the corner. On the other side of glass double doors was her new boss. He paced up and down as he spoke on the phone at the receptionist's desk. The place was completely empty except for him. She was there of course, but Zain Darby didn't know that yet. His strides were long and purposeful, though they took him nowhere further than from one side of the room to another.

As Asa stared, the adjectives she'd used before slipped back into her mind. Powerful, most definitely. Masculine. Any more and he'd have to bottle the excess, selling it to lesser men seeking some of what he possessed. All this she detected despite an entire wall of glass separating them. How was she going to handle him in close quarters? Zain, the god of all men, Zeus in his own right. But he wasn't the old guy you normally saw in Greek mythology. The "Z" was all they had in common.

Asa lowered her head, a thumb pressed against each corner of her eye, her fingers coming together pointed upward in prayer. "Lord, help me work with this man. I can tell by looking that he is not Mr. Stewart, or the nice Lance Handle. Give me some help, please." As an afterthought Asa added, "Right this minute, if you can spare the time."

Head held high, Asa walked forward, a steady buildup of confidence increasing with each step. As her hand touched the handle of the door, Asa remembered one of Brent's little stories, an image of Execute's employees lined up single file as Zain Darby marched past them military style, cracking their upheld knuckles with a thick ruler. The scene was so unreal Asa couldn't stop the smile that crept across her face. It remained in place as she walked toward her new employer.

Zain Darby had hung up the phone not a second before she walked through the door. Asa stood straight and tall, hand held out in greeting. "Good morning, Mr. Darby. I'm Asa Taylor, your new secretary and assistant."

"Unbelievable," Asa heard him mumble as he rubbed a hand across the back of his neck.

Her assumption that he was referring to whatever situation he was dealing with on the phone died as he stood staring at her. The expression on his face was not a welcoming one.

He glanced down, finally noticing her outstretched hand. He studied her face again before grabbing it. "You're two minutes…"

At his pause Asa slowly pulled her hand back. "…late," she finished for him, that one word filling the stunned silence between them. "It won't happen again," she added into the awkward silence.

Asa wanted to look up at the ceiling, down at the ground, anywhere but at the handsome brown face before her.

"This way," he directed.

Asa followed. She wanted to tap his shoulder to stop him. To ask Zain Darby if he felt the same amazing thing she had. From the hard, expressionless look he had given her, Asa assumed he felt nothing out of the ordinary. She didn't know this man, hadn't laid eyes on him until today. But when he'd touched her hand, he'd sent a storm surge of tidal wave proportions through her. That single touch had disrupted her entire body. Scary. What was even scarier was knowing the destruction a tidal wave left in its wake.

Zain Darby stopped suddenly. He pointed to a large alcove equipped with everything she'd need: a desk, computer, telephone, fax. It was wide, open and airy. Air. Asa felt as if she could use some. Instead of giving in to the urge to rush around the room to find a window to open, Asa placed her briefcase, purse and lunch in an empty chair.

"How should we begin?" she asked.

"You can begin by proving that you've got what it takes to work at Execute."

"No problem, I'm grateful for the opportunity to do just that," she said aloud, drowning out the words, "I quit," that had tried to push past her throat.

Another Lloyd Stewart after all, Asa thought as she watched Zain Darby march into his office without another word. But *this* headstrong boss was handsome, fine and the god of all men.

❋

What was Lance thinking? Zain controlled the urge to slam the door to his office. He strode to his desk, grabbed the phone and dialed the first five numbers of the hotel where Lance and Katrina were staying. He slammed the receiver down, stopping himself from dialing the last few numbers.

After the scene Katrina had made when he brought papers for Lance to sign at the rehearsal dinner, Zain didn't have the heart to call. Lance and Katrina *were* on their honeymoon. But who was the cause of the mess he was stuck in first thing on a Monday morning? Lance! Zain had no partner, no real secretary. Just a beautiful angel-faced women dressed like a sailor, who had something going on with one of his best employees. And worst yet she had no respect for being on time.

If Lance saw him now he would laugh. But it wasn't funny, that was one thing he was sure of. What he didn't know a thing about was this woman. She couldn't work here. Not with him, not when a simple handshake could have easily turned into a love wrestle, on the floor if it were up to him. No doubt about it, she had to go. Asa Taylor's involvement with Thomas and her presence outside his office would be a tremendous attraction—distraction—leading to an explosive interaction.

Zain raced to the door, his intent to fire her on the spot. He froze. *Zain, man,* he told himself, *you're not thinking. You can't simply walk out there and fire Asa Taylor because she bothers you like no other woman has ever done before,* he admonished. *You need a sane, rational, reason.*

The first step toward making a logical decision was knowing exactly what you were dealing with. Zain reread the note Lance had left on his desk, zeroing in on the last words: *Very experienced. Read file ASAP.*

Asa Taylor. Even her name grabbed at his gut. It was different, exotic, demanding that he know more about the person with such an unusual name.

Yeah, he'd read her file, right after he gave her her first assignment. Zain felt an evil grin move across his face as he contemplated the merits of the great plan that had just entered his head.

Issuing an assignment would be his first priority. Asa Taylor needed to be immersed in some real work.

Zain grabbed a stack of computer discs. They were files from the software company they'd aquired when the owner died. He'd been unable to open any of the files. Not that he couldn't; with a little bit of time he was sure he could break the passwords and security codes locked into the system. He simply hadn't had much time lately. Lance, with his head full of love and marriage, had left it up to him, of course.

If Asa Taylor *was* "very experienced," she could handle this one very small task. It would be an excellent test of her abilities, one that she was sure to fail. A case of discs containing the files of Stewart Enterprises in hand, Zain entered the outer office. He expected to find Ms. Taylor lounging at her desk chair, idly waiting to be told what to do. That would be the first negative mark against her. Instead, his eyes collided with a shapely body part that shifted right then left as she backed out of the narrow space under her work station. She stood, her beautiful eyes wide with surprise to find him standing there.

"What were you doing on the floor?" he demanded, angry because that view of her swaying hips brought back so soon and so fast those uncontrollable feelings.

"Plugging in the panel of the surge protector. I was looking for something better to do than stare at these walls."

Her voice was soft, her tone cold and precise. "So," Zain searched her face for any signs of the overpowering feelings of desire he was experiencing. "You found something to do."

"I thought I'd familiarize myself with the computer system, check out the applications, get comfortable with the desktop."

Comfortable? She wanted to be comfortable? Lazy! That's what she was! Zain mentally added another strike against her.

"Is that my first assignment?" she asked neither tentatively or forcefully, but in that same emotionless tone of voice.

His plan. Zain had almost forgotten. What was happening to the man who was always on top? The man who always knew what was happening before it happened.

"Yes, it is." His voice came out gruff and deeper than usual. "Decode these files, categorize them by the types of corporations which would require our services and give me a printout on each file."

She nodded once, taking the wide case of discs from him. There was no other reaction. No look of horror, no surprise at the mountainous task set before her.

"I need it all by noon," Zain heard himself say, prodding for some type of reaction. That single nod again was all he got.

Unable to accept her lack of response, Zain lingered a few seconds more. "Do what you can," he told her, adding in a condescending tone, "I'll understand if it's too much for you."

That was an unfair remark and he knew it. If anything, Zain had always been considered a fair employer. Demanding, but fair. Somehow, for a moment or two, a malicious part of his brain had taken over.

"Thank you, Mr. Darby."

Zain watched as she started the computer and promptly ignored him. Asa Taylor was ignoring *him, Zain Darby,* when all he wanted to do was stare into her eyes, transfer the crazy feelings he was having in his gut to her and allow them to take them both over—on the floor, right now. No one would be here for another hour. Then he remembered Thomas. He'd forgotten about her boyfriend.

"Is there something else you need from me, Mr. Darby?"

Zain blinked, shaking his head no as a response to her question. He had been daydreaming. If Lance could see him now…That decided it. Zain had to get rid of this woman. He marched into Lance's office and quickly found her file.

"Asa Taylor, age twenty-three," he quietly read to himself. She was younger than he thought. Address, education—oh, she was an LSU grad. Experience? Zain studied the list of internships and summer jobs in both Baton Rouge where Louisiana State University was located as well as in New Orleans. Asa Taylor had kept herself busy in between classes. Zain opened the manila folder once again, searching for more information. There were an application, W-2 and emergency forms, but nothing else. How could Lance consider Asa Taylor "very experienced" when her only job-related experiences were internships and summer jobs.

Zain reached for the phone again, this time placing it back before dialing. He didn't need Lance's approval to fire this woman. Her inexperience was reason enough.

As Zain gathered the papers together, the cool, crisp sheets of facts reminded him of his professional ethics, his reputation. He knew his limits, chose a path and followed it with a single-minded determination. No angel-faced woman with a strange name was going to shake him up so much that he couldn't run his own company. Folder in hand, Zain left Lance's office heading to his own, looking

neither left or right, ignoring her as she had done him
earlier.

Zain Darby was something. He had the looks and
power, but he was strange. After the first five minutes of
interaction, Asa realized that she had another Lloyd Stewart
on her hands and reacted accordingly, by not reacting. Asa
had discovered the best way to deflate or at the least mini-
mize offensive, negative remarks meant to degrade was to
ignore them. When forced to talk, she did so in the most
neutral, unassuming way possible. That's how she'd
survived before. That's how she'd do it again, despite some
major differences between her former and current bosses.
Physically, they were complete opposites.

*Where Mr. Stewart repulsed me, Zain Darby, well, let's
just say he doesn't, and leave it at that,* Asa thought as her
fingers flew across the keys. She printed out the file and
reached for the next disc.

As she worked, Asa wondered why Zain Darby had
taken such an instant dislike to her. Almost the same as Mr.
Stewart. Was it her round face with a chin that pointed
down, giving her face a heart shape? What was it about her
that made men either hate her on sight or pretend to love
her as soon as they laid eyes on her?

Asa worked methodically, knowing what keys to press
from memory. She remembered every code and password.
These files were that same she had stored and kept records
of for Stewart Software.

"Mmmm," Asa hummed to herself as she turned to retrieve another printout, put it in a folder, and add it to the growing stack of files in the metal bin beside her. Her fingers continued to move rapidly over the keys, entering 110870, the date Tom Dempsey, a field goal kicker for the New Orleans Saints, kicked a record setting sixty-three yard field goal.

Lloyd Stewart was a die-hard Saints Fan. All codes and passwords revolved around the New Orleans Saints' successes and failures. There was no systematic logic to it. Zain Darby would never have been able to open these files without her, a former employee of Stewart Software. He most likely would have lost hundreds of clients who wouldn't renew existing contracts with a company that couldn't do something as simple as access a file.

Zain Darby didn't know the good luck that had just fallen into his lap. And all after casually dismissing the staff of Stewart Software. Not that there were many of them. Still the thought of saving his hide by opening these files made her angry. Being forced to prove herself because Zain Darby had taken an instant dislike to her annoyed her even more. Then there was that hard stare and deep voice that sent those waves through her, building her anger to an even higher level, transforming it into determination. Asa didn't let the anger show, not even when he stormed from one office to another. She worked steadily, her anger pushing her to finish before the noon deadline. Her movements were efficient and steady, an 'it-doesn't-matter' expression locked onto her face as she unlocked each file.

A few hours later Asa removed the last disc from the computer and placed it into the case on her desk. She closed the application, the computer displayed the Windows desktop once again. Asa put the last printout into a folder, labeled it and placed it in the now-full bin with the others.

She let out a huge sigh of relief, rolling the kinks out of her neck.

"Gave up, I see."

Zain Darby's voice rushed across the room, splashing into her.

"You've got two minutes left if you want to keep trying. But of course you wouldn't. I understand. The job was too much for a woman of your limited experience."

Asa smiled inside. She couldn't wait to bust his bubble. She stood. That's when the dizziness hit her. Asa was horrified to realize that she hadn't eaten her morning snack, and there was only half an hour left in her scheduled lunch time. Her annoyance with Zain Darby, her opportunity to gloat, took a back seat. Asa remain calm, her response automatic. She slowly reached for a peppermint from a basket she'd brought and filled just this morning. Her unsteady fingers grabbed one of the cellophane-wrapped papers. Removing the wrapper was a slow, clumsy task. Asa could feel Zain Darby's eyes on her the entire time. Her movements were becoming shakier by the moment. The peppermint made it to her mouth. Asa knew she needed more sugar than the small mint would supply but she also needed to let Zain Darby know what she was about. Asa tried to remember the words he'd said a few seconds ago, but her mind couldn't focus. It didn't matter.

"Your files, Mr. Darby," Asa told him, pointing to the bin on the other side of the desk. That said she grabbed her purse and on unsteady legs headed out the alcove, past the receptionist's desk in search of the bathroom. Brent intercepted her there.

"Asa."

She turned toward his voice. He was at her side in an instant.

"You have a low-blood sugar, don't you?"

Asa nodded, "I've got a peppermint." Even to her own ears her speech had slurred. Asa was glad it had remained steady when she spoke to Zain Darby.

"It's lunchtime. That's not enough and you know it."

Asa leaned against him, happy to see a friendly face, even if it included a lecture. He led her to the lunchroom.

"The peppermint helped, probably saved you from passing out," Brent told her. He found the small juice box that was in her purse, opened it and handed it to her.

Asa drained it in two huge sips. The natural juice would boost her sugar quickly bringing her to a more normal level. She put her head down waiting for the rush.

"You know you need a full meal by twelve noon. I was trying to stay back, trying to give you space to take care of yourself, and look at what you did."

Asa could hear Brent rummaging in her purse. He was probably searching for the crackers she kept there. She suddenly remembered the grapes, the snack she hadn't eaten this morning.

"Asa!"

From his tone Asa knew that Brent had found them. All the time spent arguing, all the debating all weekend long was for nothing it seemed. She pretended not to hear him.

"I know that you're not still out of it. That juice should have revived you by now."

Knowing that there was no use in pretending Asa looked up. Brent held the bag of grapes in his hand. "How could you forget to eat your morning snack?"

Asa had a good reason; proving to Zain Darby that she had what it takes was more than reason enough to throw her off her schedule. But she didn't want to share that with Brent, not yet anyway. How was she supposed to be more independent if she ran to him with every problem?

And this little episode was all part of the problem. Asa rarely got a low because she followed her schedule so precisely and made necessary adjustments to what she ate or the amount of insulin she took. But sometimes a low blood sugar just happened, and Brent knew that. It would have been easier if he hadn't found those grapes inside her purse. Asa would have been happy to let her cousin assume that this low blood sugar was nothing more than one of those unexplained cases.

Now, there was nothing she could do about it. Brent would just have to rant and rave until she convinced him all over again that she alone, was responsible for herself. Zain Darby wouldn't distract her again.

"If this is how you plan on taking care of yourself, you can forget it," Brent was saying as Asa tuned in once again.

He went to the fridge, took out her lunch and set it before her, grumbling the entire time. He watched and lectured as she ate every bit of the ham sandwich, orange slices and sugar free vanilla wafers containing the exact carbohydrates she needed at lunch to maintain her blood sugar.

Zain had seen it all. Her awkward swaying movements, the unsteady walk, the way she leaned against Thomas as if she couldn't stand on her own two feet. And what was the deal with the peppermint? Something strange was going on here.

Zain stood in the exact place where he had met her. The announcement that she'd made in that dead voice of hers replayed in his head. "Your files, Mr. Darby." After about two minutes he followed the couple. They were in the lunchroom. Asa Taylor's head was on the table. Thomas was laying into her. Zain couldn't hear the one-sided conversation through the closed door but he could see them clearly through the glass window in the middle of the door. Zain heard a noise behind him. Someone was coming down the hall. He moved away from the door, passing his receptionist.

"You've got quite a few phone messages, Mr. Darby. I didn't want to disturb you. You had the sign on your door."

Lisa, his receptionist, was referring to a picture of himself Lance had taken, enlarged and mounted to warn others against disturbing him at certain times. The picture was the perfect image of what he felt when someone interrupted his flow of thinking.

"Fine," he told her.

"I'm off to lunch."

"Fine," he repeated.

As soon as Lisa was gone, Zain peered into the lunch-room again. There sat Asa Taylor, straight and proper, eating a sandwich with Thomas overseeing her every move. She looked perfectly fine now. Her abrupt departure without dismissal had irritated him. Seeing Thomas's arms around her had aggravated him even more, but he wasn't going to stand out here acting like a Peeping Tom. This was his company, his lunch room.

He opened the door. "Thomas, Ms. Taylor," he nodded to them both.

Thomas looked at him nervously, barely acknowledging him. Thomas's entire concentration was on the woman next to him, which was exactly where Zain's was centered.

"Ms. Taylor, I need to speak to you as soon as your lunch is over."

"Of course, Mr. Darby," she answered in that same monotone voice, her angelic face holding no expression whatsoever. Except for her eyes; they seemed sad.

Zain went back to his office. Along the way he picked up the bin full of the files Asa Taylor had printed. He laid them on the desk, slowly settled in his desk chair and stared out the window. None of this made sense. How could she have opened those files? And exactly what was wrong with the woman!

Suddenly it all came together in his mind. She was drunk. The unsteady movements, the uncontrollable swaying, there was even a slight slur in her speech that he hadn't heard before. He'd almost missed it, but it was there. And the peppermint, a tiny effort to hide the smell of alcohol. It worked because he hadn't detected a bit of it on her.

Zain stood and began pacing his office. Thomas had to know about her problem. He was covering for her. That would explain his nervousness just now. Asa Taylor was nothing but trouble. She unnerved him, occupied one of his faithful employee's slot and made him feel like a fool.

The files! Zain remembered. He sat on the edge of the desk. They had to be nothing but junk. He'd given her an impossible task, she'd cracked under the pressure and drunk herself silly while on the job. Either his imagination had gone wild or he was right on target.

Zain opened the first file, Bradford and Associates. Definitely one of the companies contracted to Stewart Software. He knew them all by heart. Every bit of information concerning the services provided was in the folder. Zain opened the next one. The name was also one he knew. Zain went to his desk and pulled from his personal file, there he found the acquisitions for Stewart Software. It contained a listing of clients. Zain spent the next forty-five minutes studying each and every file, comparing the limited information he had on each client to the extensive files Asa Taylor had decoded and printed for him.

Now he was confused. He'd thought he had Asa Taylor all figured out, thought he had a way to get rid of her. What excuse did he have to fire her now? And why should he even want to dismiss someone who was as capable and efficient as she seemed to be? She was a puzzle, one Zain would piece together and figure out before he made a final decision.

There was a knock on the door.

"Come in," he called, recalling his demand for her presence.

"You wanted to see me, Mr. Darby?" she asked, looking straight past him.

Zain wanted her angelic though expressionless face focused on him. How could he crack open the mystery that was Asa Taylor if she wouldn't look at him? "I'm right here, Miss Taylor." He waved a hand in her line of vision. "That's a window you're looking at. I'd appreciate you looking at me when we talk. If we are to have a decent working relationship that will be essential."

She turned to him. Zain could have sworn her eyes grew larger as they focused on him. Her facial expression, though, remained exactly the same.

"From your comments am I to understand that I have proven myself? Am I deserving of a position at Execute?"

While her words were sarcastic, her tone remained dull. Zain wanted to laugh out loud.

She had, in her own subtle way, put him in his place. She was more than young, gifted and black. Despite the sailor outfit she wore, strong, beautiful and would one day be his.

"Excuse me, sir."

Brent Thomas stuck his head inside the open door.

Thomas. Zain had once again forgotten about him. "Yes, what is it?"

"A reminder. The meeting with the geniuses, one-thirty sharp."

"Lisa would have reminded me." A sound of disgust escaped his lips. "I'll be there, Thomas."

Zain observed the nonverbal communication between the two. They were not happy with each other, on rocky ground, it seemed. Maybe Thomas was on his way out. Zain would wait and see.

Thomas hadn't budged. "Anything else?"

"Just an idea I wanted to discuss with you before the meeting."

Zain saw right through Thomas's attempt to take the heat off his girlfriend. Zain squashed the irritation and decided to be amused by his little ploy. Ignoring Thomas for the moment, he turned to Asa.

"Your assumption, Ms. Taylor, is correct." He walked toward her. "Make appointments with each and every of the companies for the files you printed. My appointment book is on my desk. I'll see you in an hour." Zain motioned for Thomas leaving Asa in his office to get the address book he had mentioned.

Asa's entire body went limp. The tension of being in his presence disappeared with his absence. This was only the first day! Asa forced her legs to move to the huge mahogany desk that dominated the room, so much like the man himself. She found the large, black appointment book. Asa grabbed it, needing to leave his office as quick as she could. He was gone, but as she stood in his domain, the tension that had disappeared with the man himself was slowly building again. She turned, bumping into the desk and knocking a small piece of paper from it. It slowly floated to her feet. Asa stooped to pick it up and without thinking read the short note. It was about her, written by the decent half of Execute, Lance Handle. She laid it on top of a manila folder. It had her name on it. Asa felt a little guilty for reading a note that wasn't meant for her. At least she now knew for certain that Zain Darby had read her files and was informed about her strict eating schedule and the reasons for it. Good. Now she wouldn't have to explain herself. The file explained enough so that even someone unfamiliar with the disease could understand the possible side effects of having to take insulin injections.

Asa replaced the note, feeling a little better about her working situation. Within the hour she had booked an appointment with a representative from each company. She was exploring the various applications on the computer desktop when she heard her name.

"Asa Taylor."

Zain Darby was sitting on the edge of her desk. He was closer than he'd been to her all day. He wasn't touching her, he didn't have to. A small pulsating wave began at her fingertips, making it impossible for her to use the keyboard. A rush of blood went straight to her head, sending larger waves of longing throughout her entire body. Zain Darby was a tidal wave, about to swamp her. A tidal wave left destruction in its path she again reminded herself. She couldn't have that. Asa quickly erected the tallest dam, a levee *and* a stone wall to protect herself. Now she was ready to face him.

"How can I help you, Mr. Darby?" Asa prayed that this rush to her system didn't deplete her body of all the carbohydrates she had consumed at lunch.

"Asa, that's an unusual name. Mind if I ask where it came from?"

He asked that question in a very businesslike manner. His voice was in no way flirtatious. He hadn't leaned in closer attempting to invade her personal space. She couldn't accuse him of sexual harassment. He was simply sitting a little closer to her than he had all day. The open feel of the alcove had evaporated. Her concentration had dried as quickly as a puddle on a hottest summer day in New Orleans.

Name. Something about her name. That's what he wanted to know. Asa took in a slow breath. Maybe he was simply trying to start over. Be friendly. Asa couldn't take offense. If Lance Handle were sitting on the edge of her desk asking the same question she would have answered it by now, and probably would have had a nice conversation going too.

"I was born in Japan."

"Funny, you don't look Japanese." He smiled, softening the remark.

That was a stupid way to answer a simple question. He was only asking about your name. You really sounded intelligent there, Asa chided herself. "I'm not," Asa gave him a little smile of her own. If he could be friendly so could she.

His expression changed when he smiled, becoming less rigid, more open. It was said that a smile could change the world. It definitely changed the face of one Zain Darby.

"You're not—"

"Japanese," Asa finished for him.

"The significance of that fact to your name is…?" he softly asked. So softly Asa found herself leaning toward him. When she realized how much closer she had inched in his direction, she sprang back.

"I was born on a military base in Japan. My father's a U.S. Army man. My mother discovered the name, fell in love with it and it's been mine ever since."

"Interesting story. You must have traveled all over the world as a child."

"Not since I was five," Asa found herself telling him, somehow wanting Zain Darby to know about her. "I was raised by my aunt and uncle once I started school."

"That must have been—"

"Mr. Darby, that call you were waiting on from Standard Industries…on line one," a short cheerful young woman announced.

"Thanks, I'll take it in my office, Lisa. Introduce yourself to Asa Taylor. I've kept her busy all morning. Show her that everyone at Execute doesn't believe that I'm a pain." Asa hid her face in her hands.

"You told him that to his face?" the excited girl asked. "Let me pat you on the back. You are one brave woman."

"I didn't. I don't know where he got that idea from."

"But it's true and Mr. Darby knows it. This is your first day on the job, right?"

At Asa's nod she went on.

"Who told you about our pet name for the boss already?"

"My cousin, Brent."

"Brent Thomas, one of Mr. Darby's geniuses? The tall, handsome one?"

"I shouldn't have said that. Brent doesn't think Mr. Darby should know that we're related."

"The secret's safe with me, sister. Tell me, what has Brent been up to?"

Their three minute conversation was cut short when Zain Darby bellowed from his office, "Ms. Taylor, I need you in here. Bring a pen and tablet."

"Duty calls."

Brent chose that moment to come around the bend. He stopped short when he saw Lisa and didn't come any closer. He pointed to his watch and then her.

"I know, I've got a whole hour before my next snack," she hissed from her desk, satisfied when he went back the way he'd come.

Lisa sighed. "Too cute."

Asa stored Lisa's comments away for later consideration.

"Ms. Taylor, tell Lisa that she has a post to man and a phone to answer," Zain Darby's voice reached out to them.

"Sounds like you have a post and phone to get back to," Asa grinned at her friendly co-worker.

"Good luck with 'the Pain'," Lisa said before rushing off.

When Asa reached his office he was all-business. Those few minutes talking to her at her desk might never have happened.

"Have a seat and let me explain how this dictation stuff works for me," he told her gruffly. "I give you the central idea, the main point of what I want to say. You convert it into letter form using appropriate wording and terminology. I'll let you know if I want it forceful, friendly, soft, or…"

"Threatening?" Asa supplied.

"No, persuasive," he corrected.

Zain paced the room as he dictated the central idea of each letter. All were directed to the former clients of Stewart Software. Asa found it amazing that he knew so much about each client. He couldn't have had more than an hour to study all thirty files. The essence of letter fifteen down, Asa glanced at her watch. It was three-twenty. Her afternoon snack time was almost over. She was not going to have a repeat of today's low-blood sugar. Zain Darby had taken a deep breath and was about to go on.

"Excuse me Mr. Darby, but I need to take a quick break."

"We can't stop. I'm on a roll and this needs to be done before the end of the day."

"While I can understand that, I don't have much of a choice. Excuse me for a moment," Asa told him quietly but firmly, her emotionless mask and tone automatically slipping back into place. She was out the door, not waiting for permission. Asa knew that *she* was ultimately responsible for her health. If Zain Darby couldn't understand that she needed a ten minute break, then he'd have to learn. She was through catering to unyielding bosses.

Asa went into the lunchroom where Brent stood in front of the fridge, arms folded, waiting. He silently watched as she ate two vanilla wafers and she drank the entire can of Choice, a nutritious liquid snack made especially for diabetics. Asa dropped the empty can in the garbage without saying a word to him.

"Asa," Brent called.

Asa went into the ladies' room. Brent called her name once more, giving the door one hard bang before leaving. Asa used the facilities and washed her hands.

Zain Darby was waiting in the hall.

"What was all that about?" he demanded.

"Nothing, Mr. Darby."

"I hope for your sake it was nothing," he told her. The way his eyes dove into hers, Asa thought there was more than one meaning to his words.

He stormed away from her, announcing, "We've got some letters to finish."

The last hour of the work day was spent in the company of Zain Darby, the demanding employer. She released a sigh of relief as she shut down her computer at four-thirty, glad to end her day.

CHAPTER 4

After a week of working for Zain Darby, Asa found that she preferred dealing with the all business Zain rather than the friendly one. When his main focus was something other than her, Asa could concentrate on her job. But when his eyes, his voice, his entire body focused on her, Asa felt so overwhelmed she could barely function.

Monday morning Asa was at her desk long before Zain made his normal appearance. She put away her purse and briefcase before moving to the lunchroom to store her midday meal. That's where she ran into Brent. They hadn't said much to each other for an entire week. Not an easy feat living and working so close to each other.

"That wasn't funny, Asa."

"I didn't mean for it to be."

"Why did you leave me?"

"You don't have to be here at seven-thirty. I do."

"But we always ride the ferry together."

"As you can see, I made it here all by myself."

"I noticed."

Asa slammed the refrigerator door. She and her cousin were going to have it out right here at work. Asa could feel it. She was glad Zain wasn't anywhere near.

She left the lunchroom, Brent right behind her.

"Asa, wait."

"Don't you get it? I can take care of myself. I took care of myself for four years in college completely out of your sight. I can do it again."

"Not really."

"What does that mean? You think I can't handle it? I've proven that I can, minus that one mistake last week."

"Yes, you have."

"And you've yet to ask me why it happened."

"No, I didn't. Tell me why, Asa."

Brent followed as Asa made her way to her alcove. She landed in her desk chair. "I can't. Not right now."

"Later?"

"Later," she agreed still not sure she wanted to let him in on her reaction to Zain.

"We're okay now?"

"We're getting there, I guess."

"You won't leave me this afternoon?"

"No, I'll wait. But Brent, no visits to my desk today, all right?"

"No visits. Just don't forget what you need to do for yourself."

"Won't," Asa told him, her usual response to his precautions slipping out automatically. Brent kissed her on the forehead before leaving. Asa smiled sadly. She never could stay mad at him.

"Good morning, Ms. Taylor." Zain walked in a second after Brent left.

"Good morning, Mr. Darby."

He stopped instead of going straight to his office as usual. He sat on the edge of her desk.

"Something wrong?"

"No, not really." Asa wasn't in the mood for sharing confidences, especially with Zain Darby in his friendly mode. At least once a day he let his guard down, which resulted in Asa letting her guard down. Asa surmised that Zain and work were the only safe combination.

"Does this 'nothing' have to do with Thomas?"

"Yes, it does, but I don't want to talk about it."

"Want me to straighten him out?"

That would be an interesting sight, but Asa didn't want Zain involved in her personal life. It was enough that she had begun to think of him as Zain. Never out loud, but in her mind he was Zain just the same.

"No, thank you," Asa answered, using her usual business tone.

"Let me know if you change your mind." He went to his office without another word.

Asa spent the morning attending scheduled meetings and keeping track of the changes in contracts for the Stewart acquisitions. She took notes, gave her input, depending on various quirks she remembered about the clients. Mr. Stewart had never involved her in meetings like this but she had learned a great deal despite his secretive nature.

Zain and Asa worked together as if they had been at it for years instead of days. There was that spark between them. Asa focused on the smoothness of their working relationship preferring to deal with what was most comfortable between them.

At the end of one meeting a long-winded client began a story of a recent fishing trip. Asa quietly excused herself. As she sat in the lunchroom eating a bag of grapes for her morning snack trying to get the image of Zain out of her

head, Asa attempted to concentrate on Brent. She had to do
something about him.

Before returning to the meeting Asa stopped at the restroom. In the office she rushed past Lisa who was always
ready to talk and went into the alcove to find Zain waiting
for her. He sat on the edge of her desk. Business Zain gone,
friendly Zain waited with a purpose. Now she wished she
had stopped to talk to Lisa.

Asa slowly went to her chair. "Can I help you with
something, Mr. Darby?" Asa sat with her fingers over the
keys, trying to look busy.

"No, we've got about fifteen minutes before the next
client's due. I want to talk to you, to ask you something."

"Certainly," she told him, her body language conveying
exactly the opposite. Zain didn't seem to care. The tidal
wave inside her began to build once again.

"I've noticed some things."

Asa nodded. She had too. Like how the deep brown
color of his eyes when he spoke to her seemed to turn into
melted chocolate. That he had thick even-spaced-eyebrows
that begged her to trace them, straightening the tiny hairs
that tended to go wild sometimes.

"This nine-thirty break time."

"Do you have a problem with that, Mr. Darby? Aren't I
allowed a break at that time?"

"Yes, you are and I don't have a problem with it unless
it interferes with work."

Asa was disappointed. When he hadn't made negative
comments last week about her break times and eating
schedule she'd thought he understood.

"Are you saying that today I wasn't allowed to have my morning break?"

"Not in the middle of a meeting."

"The meeting was over, Mr. Darby."

"The client was still here."

"What you're saying is that *all* other things should be put on hold if they interfere with work."

"Exactly!"

Asa was dealing with the Stewart experience all over again. Zain wasn't being rude and obnoxious about it, but his attitude of work above all else was exactly the same. She wouldn't have it. "I'm sorry, but my nine-thirty break is a necessity."

A flash of surprise crossed his face but it was gone in a moment. A hard look came into his eyes as he asked, "Do you have any other *necessities* I should know about?"

He knew exactly what her necessities were. They were all in her file. Asa started to wonder what game Zain was playing. Game or not if he wanted to hear her necessities from her own mouth then she was more than happy to oblige. "Lunch no later than noon, an afternoon break, notice ahead of time if you need me to work late." They were no different than the standard amenities granted to office staff.

The hard stare remained on her, his chocolate gaze pulling her inside him. The wave inside her rose higher.

"I can deal with that."

He went back into his office. By the time the next client came, business Zain was back.

The last meeting of the day ran longer than expected. Asa quietly excused herself and left just before twelve. Her stomach growled empty and hollow, a sure sign of an impending low if she didn't eat soon. She even felt a slight dizziness. Asa popped a peppermint into her mouth and headed to the lunchroom with only a slight tilt to her walk.

Asa found Lisa in the lunchroom. They ate and talked together. Brent came in once, saw her companion and quickly left.

"He gets cuter everyday," Lisa commented.

That's when it hit her. Brent had been avoiding Lisa. Whenever Asa was anywhere near the reception desk, Brent had made himself scarce. Lisa was the answer to her problem with Brent.

"You really think so?"

"I've only said it a million times."

"Yeah, but what does that mean? Do you like him or what?"

"Like him? He's gorgeous, funny, and so sweet."

"Why don't you do something about it?"

"I did, once. We went out, had a good time and all, but he never asked me out again. Some mess about office relationships."

"Around Christmas?"

"Yeah, it sure was. Right after, in fact. Did he talk about me? Please tell me he talked about me!"

"Once, but that's saying a lot for Brent."

"Good news. Tell me some more!"

"The problem with Brent is that you are going to have to do the pursuing."

They spent the next half hour discussing plans for Brent and Lisa to get together.

Asa went back to work, her mood lighter because she now had some direction, a plan that would take Brent's focus off her. Asa found herself humming as she logged in new information for each of the clients they had met with today.

Suddenly Zain came bursting out of his office. "Come with me, Ms. Taylor. I need your help." His handsome face held a mixture of worry and urgency. Asa quickly complied, grabbing her purse before following Zain out of the building.

Zain couldn't believe he was doing this. His grandmother had locked herself in the bathroom and refused to come out to take her medication until he came over and introduced "that nice girl" to her. Zain had no idea what nice girl Grammy Dee meant. He couldn't remember introducing any girl to her since he was in high school. The women he dated couldn't be considered "nice girls".

Now Asa Taylor, she fit that description. She had some strange habits but she was a nice girl. Zain still suspected that she was a nice girl with a drinking habit, but a nice girl just the same.

They were in his Lexus and driving toward the ferry in no time.

"Where are we going?" she asked.

"This is going to sound strange, but I need you to pretend to be my girl."

"As in *girlfriend*. You can stop the car right now, Mr. Darby. Acting is not in my job description."

"Too late, we're on the ferry." His face showed no remorse. When it came to his grandmother, Zain did what he had to do to make her happy. She had been there for him when he needed love, a home. He would be there for her too.

"It's not what you're thinking. It's for my grandmother's benefit," Zain went on to explain.

"Do you really have a grandmother?" Asa asked, her voice carrying some inflection.

"You'll meet her soon."

She stared at him a good, long time. "Then I'm doing this for her sake."

"Which means you're doing this for me, Ms. Taylor."

Having reached the west bank, Zain drove down the ramp of the ferry, arriving at the assisted living apartment building a few minutes later. Not waiting for the elevator, Zain took the stairs two at a time, grabbing Asa's hand, pulling her behind him. They stopped on the third floor. Zain went straight into his grandmother's apartment, knowing Rose, the nurse who'd called him, would be waiting inside for him.

"Has she come out yet, Miss Rose?"

"Now, you know better than that. When has Grammy Dee caved in after giving an ultimatum?"

"Never."

"So you got your answer. And you've got a nice girl, too."

"Miss Rose, Asa Taylor, my secretary and assistant. Asa Taylor, Miss Rose, one of the nurses on staff who almost exclusively takes care of Grammy Dee."

The older woman laughed. "True, but let's work on getting her out. She's already late for her medication. This little episode is going to throw her schedule way off."

Zain pulled Asa behind him toward the only closed door of the apartment. He was surprised to still find Asa's hand in his own. He had only grabbed hers to get upstairs faster. Now he didn't want to let it go.

Miss Rose knocked on the bathroom door. "Grammy, your grandson's here."

"Zain? Come closer to the door, boy."

"I'm right here, Grammy Dee. Come on out."

"Not unless you got that nice girl with you."

"I sure have." Zain looked over at Asa. Her prim and proper black skirt and peach button-to-the-top blouse couldn't be nicer. And the tight bun at the top of her head couldn't scream it any louder. Just as her niceness couldn't hide how beautiful and sexy she was.

"You better not be fooling this old woman, Zain Darby."

"He's not," Asa called out, talking for the first time.

Zain gave her hand a squeeze of appreciation. The bathroom door opened a crack. "That's the one. Round face, the look of an angel."

Zain's insides churned at his grandmother's words. What was she talking about? How did she know what Asa looked like? He glanced at Asa to see her reaction and was satisfied to find her normal cool-as-a-cucumber expression. Zain fixed his face to show none of the surprise he was feeling.

The bathroom door opened wide. Grammy Dee stepped out. "Why all the gloomy faces? You two should be happy that you finally found each other. You *are* happy?" Grammy Dee stared up at him. She didn't have to look too far up. She was almost as tall as he was. She always claimed that he got his height from her side of the family.

"Oh, yes indeed, Grammy. We're more than happy," Zain told his grandmother. Now that she was out he didn't want to do or say anything that would make her barricade herself inside the bathroom again. She still needed to take her medication.

"Then prove it to me. Kiss the girl."

"Now, Grammy."

"Don't 'now Grammy' me. Do it now." She stood straight and tall, a thin finger wagging in his face. "Or I won't be swallowing no green pill or blue pill or that nasty orange one either."

"Come on, why don't you kiss her?" Miss Rose added, folding her arms, waiting for the show.

Zain had had thoughts of doing just that, daydreams even. More than once he had fallen asleep at night thinking about kissing Asa Taylor. From the moment he'd seen her with Thomas in that elevator he'd thought of it. But not like this. Not with an audience. Her fingers wiggled in his hold. Their entwined hands were slick with perspiration. His or hers he didn't know. Zain loved Grammy Dee, but she was asking a lot of him. She wanted him to kiss a woman who wanted nothing to do with him, who barely tolerated working with him, a woman who made him crazy inside. A woman who was kissing him...

Her lips, Asa's lips, were on his. Soft, full, sweet. As soon as his mind registered the feel and taste of her they were gone.

"You can do better than that, Zain," Grammy Dee said as she moved to sit in the open dining area. "Don't you think so, Rose?"

"That I do," Zain heard the nurse say.

He looked down at his secretary. Asa's face was stunned instead of blank. She'd felt something. "Yes, I can do better than that," Zain heard himself whisper. He lowered his mouth to hers.

A low raspy "no" reached only his ears. He pulled the word as well as the essence of Asa Taylor toward him. He softly delved and searched with gentle movements of his lips and tongue, discovering that she wanted him too.

Asa was pulling away, trying to end the searching kiss. He didn't want it to end, but suddenly her lips were gone.

"Better," Grammy Dee announced.

Zain had forgotten his audience. Asa began talking with more expression and speed than he'd ever heard from her before.

"I'm Asa Taylor, Grammy Dee," she was saying in a rush. "Do you want me to get you some fresh water to take your medicine?"

"What a nice girl. Yes, I'd like that. Make it nice and cold, will you, sweetie?"

"Sweetie"? Zain couldn't remember his grandmother ever calling any girl he knew sweetie. And "sweetie" was moving as fast as she could. She probably couldn't wait to get away from him. That was okay. Her run-away tactic couldn't hurt his pride, Zain knew. With that kiss had come a brand new discovery.

"Ow! Why'd you pinch me, Grammy?" Zain howled, surprised at the unexpected attack.

"For embarrassing Asa that way."

"You're the one who told me to kiss her."

"Kiss her, not get down and dirty."

Miss Rose laughed. Zain shook his head at the speed Grammy went from approval to disapproval of a kiss she had demanded.

Asa returned with a glass of ice cold water and Zain kept his mouth shut. Grammy took all of her medicine without a problem. Asa, he could tell was ready to bolt.

"You come visit me again, sweet angel," Grammy told Asa. "Be good to that one, she's a keeper," his grandmother whispered to him.

Asa was down the steps, out the building and a half a block away before he caught up with her.

"Asa, stop!" He demanded. She kept going. Zain wasn't used to dealing with people who didn't follow orders. Asa never did, so why was he surprised when she kept going?

Zain sprinted, catching up to her in no time. He slowed to a walk, keeping pace with her. "Don't run away. We need to talk."

Asa surprised him by stopping cold. He was already two strides ahead of her before he realized it. Must this woman constantly make him feel like a fool? He walked back to where she stood.

"You should not have kissed me!" she told him, her hands moving to the rhythm of the words, her teeth clenched. He'd never seen so much emotion on her face. She was even more beautiful.

"You kissed me first," Zain reminded her.

"But you didn't have to reciprocate. Oh, look at what you did!"

She was staring at her watch. "Look at the time! It's three-thirty and it's all your fault!"

Zain was amused. He was now responsible for the movement of time.

"Where's my purse? Zain, you made me forget my purse!"

She was angry. Amazingly upset, but all he could think was, "She called me Zain."

Asa took a peppermint out of her skirt pocket, pulled off her shoes and ran back toward the apartment building. Had the woman gone crazy? Maybe he shouldn't have kissed her. No, he was glad he did. Asa just wasn't used to showing her feelings, any feelings. He would catch up to her after giving her a moment or two to breathe.

By the time he reached the building Asa was out again, purse in hand. "I think I've more than earned my pay today. Take me home, please."

She stood before him cool, calm, and with absolutely no expression on her face. The Asa Taylor he knew was back. In the last hour he had experienced a stunned Asa, a melting-in-his-arms Asa, as well as a panicked, angry Asa. If he hadn't seen it himself he wouldn't have believed she was capable of expressing so many different emotions. But Zain wouldn't push it today. There was always tomorrow.

CHAPTER 5

Too late, Asa realized that she'd led Zain right to her house. Now he knew where she lived. Not that he couldn't look it up it up in her files. But knowing someone's address was different from knowing exactly where someone's house was, the color, the shape and the size. Zain Darby knew too much. Way too much.

Asa felt his eyes on her as she walked up the steps to the porch, even as she unlocked the door. She quickly closed it against his stare, against the power that was Zain. Zeus the god of all men put women in a trance when he found one he wanted. Zain the god of all men must have the same power. Asa didn't know if she could resist it.

Asa peeled away her office wear, the clothes much too tight and confining after having Zain's arms around her, surrounding her, pulling her inside him. That's how it felt. That's how he'd kissed, as if he wanted to have all of her. He would have had all of her passed out at his feet if she hadn't remembered her snack time. Zain once again had caused her to forget about her health, her needs. And if Brent knew—Brent! She'd promised to ride the ferry home with him today! Asa went to the phone and dialed Execute's number.

"Good afternoon, Execute, the answer to your anti-virus software needs."

"Lisa, it's Asa. Let me talk to—No, I've got a better idea. Give Brent this message." Asa left a message explaining her absence. "Why don't you ask Brent out tonight? He won't have any excuse not to go."

"I don't know. You've seen the way he's been avoiding me."

"Don't think negative. Go for it!"

Asa hung up. At least one good thing had come out of this. Operation Keep Brent Occupied could go into effect immediately. Now she had to find something to do with herself. Asa didn't want to be home when Brent got here. He would come to check on her.

Asa went into the bathroom, turning the shower on full blast. She stood under the heavy spray, eyes closed. Zain immediately came to mind. His hard body leaning onto her, those amazing lips, that searching, grasping, give-it-all-to-me tongue. Her eyes sprang opened. Thinking about it had projected the vivid image in her mind.

Asa slipped on a pair of jeans and her Dry Dock Cafe t-shirt advertising a neighborhood restaurant and bar in Algiers Point. That was where she'd go, the Dry Dock Cafe. She and Brent hadn't been there in months. She could sit at the bar, drink some water, talk to Ernie the bartender, if he still worked there. She could even get something to eat.

Refilling her medicine pouch with another cold pack, Asa made her way to the Dry Dock. It was only a few blocks from her house, near the ferry landing. Asa hurried. She didn't want Brent to catch her on his way home from work before she got inside.

The Dry Dock looked the same as always with its white paneled doors. At the entrance of the pale blue house-turned-restaurant were three sets of plastic green patio-style tables and chairs for those who wanted to catch the evening spring breeze from the river.

Asa sat at the bar. She was so happy to see Ernie she gave him a big hug and a kiss on the cheek. "You cut off all your hair, and bleached it blond."

"It was getting too long. Sherry said I was looking better than her. I thought it was time for a new look anyway."

"It doesn't quite go with that tatoo on your arm."

"It'll grow out."

Ernie brought her a glass of water just the way she liked it, in a martini glass with an olive. It was a drink she and her roommate at LSU had created. Both of them were non-drinkers and got a kick out of creating their own drink. They even named it: the Vodka Kiss.

Asa talked to Ernie as he served drinks. He refilled her glass over and over again even adding an extra olive once in a while. He clowned with her, even flirted a bit, but it was all in fun. Asa hadn't laughed this much in a long time.

After an hour or so in Ernie's company, Asa went up the small set of steps leading to the restaurant. She found a seat at one of the tables and studied the menu she already knew by heart. She ordered her food and went to the ladies' room to take care of her medical needs. Sugar reading done, insulin drawn and shot taken in her left thigh, Asa returned to the dining area. She sat, then remembered something she wanted to tell Ernie.

Asa was leaning over the bar whispering in Ernie's ear when she spotted Brent and Lisa through the paneled doors of the cafe. Asa didn't know how Lisa had talked him into it, but she wasn't going to spoil things by being noticed.

"Don't tell Brent I'm here," Asa hissed, spinning around to find a place to hide. Behind her was a little niche where the video poker machines were kept. She slipped between the old-fashioned wooden swinging doors. Asa felt as if she were hiding out in some old western bar.

A man was sitting in the dark corner of the small room. He looked somehow familiar. She peered at him as her eyes adjusted to the dark room, and he absently moved closer. It couldn't be, but it was. What was Zain Darby doing here? Asa was about to ask him that question when his hand shot out, pulling her toward him.

"Shhh, Thomas is talking to your bartender friend."

"Well then, thanks," she whispered, sitting down on the stool next to him. "I didn't want Brent to see me here."

"I figured that out by the expression on your face," he told her in a low voice. "Strange, when you're around me I can rarely tell what you're thinking. Just now I could read every thought that ran through your head. And when you were at the bar, every move, every little twitch showed that you were enjoying yourself."

"You've been here, watching me?" Asa didn't like what she was hearing. She liked even less the soft seductive tone of his voice as they sat in the dark little room together.

"I was. I couldn't help it. You came in not long after I decided to try my hand at video poker."

"You could have come out, said something."

"And miss this wonderful opportunity to see the cool, calm Asa Taylor act like a normal woman?"

"Normal woman?" She *was* normal. All her life her aunt and uncle, Brent, doctors and nurses had drilled into her head that she was normal. Her diabetes didn't make her any different from anyone else. She just had a few extra things to do before she ate, a few extra precautions she had to take into consideration every day of her life. What was normal to him? A perfect woman? Someone who would bow to his power, his kisses? Not her.

"Was it the alcohol?"

"What?" Asa only vaguely heard the question because she was trying to listen to what Brent was saying. How would he introduce Lisa to Ernie? She twisted around peering at the couple through the wooden slants. She was thrilled that Lisa and Brent were out on a date together but disgusted with her present situation. Not only was she stuck in this small room with the only man alive who could insult her and at the same time make her feel again the power of his kisses without even touching her, but she'd already taken her shot and the fast acting insulin would quickly do away with the few carbs she still had in her system. Not more than fifteen minutes ago, her sugar was eighty. A perfect reading before mealtime but her meal was out there and she was stuck in here. Somehow this was all Zain Darby's fault. He was always nearby when something stopped her from doing what she needed to do for herself. He was bad luck.

A hand touched her bare arm. It was warm, firm and sent a huge wave of pure longing straight to her head, activating her memory and transferring a throbbing need to her lips.

"Was it the alcohol? Was that what made you come alive?"

Asa stared at Zain, not believing the question. She didn't want to deal with him or these feelings his presence was bringing out in her. Suddenly she felt dizzy and shaky, her thinking unclear. Was it just the low blood sugar coming on or was Zain making this whole situation more difficult.

"Okay, fine, sure. If that's what you want to believe," Asa told him, not bothering to turn around. She took a peppermint from the pocket of her jeans and plopped it into her mouth.

"Peppermints again?" he whispered into her ear.

"Yes, peppermints, again!" Asa placed her thumbs in the corner of her eyes, said a quick prayer, then looked Zain Darby in the eye. "I need you to do me a favor. Go over to that table. The one under the picture of the Natchez steamboat and get me the food the waitress has probably already put there."

"Why?"

"Why? Because—I—need—it," she enunciated slowly.

"To soak up all that alcohol you drank. You know, most people eat *before* they drink. It works better that way."

"I've heard. Bring me the food, Zain, please."

"I can do that," he paused to stare at her lips, "for a kiss."

Asa shook her head in disbelief. Here she sat with a low blood sugar, the possibility of passing out very real, and he was bargaining a simple act of charity for a kiss. Asa couldn't think anymore. Her own speech inside her head was slow and distant.

"Okay, whatever you want,"she dragged out.

"Just a kiss."

Zain left but was back quickly, carrying two plates of food in one hand and a glass of milk in the other. He placed the food on a stool before her and handed her the milk. Asa drained the glass, knowing lactose in the liquid would work the fastest in her system. Zain watched her every move.

"They saw me. Thomas thinks I'm eating at the bar. Be right back. He took her plate of chicken divan, a delicious-looking chicken breast covered with asparagus and cheese. He left her with the cup of crawfish bisque and a slice of french bread.

Asa could see him through the slants. She dipped her spoon into the creamy soup as she watched Zain sit at the bar. Lisa and Brent came walking toward him. Asa paused listening intently, hoping Zain wouldn't give her away. She absently lifted the spoon to her mouth. The taste of food was like heaven when her sugar was low.

"Hey, boss, what are you doing on this side of the river?" Asa heard Lisa say.

"What do they say?" Zain's strong voice rung loud and clear. "The west bank is the best bank."

"True," Brent agreed. "But don't eat at the bar. Join us."

The peppermint, milk, and the now-empty soup cup had worked wonders. Asa felt much better. She had to stop herself from yelling aloud to Zain, "No, no, no!" Instead she concentrated on willing him to say that one word.

"No thanks, my food's here. You two don't have to entertain me. Enjoy yourselves."

Brent and Lisa were walking away when Asa heard Zain ask, "Is this a first date?"

"More like a get-together to find something to eat kind of thing, right Lisa?"

"Yeah, that's it."

Asa giggled when she heard Lisa's none too cheery response. "That's what you think, Brent," Asa mumbled just as Zain came back with the rest of her food. She still felt as if she was starving.

"Thomas is in trouble then?" Zain set the plate before her.

"He doesn't know it, but yes." Asa had no shame in digging in right in front of him. She cut the chicken in small pieces, eating a forkful of rice and asparagus with every bite. He watched as she consumed the rest of her estimated seventy-five carbohydrates.

Plate empty, she leaned against the video poker machine behind her. A sigh of satisfaction and relief escaped her lips. She'd got food into her system and Brent hadn't spotted her.

"Asa."

She looked up. How could she have forgotten that the god of all men was standing before her. The joy of the moment disappeared. She wasn't ready to deal with this, but she had to. Asa pulled herself together. Zain moved the empty plates and sat on the stool before her, his back facing the far wall. This way he could see through the swinging door while still facing her. He leaned in close. Asa could feel his warm breath flow across her face.

"Don't do that," he said low and serious.

"What?" she squeaked.

"Fix that blank look on your face. It's so beautiful when you let it come alive."

"You shouldn't be saying that to me, Mr. Darby."

"Zain, like before, we're not at work." His hand gently cupped the side of her face. "I saw so many expressions on this face tonight. Do you save the blank one for me?"

She did, but Asa didn't want to tell him that. Instead she found herself saying, "Maybe."

"I'm going to have to do something about that."

His hand was gone. Asa wished it was back, warm and gentle on her cheek. She also wished it would never find its way there again. Zain Darby was too much of a man for her. He'd shown her that earlier. Add to that the fact that he was too self-centered, too dominating, just too much.

"They probably aren't gone." Asa tried to change the subject, wishing Brent and Lisa *would* leave.

"No, they're at the juke box." Zain leaned forward to peer at them. "Mmmm."

"Mmmmm, what?"

"Thomas is coming this way, probably to play some video poker."

"Zain, do something."

"What?"

"Anything. I don't want Brent to see me!"

"*Anything?*" he asked.

"Yes!"

Zain swallowed that word whole just as he'd done with the no she'd given him earlier.

"From what I can tell the video poker machines are full. And not exactly with poker players," Asa heard Brent say as if he were speaking through a hollow tube, the sound of the swinging door squeaking as distant and hollow as his voice. "Let's get our food to go. I'll show you the house I'm renovating…" Her cousin's voice faded, drifting away like the last soulful note from a trumpeter's song.

If Brent's voice was drifting, Asa, herself was riding the crest of a tremendous wave. It was drawing her in, persuading her, begging her to give a little of herself. A nip at her bottom lip, the top. A gentle deepening that washed over her, turning into more, so much more. He ended the kiss. Not suddenly, but with a trio of tiny lip-pressing caresses before slowly moving back.

"How was that for *anything?*"

"More than I wanted. I need something to drink." Asa peered into the bar just to be sure that Brent and Lisa were actually gone. "My usual, Ernie. "

"You don't need that," Zain told her sitting next to her at the bar.

"Yes, I do." Ernie put the water in front of her.

"If my kisses drive you to drink I can fix that."

"By not kissing me?"

"By never stopping. If you get high on me, you won't need anything else."

Asa took a gulp from her glass nearly swallowing the olive. "Zain—Mr. Darby."

His eyes narrowed at her.

"Mr. Darby," she repeated, "we can't do this."

"Why?"

Asa didn't want to tell him the truth, that she couldn't handle the power he had over her. Lisa's words about Brent's reasons for not asking her out again came to mind. "I don't believe in office romance."

"What about Thomas?"

He had her there. It was obvious. Zain had eyes. Of course he realized that she was trying to set Lisa and Brent up. Asa had spent the evening in the close confines of a video poker corner, promised to kiss her boss, and goodness knows what else all for the sake of an office romance. Brent. Too bad he didn't know all she'd done for him.

"That's completely different."

"Two people working in the same office, going out together. I'd consider that an office romance."

"All right, let me be more specific. I don't believe in office romances involving the boss."

"Okay, I fire myself."

Asa laughed, "Don't be ridiculous."

"I love that sound."

Asa swallowed the bubbles of laughter that had risen in her throat.

"I haven't heard that laugh since the first day in the elevator, when you tried to hide it from me. The sound exploded through the elevator door before the car could even begin to move down."

All amusement vanished from her face at his words. "This has gone far enough, Mr. Darby. It has to stop or I will have to quit."

Zain Darby's chocolate brown eyes gazed deeply into hers. He must have seen that she meant what she said because his face turned completely serious.

"If that's the way you want it, Ms. Taylor."

Asa drained her glass. "That's how I want it, Mr. Darby."

"How about one for the road?" Ernie asked.

"That's not a good idea," Zain Darby said before she could answer her friend.

"No, thank you, Ernie," Asa said clearly before retrieving her purse and walking out the white paneled door.

CHAPTER 6

"When is Mr. Handle due back?" Asa whispered to Lisa on her way to lunch. "Not for another week or so."

"A month-long honeymoon? What a luxury."

"He can afford it. I don't know if your nerves can take being around the boss nowadays."

"It's been rough but…"

"You're dealing with it. A whole lot better than I could."

Asa nodded, agreeing with Lisa. What she was actually thinking was that dealing with Zain Darby's foul moods was better than holding off his amorous advances.

"Hey there, good looking." Brent came over and landed a kiss on Lisa's lips.

"I don't know what to say about you two," Asa gushed.

"How about, have a good lunch?" Lisa suggested.

"Have a good lunch," Asa repeated, waving them off. "I am so jealous," she whispered to herself, watching Brent and Lisa walk into the elevator.

"No need to be jealous, Ms. Taylor. I'll have lunch with you," Zain Darby announced behind her.

"No, thank you. I'm headed to the lunchroom and I know the way."

"So am I. Why don't you lead."

Asa did lead the way, not wanting to annoy him. Since the night she'd threatened to quit Zain Darby had been acting like an alligator with a toothache. For the last two weeks she'd walked a fine line for sanity's sake. If she shifted, if the least thing went wrong, Zain Darby exploded as if he, the alligator, had slammed his mouth shut banging that aching tooth of his. He then shared the pain with her and everyone else.

Asa got most of it. Grammy Dee, who called almost every day, got none of it. Asa couldn't understand how a man who was so giving, respectful and genuinely caring for his grandmother could be so unsympathetic toward her.

Zain Darby had tried to disrupt her schedule in any way he could. He called her in to dictate at her snack times, rescheduled meetings with clients that overlapped her break or lunch times. He even took to throwing a comment or two at her. "Peppermints will rot your teeth." And her favorites, "It's not healthy to be so rigid," and "Inflexible people live shorter lives."

If that were true, his inflexible attitude toward her schedule would have him gone way before his time. Asa felt as if he were trying to shake her up to get her attention. He even went as far as changing the times on all the clocks one day. Asa wished that Zain Darby would fixate on something other than her.

Asa took her lunch bag from the fridge. She ignored his staring eyes as she opened a container of plain yogurt, added fresh strawberries and a packet of sweetner.

"That's your lunch?"

"A part of it."

"Telephone, Mr. Darby." Trisha, the girl who covered the desk while Lisa was at lunch came to say.

"That's probably Grammy Dee. I talked to her earlier. She wanted to speak to you, Ms. Taylor, but you were on your morning break. I knew that I couldn't possibly interrupt that."

"If it is Grammy, Mr. Darby, please tell her that I'll call her after lunch." Asa had spoken to the nice lady each time she called, keeping up the facade, not having the heart to tell her the truth.

"That might not work."

"Yes, it will. I'm her sweet angel."

Zain Darby actually smiled at that. "Yes, you are," he agreed, his smile turning sad before leaving to answer the phone.

Asa finished her yogurt and strawberries, refusing to speculate on the reason he might be sad. She reached inside her lunch bag for the tuna sandwich she'd made this morning.

"Asa!" Zain stormed back into the lunchroom. "That was Mr. Vallet. He's got an out-of-town emergency and can't make tomorrow's meeting. He's rescheduled for lunch today. We have to leave!"

"But I'm eating lunch right now!"

"You can start all over again at the Dry Dock Cafe."

"The Dry Dock?"

"That's where he wants to meet."

"You planned this, didn't you."

He shook his head. "Client's choice. Why would *I* sabotage your rigid schedule?"

"All right, give me a minute."

"You've got two."

Zain Darby seemed suddenly very pleased with himself. She hadn't seen him this happy since before she threatened to quit. Asa smelled a rat. She counted the carbs she'd eaten in her head, replacing her afternoon snack for the rest of her lunch. By the time she got to the Dry Dock it would be way past her allotted lunch time. She would have to consume the rest of her carbs as quickly as possible. She went to her desk, grabbed her purse and drained the contents of a can of chocolate-flavored Choice beverage. That would do it. Now, when everyone else was eating lunch, Asa wasn't sure what she would be doing. Maybe pretending to eat a salad. That should work, lettuce had little or no carbs anyway.

They walked the short distance to the ferry. It felt strange sharing this walk with Zain. Um, Mr. Darby, she reminded herself. Although he slipped and called her Asa, she would not do the same. Especially since they were going to the Dry Dock.

"I've seen you walk this way almost everyday."

"It's the way I go home."

"With Thomas."

"It's the way he goes home."

Zain was quiet for the next block. He said not a word as they climbed the steps to the ferry's pedestrian entrance. They stood at the rail, both of them, it seemed, wanting to stand outside to feel the breeze from the water. April's heat was too much to bear in the stifling indoor section.

"So, are you okay with how things have worked out?"

"What things?"

"With Thomas."

"Brent?" Asa was leery of answering his question. He was getting a little personal, but this one didn't directly involve her so she felt safe enough to say, "I think he and Lisa are good for each other."

"And you're okay with that?"

"Mr. Darby, you are getting too personal."

"Sorry, I didn't mean to. I don't want you threatening to quit on me again."

He stared out at the muddy water. Asa turned toward the eastern bank of the river, her favorite view. She searched the shoreline trying to find something new. Asa always discovered something she'd missed before, no matter how many times she searched.

The ferry docked. The ramp was lowered, and Asa had not made one new discovery. She knew why. Zain Darby was standing next to her, destroying her concentration.

Disgusted with herself, Asa walked down the steps and crossed the street to the Dry Dock Cafe. Mr. Darby opened the door for her.

"Don't you think this is a strange place to have a business lunch?" Asa asked, waiting at the door for her eyes to adjust to the dim lighting inside the neighborhood restaurant.

"This is where Mr. Vallet wanted to meet. What can I say? The food's good, right?"

"But some of the memories aren't." Asa avoided even glancing in the direction of the video poker machines where Zain had kissed her with so much power and passion less than two weeks ago.

Zain didn't have that problem. His eyes had been scanning the restaurant for their client, but they strayed to that corner more than once. "He isn't here yet."

"There's my friend Ernie. Let's sit at the bar." Asa moved in that direction.

Zain reached for her arm, grabbed her purse instead, breaking the strap. The entire contents of her bag were spread across the floor.

Asa bent to retrieve her personal belongings.

"I didn't mean to do that." He stooped to help her.

Asa quickly grabbed the small medicine pack with her insulin, shoving it inside the bag, not wanting him to ask questions or even mention her medication. His attitude towards her diabetes was a sensitive issue with her.

Asa took her lipstick, mirror, and change purse from his hands and put them back into her purse.

"You all right there, Asa?" Ernie asked.

"Just a little accident," she told him.

"What's this?" Zain asked, holding a battered plastic cylinder-shaped container out to her. It held glucose tabs. Asa grabbed it from him, hoping he didn't know what they were. It wasn't easy to tell what was inside the white, plastic container. The outer covering had long ago worn off. She must have had that pack of glucose tablets in her purse for a year. She'd rarely had any low-blood sugar episodes until she met Zain, and preferred to handle them with juice instead of the big chalky tablets. They were her backup.

Zain's chocolate-colored eyes bore into her. Asa could feel the questions he didn't ask. Hopefully the ones he wouldn't ask. Why was he so weird about her needs?

"I'm going to the restroom. Maybe Mr. Vallet will be here when I get back."

"Hey, Asa!" Ernie called as she passed the bar. "The ususal?"

"When I get back, but make it a double, and add an extra olive."

Zain headed straight for the bar, ready to knock some sense into that blond-headed bartender.

"Mr. Darby, good afternoon."

Zain turned to find his client at the restaurant door. "Mr. Vallet."

"I hope I didn't keep you waiting too long. I had a little trouble finding the place."

"Not at all. I'm just glad you did."

"Giving you the option of choosing the meeting place was the least I could do, having to change our appointment at the last minute."

"Don't mention it." *Ever again*, Zain added to himself, searching for Asa, expecting her to return any minute. Hopefully after Mr. Vallet stopped commenting on the fact that *he* had chosen to meet here.

"Let's have a seat." Zain led him to an empty table. Asa came out of the restroom a moment later. Zain watched her walk down the steps to the bar, talk and smile with Ernie the enabler, before coming to the table. Both Zain and Mr. Vallet stood.

"This is Asa Taylor, my secretary, Mr. Vallet."

"Pleased to meet you, Mr. Vallet." Asa had a smile for the client. She had a smile for everyone except him.

"Same here, Ms. Taylor."

She frowned at him, Zain noticed. The waitress came to take their drink order.

"Ernie already has my order," Asa told the waitress, making Zain's stomach twist, wishing he had gotten his hands on Ernie.

Here was a bartender no more than three blocks from her house, encouraging her to drink, probably making it easy for her to get wasted. Maybe he took her home every night and was even taking advantage of her. That thought send a furious need to land his fist in the bartender's face, but Zain didn't give into it. He was handling this whole situation with Asa his own way. Zain had learned all about enablers at the first Al-Anon meeting he'd gone to last week. His strong suspicion that Asa was an alcoholic drove him to act, that action being joining a local Al-Anon group. He would attend the weekly Al-Anon meetings in order to understand more about the addiction. The people there would help him to help her. Zain needed to do this for Asa because already she had gotten to him.

Thomas, he thought as Asa conversed with the client, might be an enabler too. Zain wasn't sure. But that Ernie guy...Zain stared at the bartender from his table. He was adding two olives to the martini he had just placed on the bar. Who drank martinis nowadays anyway? Asa did, it seemed.

Zain turned toward her just as Mr. Vallet asked, "Do you come here often?"

"I live close by, so I stop in once in awhile."

More than once in awhile, I bet, Zain said to himself.

"Then perhaps it was you who suggested—"

"Our drinks are here!" Zain interrupted.

The waitress served the drinks. Zain had ordered a Coke, not wanting to encourage Asa in the least. He wasn't much of a drinker anyway. Mr. Vallet had an iced tea, and Asa of course, had the double martini. She raised her glass as a toast to Ernie across the restaurant, the bar visible from where they sat. Then she smiled that beautiful smile at him.

"Why don't we get down to business," Zain suggested after they each gave their order.

On cue Asa took out her pen and pad, ignoring the glass before her. He had to hand it to her, Asa was always serious about work. If her hands were busy, she couldn't drink.

She kept a record of the specifics Mr. Vallet was looking for as protection for his computer files. Zain kept the conversation going, dragging out each and every detail as he waited for the food to come. The waitress had come and gone twice, refilling Mr. Vallet's glass. Zain didn't touch his and, surprisingly, neither did Asa. At least not until they were done. Once the deal was set, Asa lifted the glass draining it in one swallow.

"Careful, that stuff goes right to your head," Mr. Vallet warned.

"No need to worry," Asa told him.

Denial. Asa was in denial. She was a functioning alcoholic. How did she do it? He had no idea. How could such a beautiful, gifted young woman do this to herself?

Business done, they sat at the table chatting about various things. Asa had two more martinis before the food arrived. A small salad was all she had ordered. Mr. Vallet had the seafood platter, and Zain the oyster plate.

"Surely that won't fill you up," Mr. Vallet commented.

"This is more than enough."

Zain wished she felt that way about the amount of alcohol she was consuming. Before the waitress could leave, Zain heard Asa request, "Could you ask Ernie to fix another one of my special drinks, please?"

Zain had had enough of this. "Excuse me," he told them, heading straight to the bar.

"Ernie," he called.

"How can I help ya?"

"You can help me by forgetting that last drink order."

"But it's for Asa."

"Not anymore." Ernie had the nerve to try to stare him down.

When Zain didn't back down, the enabler opened his mouth to say, "If you got a problem with this, you better take it up with Asa. She asked for a drink, I'm going to give her a drink.

"Besides it's only—"

"Something wrong?" Asa came up behind him.

Ernie kept his eyes on him, Zain's look an order the other man ignored.

"Nothing. Here's your drink, Asa."

"Three olives this time. You're too good to me, Ernie."

"I aim to please. You especially, beautiful lady."

"Don't let Sherry hear that."

"She won't, she's off today."

Asa laughed. The laughter died as soon as her eyes settled on him again. "Can I have a word with you, Mr. Darby?"

"Would you like to go to our corner?"

"I didn't know there was such a thing. Right here will do."

"Mr. Vallet just left. He had an emergency. He said to thank you for introducing him to another fine New Orleans restaurant."

"Oh, he did?" was all Zain could think to say. He was trapped and he knew it.

"I've discovered many things about you, Mr. Darby. You're a bully, a grouch, and a liar. I can't work in this kind of environment anymore."

"Asa—Ms. Taylor," he amended at her hard look.

"I'm going home now. I'll see you the day after Easter when I turn in my resignation. Forget about a two week notice. I'm sure you'll agree that under the circumstances it should be waived. Either way, I won't be coming back."

Zain stood in front of the Dry Dock. This had to be the lowest point of his life. He, the master of everything he touched, had masterfully destroyed his chances of ever making Asa Taylor see him as anything other than a bully, a grouch, and a liar.

Oh, he'd lied, but it was out of necessity and desperation. By bringing Asa back to the place where they'd shared that soul-searching kiss, Zain thought he might get her to remember it. It didn't work. She hated him, thought he was the lowest of the low.

Zain peeled off his suit jacket and walked up to the top of the levee overlooking the river. The ferry had just landed on the east bank. Another was making its way toward him. He wouldn't go back to work. Zain wasn't in the mood for work. Another first. He finally understood his partner. This was what love could do to a man.

Zain stood in that one spot watching a tugboat push a laden barge down the river. Love was like that tugboat. It pushed you. It didn't matter how big or heavy the load was, the tugboat exerted enough force to push those barges down the river. No matter how much he resisted, love pushed him toward Asa Taylor, drove him to act like a fool. But Zain wasn't a fool. He'd find a way not only to have her, but to save her from herself.

Zain walked along the gravel-topped levee letting his mind wander through his options. It was obvious Asa was attracted to him as much as he was to her. It was just as obvious that she didn't want to be. Zain needed to find a way to show her his best side. Even he had to admit she had seen only his worst. The levee became his thinking ground as he walked from one end to the other. The sun had gone down, the hour was late as he finally boarded the ferry heading back to the CBD and his office.

CHAPTER 7

"Stop your moping. You've got a Friday off. How often does that happen?" "It's Good Friday, Brent. I have just been in a prayerful, reflective mood." Asa dipped her pancake into a puddle of sugar-free syrup. She hadn't told Brent about quitting yesterday. She had never told him about her trouble with Zain, her silence, consequences of exerting her independence. She would have to tell him about quitting but decided to wait until after the holiday was over.

"Don't get too reflective, it might turn into depression. It's a good thing Easter's only three days away so that you won't have long to wallow in this reflective moping."

"We'll be in Florida then."

"Visiting our wonderful parents."

"Reason enough to mope."

"We haven't seen them since Christmas."

"Don't get me wrong. I'm dying to spend time with Auntie Reenie and Uncle Boyd. It's my own parents I'm dreading to see."

"It won't be so bad."

"You weren't on that ski vacation they convinced me to go on after Christmas."

"It won't be so bad, cuz. Lisa's coming along."

Asa perked up at that. "Oh, you're moving in that direction, are you?"

"Maybe," was all he would say.

Brent cleaned up the dishes since it had been Asa's turn to make breakfast. "What are you doing with yourself today?"

Asa smiled to herself. He hadn't assumed that she would be spending her day with him. Brent had come a long way in the last few weeks. "I don't know, hang around, clean, go to the post office and church. There's a prayer service at three o'clock."

"Don't forget—"

"—to have a snack beforehand," they said together.

"Won't," Asa grinned at her cousin.

"That's the first time I said anything today."

"You're right, and thank you."

Brent went back to his side of the house, closing the kitchen door behind him. He would probably be spending the day with Lisa. He had been spending a lot of time with his new girlfriend and less and less with her. Which was good, Asa reminded herself. Brent was finally in a real relationship. Asa, on the other hand, had nothing. No man, no job, nothing. Well, she had her health and that was a good thing. Always focus on the good things in life, Auntie Reenie had always told her. Too bad her own mother had a problem living that adage.

Asa hung around the house, cleaned, and walked to the post office two blocks away to mail a few bills. The neighborhood post office was actually a quaint little card and gift shop as well as a contracted post office. Asa loved browsing in this little store. The smell of scented candles hit her nostrils as soon as she walked inside. Cards, stickers, stuffed animals, picture frames and all sorts of knick-knacks sat on shelves waiting to be bought.

Asa took her time looking around, studying the many familiar postcards depicting New Orleans scenes, reading cards, and getting a closer sniff of the candles that hung from one of the walls, finally making her way to the counter. The friendly gentleman sold her some stamps and Asa left her bills to be mailed. She then walked three blocks over to church.

Asa loved living in Algiers Point. The Point, as it was called, couldn't be classified as simply a neighborhood or even a subdivision. It was more like a little town all its own within the big city.

The prayer service wasn't very long but helped Asa put things into perspective. Her depressing mood lifted a bit. Zain. There, she'd said his name. Asa hadn't wanted to even think it this morning. Zain was not worth being depressed over. Jesus had died with grace, giving up his life for humanity. What had she given up but another intolerable job with an insufferable man? That's what Zain Darby was, that's exactly how she had to think of him, not remembering a thing about his powerful kisses or his deep, chocolate-brown eyes.

Asa was nearly home when she spotted the insufferable man on her porch. She almost turned back to seek the sanctuary of the church, its beautiful stained glass windows and soothing blue interior always having a calming effect on her. She decided not to run. She could be an adult. That meant facing people or situations that were uncomfortable. Not that Zain Darby ever made her feel comfortable.

Asa stopped in front of her house. "What are you doing here?"

"Hoping to see you," he turned to tell her.

The roaring of waves in her ear, the rising of her blood that had started long before she stood before him, increased with the sound of his voice. The storm was surging once again. He looked so-o-o-o good. Not grouchy, not full of himself, simply charming, as corny as that sounded.

But Zain was no Prince Charming. The charming god. Yeah, that was more like it.

Instinctively Asa knew what he was about. Zain Darby stood on her porch, oozing charm all right but only because he wanted something. Whatever it was, he wasn't going to get it.

"You have seen me, you can go now, Mr. Darby." Asa used her calmest, driest tone. It was a false calm, a calm she didn't feel, like the calm before a storm which was sure to be intense.

"Let's start over. I came to talk to you." Without hesitation he asked, "Do you mind if we go inside?"

"Yes, I mind."

"The porch will have to do then," he conceded.

"It's as good a place as any to...talk."

He nodded once. "I want to talk to you about yesterday."

"Yesterday you were no different than you've ever been since the moment I met you, Mr. Darby." Asa's words were directed at him but her eyes were trying to focus on something besides his handsome brown face. They finally strayed to the house across the street. It was the one Brent had been working on. He was there now. She could tell by the loud hammering noises coming from inside.

"That's not fair, Asa."

She turned at her name the sound of it from his lips building a wave of desire inside her. "It's more than fair, Mr. Darby." She turned to look across the street again, unable to hold his gaze as the waves increased, and the storm moved in closer.

"I have some things to say to you, but I can't say them standing out in the open on a porch."

"Then you won't be saying them at all."

Asa was moving up the steps, planing to go inside alone when Brent came jogging across the street. He hopped onto the porch and in one breath asked, "The door open? I forgot my keys."

Asa shook her head before tossing the keys to him.

"I'm glad you're here. We need a little water. It is hot in there." He threw Asa's keys back to her, just then noticing Zain. "Hey, Mr. Darby, what are you doing in our neck of the woods again?"

"Business."

"Thought it was a day off. Things as usual then, huh?"

Brent ran in and out in a flash, carrying two bottles of water. He gave her a quick kiss on the forehead as he passed. "Thanks, Asa girl." He was across the street and out of sight a second later.

"He's so happy," Asa whispered, forgetting Zain Darby was still on her porch.

"He has a *key*?"

"Mr. Darby, you're still here?"

"Five minutes inside. You can time me."

Asa looked straight at him for the second time today. She knew it was a mistake the minute she heard herself say, "Five minutes is all you'll get."

He followed her inside.

Her living room, the first room in the house, was sparsely furnished. A sofa, a few paintings, that was about it. Zain and his power filled the entire room. With a wave of his arm he directed her to sit on her own sofa. Only after she sat did he find a place at the other end of the sofa. That move surprised her. His entire manner was throwing her completely off guard.

"For the next five minutes, please call me Zain."

Asa nodded.

"Forgive me."

Those were the last two words Asa expected to hear come out of Zain Darby's mouth, ever!

"I've been a sorry excuse for a boss, for a man with principles." He was staring into her eyes, his own troubled as if he was worried that she wouldn't believe him. "This is hard for me, Asa."

"Me, too. You've got me wondering if this is all some sort of line."

"No—no." He paused for a minute, almost as if he didn't know what to say next. "These are the heartfelt words of a man falling in love, Asa."

She stood. "You didn't say that!"

"I did."

"You didn't mean that." Asa sat back down since standing was much too difficult for her to do right then.

"I have never been more serious about anything in my life."

"How can I believe this? You have been nothing but horrible to me!"

"Always?"

"No, not always," Asa reluctantly agreed, remembering his overpowering kisses, "but mostly."

"It was only because you've been twisting me up in knots."

"You haven't been making me feel too great either, you know."

He smiled at her, the charm, the power of Zain Darby increasing the storm's potency and possible destruction. "Seems like we have something serious going on here."

"Sounds like some kind of deadly virus, don't you think?" Her little joke didn't seem to bother him much because that smile of his didn't leave his face for a second. His reaction bothered her, everything about him bothered her. Asa began to pace, just as Zain did when he gave dictation. But in her living room she had limited space. She brushed past him twice, the storm rising each time she made contact. "Your stomach is twisting, my blood is rising, making me feel—"

"—hot all over? That's encouraging." Zain was right in front of her. His arms had landed on her shoulders. Asa stood trapped by his melting chocolate gaze.

"Zain, you don't understand."

"I do." His head leaned down toward her neck. Then he did the strangest thing. He took a deep breath, then released it, letting the warm air caress her neck before kissing his way under her jaw, her chin and then finding her lips. Lips that were ready this time.

Asa experienced a wave of passion that would not allow her to deny that Zain was what she wanted. He was hers for the moment. She kissed him, really kissed him, with her entire being. Her lips pulled his inside where her tongue claimed possession of him.

It was Zain who pulled back a breathtaking, disappointing moment later.

"Breathe, Asa, breathe," he whispered into her ear.

Asa released a pent-up breath she hadn't realized she had been holding.

He held her then. Asa slowly felt the storm inside her quiet, only to rise again at the sound of his voice.

"What don't I understand, Asa?"

Quickly, naturally, and without thought, Asa answered, "You make me feel so uncomfortable."

Zain laughed. "That could be considered an asset."

"That's not what I mean." Asa broke out of his arms. "It's more than this sexual tension. Don't you see? I'm simply not comfortable around you."

"That's because you don't know the real me."

"I've seen enough."

"Only my bad side, and that was because you had me so tied up." When she said nothing to this, Zain continued, "You've got to admit, Asa, that you've seen glimpses of the better side of me."

Asa remembered their little conversations at her desk and his kindness for Grammy Dee. "So you're telling me there's more to know."

"Yes, a whole lot more."

Asa needed to think on that a second. Her blood was still moving in waves but her head was clearer. Without saying another word she walked to the back of her house toward the kitchen. He followed. She grabbed a bottle of water, silently offering him one.

"No, thanks."

"Then what do you want, Zain?"

"For you to be a part of my life. For you to come back to work."

"I meant to drink."

"Nothing. I want you."

"To come back to work." Asa questioned.

"That, too."

"Why, when we have all this tension between us?"

"So that I can be with you all the time. So that I can prove to you what a nice, fair, decent guy I am."

"Is that all?"

"So that I'm not left hanging without the best secretary/assistant I've ever had."

"Nice try."

"It's true. I need you."

"Is that what this is all about, me coming back to work?"

"No, I told you, I think I'm falling in love."

Asa still didn't want to deal with that declaration. Zain, she felt, didn't know what he was saying. She didn't know how she felt about him yet, so how could he know that he was falling in love with her? "Then how can we have a working relationship?"

"It's possible." At her skeptical look he continued, "Let's make a deal. Come back for the next two weeks, just until Lance comes home from his honeymoon. Then we can find someone else; that is, if you still want to leave."

"What about this other thing between us?"

"I was hoping we could start anew. Take it as slow as you want."

"No fooling around at work."

"If you say so."

"I don't want anyone to know."

"It'll be our secret."

Asa felt his arms around her. She hadn't even seen him move close enough to touch her. Funny how they suddenly felt so comfortable there.

"Let's seal this deal with a kiss."

Asa did, this time ending before they could get carried away. She walked with him to the front door.

"I'll call you tonight?"

Asa nodded. Zain gave her one more quick kiss. He was halfway out the door but came back, pausing a minute before he said, "About Thomas."

"Brent is nothing to worry about."

Zain looked as if he was about to say more when Brent and Lisa came up the steps, both sweaty and laughing.

"Come to the car and I'll get those files for you." Zain made up a quick excuse for their benefit, already easing Asa's mind, assuring her by his actions that she had made the right decision.

"Hey boss," Lisa called. "Brent said that you were here."

Zain gave a nod of acknowledgment.

"Excuse us," Brent said, moving into the house. "I mean to spend some time in some good old modern air-conditioning with a beautiful woman at my side."

Lisa giggled. They went into the house, leaving Asa and Zain alone.

"I see what you mean."

"Lisa has him completely occupied now."

"Do you like it that way?"

"Yes, I do."

"Me too."

Zain leaned over to kiss her again. Then before she knew it, Zain was in his car and driving away. Asa stared at the retreating car. One conversation, one kiss had changed so many things. Change was usually good. But would it be good for her in this case?

❉

"You sure are in a good mood, boy."

"So are you, Grammy Dee." Today was one of her good days. Miss Rose had informed him of that as he was coming in and she was leaving. She had also invited him and Grammy for Easter Sunday dinner with her family.

His grandmother stared at him a good, long minute. "More than a good mood."

"I'm happy."

"Then get your happy self over here and play a game of Boo-ray with me."

"That's exactly what I want to do."

Zain played cards with Grammy for an hour or so, leaving just before the evening nurse came in with her medication.

"Last dose for today!" the cheery lady told his grandmother.

"I know, it's the same time every evening," Grammy complained eyeing the clock on the wall.

Zain bent to kiss her. "I'll leave you to take your medicine."

"You're not getting away that fast. Before I swallow these pills tell me where you've been hiding my sweet angel. I haven't talked to her in days."

"You talked to her the day before yesterday, and she's not hiding."

"Then bring her over tomorrow. I'll be waiting. We can play some cards."

"Whatever you say, Grammy."

Zain left his grandmother, dying to turn the car in the direction of Asa's house. But he wouldn't. Not when this afternoon had gone so smooth. Zain wasn't going to ruin a relationship that had barely begun by being pushy, despite that being a known trait of his.

Too impatient to wait for the ferry, and knowing that route took him too close to Asa, Zain drove toward the Crescent City Connection, one of the twin bridges spanning the Mississippi. Traffic was light this late in the evening and he was home in no time. Zain drove into the parking lot of his condo on Lake Ponchartrain, not far from the Orleans/Jefferson parish line.

Asa seemed to love the river. Zain had a deep appreciation for the lake. It was much wider, calmer, and at least
appeared to be cleaner than the river. Lake Pontchartrain
wasn't quite clean enough for swimming but Zain had a
boat docked at the marina near his home. When he had
time he spent an hour or two out on the lake.

He went straight to the balcony overlooking the wide,
blue water. The cordless phone that he picked up along the
way was in his hand. Zain dialed Asa's number, having long
ago memorized it.

"Hello."

Her voice sounded breathless, as if she'd been running.
Zain wondered if her voice would hold such a raspy sound
when he made love to her. The few kisses they'd shared had
quickened her breath, he'd noticed. Zain bet that he could
make her lose it entirely.

"Hello," she said again.

"Hello there, yourself." Zain finally answered, his mind
refocusing, concentrating on speaking to her now, instead
of his wishful fantasy for later.

"Zain?" Her voice had lost that breathless quality.

"Were you busy?"

"No, I just finished a workout."

"You work out?"

"Treadmill. Almost everyday. I have to stay in shape.
Keep healthy."

Zain was pleased to hear this. If she was interested in
staying healthy, then she should be able to recognize the
dangers of excessive alcohol consumption. "You're in pretty
good shape already," he found himself saying.

"Nice of you to say so. It's because I work out."

"See, you've used the word 'nice' while referring to me already."

"That was very humble of you to mention."

"I've never claimed to have humility. The faults I can admit to are pride and a strong sense of confidence in myself." Zain knew this was true, but had never said as much to anyone.

Asa laughed. "Overconfidence, perhaps."

"I like that sound."

"Me? Laughing?"

"You laughing, and being able to detect an actual inflection in your voice."

"Since you confided a secret, I'll uncover one of mine."

"I can't wait."

"My lack of inflection, my calm business voice, I knew it drove you crazy. That was my main reason for using it so often."

"What's the other?"

"One secret at a time. I might let you in on the other one tomorrow."

"That's how it's going to be? A secret a night?"

"That sounds like a good way to start."

"Asa, I love that idea. It'll give me the opportunity to uncover the real you." Zain found himself intrigued and couldn't stop himself from visualizing a prim and proper Asa standing before him as he peeled away each layer of her ordinary clothes, uncovering the extraordinary body he knew must lie beneath.

"Then maybe I'll eventually discover this nice guy you keep telling me about." Asa told him, dispersing the vision.

Zain laughed.

"I think I like that sound," she told him. "You don't laugh that much yourself."

"Then we should be good for each other."

The line was dead quiet for a minute.

"Asa."

"Zain."

They spoke at the same time.

"Go on," she said.

"What are you doing tomorrow?"

"There's an Easter egg hunt at church. I'm volunteering. Would you like to come?"

"Yes." Zain jumped at the idea. Nice guys went to things like Easter egg hunts for kids at churches. Any chance to be with Asa was reason enough. He felt empty when she wasn't around.

"I haven't been to one in years. You'd have to show me what to do."

"You hide the eggs and stand back."

"Sounds easy. What about after the hunt? Care to visit Grammy Dee?"

"Oh, sure." She sounded a bit disappointed. Zain was pleased that Asa had shown that she actually wanted to be with him.

"Grammy has demanded your presence."

"I'd like to see her again."

"Afterwards we can go out, get some dinner, spend some time together."

"Sounds like you have our entire day planned."

"I thought we were planning it together."

"A good thought."

"Asa."

"Yes."

"Say my name."

"Zain."

"A good sound. What time should I come over?"

"Nine o'clock. The hunt's for twelve but we're dyeing eggs first and have to get things together."

"I'll be there."

"Goodnight, then."

"Goodnight, Asa." Zain hung up. "I love you," he whispered to himself. He laid the phone on his chest and wallowed in the idea that he had an entire day with Asa that had nothing to do with work.

CHAPTER 8

"Where are you going so early this morning?" "The Easter egg hunt," Asa told Brent. "That's not till twelve."

"I have to be there early. We're dyeing eggs and setting up before the place gets mobbed."

"Then I better get myself together."

Brent went into the backyard and into the shed. A few years ago he had designed and painted wooden cutouts of bunnies, rabbits, baskets, and other springtime characters for the hunt. He came back into the house as Asa stood in the kitchen filling a backpack with some boxes of dyes and plastic cups.

"I think I need Lisa's help."

"I bet you do."

"Thanks, Asa."

"For what?" she asked absently, searching the contents of the fridge to find something to make for lunch.

"Lisa let the cat out of the bag and told me about your little help in getting us together."

"She did, huh?" Asa cautiously peeked over the fridge door to ask, not sure how Brent felt about her interference.

"I don't know how you found out that it was Lisa I took out last December, but I'm glad you did. I've been pushing you around for so long I guess I needed a push in the right direction myself. Lisa's the best thing to happen to me in a long time."

"I agree. Go call her."

"Wait a minute, I have something for you." Brent went into his kitchen. He came back with a small container in his hand. "Fresh pineapple would make a good morning snack. I just cut it last night."

"About fifteen carbs, I bet."

"Exactly."

Asa couldn't be upset with him. Brent had really shown a lot of restraint lately. "Thanks, cuz."

"Old habits die hard."

Asa put the pineapple into her lunch bag and proceeded to make a sandwich for later. "See you at the church," Asa yelled into Brent's side of the house before she left.

She sat on the front porch to wait for Zain. A few of her neighbors passed by, walking their dogs or themselves. A family rode by heading toward the bike path on the levee that began near the Dry Dock Cafe.

Zain wasn't long in coming. He parked his Lexus at the curb near the house. "This is a welcoming sight." he said coming onto the porch.

"Good morning to you, too."

"Good morning," he said laying a soft kiss on her lips.

The kiss was quick and sweet. Asa stopped herself from reminding him that they were out in the open where anyone with eyes could see, making their secret relationship not much of a secret. It wasn't worth it. That brief connection warmed her, softly churning a tiny wave inside. "Ready to get started?" she asked instead.

"I'm ready for anything today."

"Don't be so sure about that." Asa watched Zain go to the passenger door of his car. She stopped him before he opened the door for her. "Oh, no, we're walking."

"We are?" He opened the door anyway and pulled out a backpack much like her own.

"It's only a few blocks away. Not far enough to get your blood pumping, but a good start."

"Mine's been going double time since the second I pulled up to see this beautiful woman waiting for me."

Asa stopped midway down the steps. "Zain, please," she said, a hand on her hip.

"I know how it sounds." He stood in front of her looking directly into her eyes, her position on the steps bringing them on eye level. "I'm serious. Being with you does things to me, Asa."

"I understand and completely empathize. But you need to remember that we're going to a church function—with children. There is a certain type of behavior that is expected of adults," she told him, holding in a laugh.

"As if I didn't know."

His eyes still held hers. Asa thought that he was about to kiss her again. She was sure that it would be just as sweet as the one before but nowhere as quick. She moved past him and began to walk down the sidewalk, not wanting to give in to temptation.

Zain was at her side. He took one of her hands in his. "Is this acceptable?"

Asa looked him up and down, taking in everything about him, his handsome brown face, his attire, the firm yet gentle grip he had of her hand. "More than."

They walked the next two blocks in a comfortable silence. Asa mentally compared the casual Zain to the business Zain. He was always absolutely gorgeous, powerful, in those business suits he wore. But Zain in a pair of tight jeans, tennis shoes and a pullover was just too much.

"What's in the bag?" Asa asked, remembering the back pack he'd gotten out of the car that was now slung over his shoulder.

"Execute's contribution to the Easter egg hunt." Zain released her hand and slowed as he pulled out a metallic-coated plastic egg.

Asa felt a strong sense of loss now that the warmth of his hand was gone, but was working on dealing with it as Zain opened the egg and began to tell her about his contribution to the egg hunt.

"Inside each of these eggs is a crisp one dollar bill. I've got five dozen. Do you think that will be enough?"

"It should be. That's very generous of you, Zain."

"Just a little something extra." He shrugged his shoulders as if it didn't matter. Something a nice guy would do. Zain Darby was either playing a part or really showing a side of him she didn't know. "After talking to you last night," he continued a moment later, "this old brain of mine—"

"Old?"

"Pushing thirty-three. I'm getting there."

"Far from old."

"We won't discuss that right now. What I was about to say was that I remembered going to one of these Easter egg hunts when I was a kid. I couldn't have been more than ten."

"Twenty-three long years ago."

"Yeah," he laughed.

He'd laughed at himself. Asa smiled. She liked a man who liked to laugh, one who could laugh at himself. She had known almost from the moment she met him that she was attracted to him, but to like him? Asa was finding herself doing that quite easily.

"—at a church function like the one we're going to," his voice rolled on. Asa took her head out of the layer of niceness surrounding Zain to listen to what he was saying. "Grammy Dee took me."

"She did a lot with you, didn't she?"

"Everything. She raised me."

"We've got something in common then. Neither one of us was raised by our parents."

"Mine died," Zain said matter-of-factly.

"Mine didn't have time for me."

"Sorry, Asa."

"Not your fault. Go on. You were at an Easter egg hunt…"

"Right. There was a special egg hidden with money inside. I was the lucky one to find it."

"Let me guess. You bought ice cream and candy with it."

"No, I felt bad that all the other kids didn't have one so I put it in the poor box."

"You're pulling my leg."

"Ask Grammy Dee when you see her today."

"I will," Asa promised, needing confirmation on a tale that smacked of niceness.

"I brought enough to make sure that everyone gets one special egg. When they find one, they can't keep another. That's why I got the shiny ones."

"Sounds like a good plan."

When they reached the churchyard a few parishioners were already there setting up tables. Zain joined in carrying out a few more, helping her lay newspaper on the tables and prepare the dyes.

"I can't remember having so much fun playing with vinegar."

"I can see that," Asa said, watching him measure a tablespoon of the acidic liquid and study the tablet as it dissolved. She was still amazed at the difference between the business Zain and one here with her today. Tearing her eyes away from the handsome relaxed Zain, Asa glanced at her watch, ten o'clock, snack time. "Be right back, I have to take a little break."

"A break?" He looked up from staring at the dye changing from a pill into a bubbly green liquid. "You take those on a weekend too?"

"It's a necessity. Go back to playing with your vinegar. I'll be back in a minute."

"This is not playing," Asa heard him shout. "It's science. I'm studying chemical reactions."

Zain watched as she ran into church's rectory. Ten o'clock he noticed on the clock tower. What was it with Asa and schedules? Did everything have to be so precise? He certainly hoped she didn't have any intention on timing the intervals of when he could kiss her or when they made love. *Whoa, man! You're getting a little ahead of yourself.* Zain went back to conducting his little experiments.

Two ladies, each holding a huge colander, came outside. The sight of wispy smoke rising from the colanders told

Zain they held eggs, straight out of boiling water. Zain rushed forward to help them. He set the eggs on two separate tables. The ladies nodded their thanks and went about setting spoons and paper plates, stickers and wax crayons on the tables. Zain hoped the kids wouldn't come too soon because those eggs looked like they needed some cooling. He did too. He was surprised but relieved that Asa had taken her scheduled break. Being around her all morning with nothing challenging to distract his mind beyond vinegar, dye and water had him as hot as those eggs. Which explained his fascination with making dyes. While those eggs' futures involved being dipped and colored, Zain hoped his would be more promising. He wanted Asa in his life. He could already imagine himself changed because of Asa. She was one woman he felt could change his life. What did he mean *could*. She *was* changing his life, adding color and meaning to his world. Aw, he was starting to sound like Lance again. But just the idea of wanting to come to an Easter egg hunt, of all things, and then actually remembering that one so long ago surprised him. His plan was to be a nice guy, to show Asa that he wasn't a grouch. Problem was, he was starting to feel like a nice guy.

"Isn't Asa wonderful!"

Zain's ears zoomed in on the sentiments he completely agreed with. He unashamedly listened to the older ladies' chatter.

"I know, she always helps out and she doesn't even have any kids, no nieces or nephews, no one that would make her feel obligated to be here."

"True, but I meant with her little problem."

"Oh that, I know what you mean. It must be a daily struggle."

"Brent's a big help, but you have to admit, that girl's strong and Asa knows what's good for her."

"Mmmm-mm I know ya right. We raise 'em like that. Today's woman has to be strong. And I can tell you this much, she does a whole lot better than my nephew. He has the same problem, but refuses to do anything to help himself."

Both women made tsking sounds. Zain poured his last tablespoon of vinegar. So other people knew about Asa's drinking problem. It sounded as if she was trying to get help. And Thomas? Zain supposed he could strike him off his short list of enablers. Zain wondered if Thomas or these ladies knew about her recent lapse at the Dry Dock. Probably not. Having listened to the two women, Zain was even more determined to be there for her. He suddenly needed to see her. It didn't matter that she had been gone for no more than ten minutes. He spotted her backpack on one of the tables. Maybe she needed something from it.

Zain found her sitting crossed legged in a chair eating something from a little plastic container. She was adorable, gorgeous and the woman he didn't know he'd been waiting for. He wanted to tell her about the feelings that grew inside of him whenever she was around but knew better than to voice them. She hadn't been too receptive when he told her about the possibility that he was falling in love with her. Instead he found himself saying, "What do you have there?"

"Pineapple slices, fresh."

"Smells good." Asa's unique scent mingled with the sugary smell of the fruit.

"They're very sweet."

"So are you." Her eyes widened a bit at that. "But since I've been warned about proper behavior at church functions I'll have to be content to sample the fruit instead of you."

She had just popped the last piece into her mouth. Despite the reminder about proper behavior Zain very improperly caught the end of the yellow fruit, and pulled it into his mouth, tasting it's sweetness as well as Asa's. He lingered a moment before slowly moving back to smile at her. That simple sharing had outdone him. She had to have felt the same power, the pull, just as he had. Zain wanted to see it in her eyes, but they were closed. She slowly opened them.

Her eyes didn't hold the soft or sleepy glow he expected. They were stormy, upset. "Why did you do that?" she gasped.

Why? Because your mouth was there and I had to taste it, because you are mine he wanted to say. From the look in her eyes Zain knew those were the last words she wanted to hear. "Asa, I was only—"

"Don't ever do that again." She stood and moved past him to storm outside.

Don't do what? he wanted to ask. Don't kiss her when nobody was around? Don't enjoy the taste of her? Don't eat her food? She did seem picky about that. The only way to find out was to ask. Just watch it, man, he told himself before following her outside.

Asa was surrounded by children. She was directing them to various tables full of the dyes he'd help to prepare. Zain walked to her side. "Don't be mad at me." He hadn't expected to say that but was glad he did when a smile lit her face.

"I'm not mad. I may have overreacted." Two eggs in her hand, she spun around on her heel and announced, "It's time to dye some eggs!"

Zain was amazed at himself. He had never cared if a woman was angry at him. Asa's feelings, her opinion of him, mattered. Maybe she had been testy because of her daily struggle with alcohol. Yeah, that had to be it. Zain decided not to think about it anymore. Instead, he helped a little girl who looked to be no more than three draw a happy face on an egg with a wax crayon before dropping it into a cup of yellow dye. A harried woman with a set of twins, one sleeping in a stroller, another fidgeting on her lap, gave him a smile of gratitude.

Zain went around the tables catching Asa's eyes once in a while, sharing a look or a smile as they oversaw the vast artistic creation of over fourteen dozen eggs. When done, the children held egg cartons cut into fours and labeled with the owner's name. Asa and the two women whose conversation he'd overheard earlier led the children away to play games.

Not long after, Zain could hear "Peter Cottontail" coming from the direction they had disappeared in as he helped to dismantle the tables.

"Mr. Darby? What are you doing here?" Thomas grabbed one end of the heavy tables helping him to flip it onto its side.

Zain was stumped. Yesterday he'd had a ready excuse. Today his mind was a blank, a very unusual experience. Asa wanted their relationship to be kept quiet, but Zain wasn't used to hiding what he wanted. He bent to fold the legs on his side of the table.

"Hello there, boss, what's going on?" Lisa peered around Thomas to ask.

Thomas stood from folding the legs on his end of the table. "That's what I just asked."

Zain didn't respond. He pointed his chin up, indicating that Thomas should lift his end of the table. Zain walked backwards, concentrating on what he should say and trying to avoid a collision. They laid the table on a stack in a shed. Lisa and Thomas looked at him expectantly.

"Asa," was all Zain got out before Lisa jumped in.

"She got you too, huh?"

Asa had him all right. That was an understatement, but he'd take that.

"She asked you for a donation for the hunt, then convinced you to donate your money *and* your time."

"That's about the way it went."

"Where is Asa?" Lisa asked, her eyes scanning the area.

"Follow the music and the sound of happy kids. That's where you'll find Asa." Zain liked that idea. Asa and kids.

"Gotcha, boss," Lisa said before sprinting off.

"She is so cute," Thomas said, watching her run across the field.

"Cute" was the word for Lisa. "Cute" was what Thomas would need. Not Zain. He needed Asa. Beautiful, graceful, smart, and wonderful with kids, the perfect woman for him. She could, would, someday be his wife and the mother of his children. *Whoa!*

"Mr. Darby?"

Double whoa! What had happened to that anti-marriage virus he'd stored in his head ten years ago. Asa Taylor had hacked into his brain, infiltrated his system and had gotten into his blood in less than a month's time.

"Hey, Mr. Darby!"

"Yeah, what is it?" Forgetting where he was, the sound of Thomas's voice automatically had Zain responding in business mode.

"Give me a hand with these cutouts. We hide eggs behind them for the little kids. Makes it easier for them to find."

Zain shook his head, realizing where he was once again. He let that marriage thing flow to the back of his head. Using the physical exertion of lifting the wooden shapes of bunnies, chicks, giant eggs and baskets to clear his mind worked off the sudden tension those thoughts had brought on.

Everything in place, eggs hidden with the help of some other volunteers, Thomas announced. "I'll go tell Asa we're ready."

A huge group of small children holding Easter baskets came racing around the bend. Zain stood in the middle of the chaos searching for Asa. The direction of his thoughts should have had him leaving, running as far and as fast as he could. He'd known he wanted Asa in his life, but he hadn't realized he wanted her for life. Funny, he didn't want to run; instead he found his eyes scanning the crowd for her. He couldn't find her anywhere. Zain moved out of the path of little arms and legs determined to find all the goodies they could get their hands on. Suddenly a little hand attached itself to one of his. The little girl he had helped earlier, her hair in two shiny plaits on each side of her head, asked, "Can you help me? I can't find any eggs."

"Where's your mommy? Can't she help you?" Zain knew that the little kids could have a little help.

"Changin' diapers. Mommie's always changin' diapers."

"I bet." Zain felt sorry for the mother as well as the cute little girl. He walked her around pointing out an egg or two until she got the hang of it. Soon she was running around just like the other kids, trying to gather as many eggs as she could. Where was the kid's dad? He wondered. She was such a cute little girl. He and Asa could make one even cuter. This time the thought didn't scare him as much.

Zain went into the church hall. That's where he found Asa. She was putting a huge number of hot dog weiners into a gigantic pot..

"Getting ready for when the mob finds the last egg?"

"That should be soon. Would you like a hot dog before the crowd gets here?"

"If you sit with me."

"I already ate."

Zain felt disappointed that she'd eaten without him. "I guess I'll take one anyway."

She grinned at him. "I'm sure it'll taste just as good."

"I wouldn't bet on it," Zain said as he took the sandwich from her hands.

A half an hour later they waved good-bye to Lisa and Brent as they prepared to leave.

"What about these older kids?" Zain asked as two zoomed past him on bicycles.

"They're with the CYO, the Catholic Youth Organization, and they've got plans that have nothing to do with us. We are done."

"Good."

"And I must say," she looked at him sideways as they walked across the church grounds "you were wonderful today, Mr. Zain Darby."

"Thanks, I had a good time." Zain was surprised that he actually meant it. He did have a good time. Just being there with her even when she was nowhere in sight gave him a sense of satisfaction he had never felt before. He was feeling a lot of things he'd never felt before. Doing a lot of things that he had never done before. For example, what he was about to do now.

"Hey, what's that on the ground over there?" Zain stopped in his tracks. Could he have possibly sounded more phony? Romantic, sweet, that's what he was trying to be. Asa stood beside him looking down at where he pointed. "A huge, golden egg. Maybe from a giant Easter bunny."

She stared up at him. "Maybe from a giant without long fuzzy ears or a tail."

"Close."

"From you."

"Open it."

Asa gave him a leery look but bent down to pick up the huge metallic egg. Before it opened it Asa warned, "I don't like the idea of accepting gifts from you, Zain."

"I'm sure."

"I'm not that kind of woman."

"I'm more than sure about that. It's not that kind of gift."

She opened the egg slightly and stared at the contents for a moment that dragged on longer than he could tolerate. She hated it. Probably thought it was a stupid gift. He felt ridiculous. This whole idea was ridiculous, all stemming from these feelings he had never experienced before. No more he supposed, then the instant need, the attraction he felt for her. Which was exactly what he was feeling now, what he felt when she was nowhere near him, what he felt when they were at work. Even doing something as mundane as taking her scheduled break activated the need inside him. Plopping a few grapes into her mouth, biting into an apple, or heaven forbid, eating a banana were all acts of enticement. Ridiculous. Ridiculous but true. He couldn't take this a second longer. "You have to take it out to look at it."

"I *am* looking at it."

She was looking at it all right. Asa was eyeing the egg as if it held a deadly snake instead of a gift. The egg didn't hold diamonds or gold, although he wanted that for Asa. It seemed as if she were having a hard time accepting this simple gift. But it wasn't simple. That was the problem.

It was too much too soon, but he had nowhere to go but forward. All this uncertainty was new to him. He knew about pushing a situation even when it was risky. Zain took the egg out of her hand and lifted the golden key attached to a wooden key chain that spelled her name. "Take it. Keep it so that I can be honest when I tell people you have the key to my heart." He placed it in the palm of her hand. *Play it light, easy,* man, he told himself. Then Asa would take it the same way.

She turned the key over in her hand and silently mouthed the words "my heart" he had engraved inside a tiny heart. "You're serious."

So she wasn't taking it lightly. "I wanted to show you how much I want this relationship to work."

"Zain this is so…"

"You better not say nice." He had been shooting for nice, but he didn't want this gift classified as nice.

"It is, but also irresistible."

"Irresistible. I like that. Another fine adjective you've attached to me."

"Maybe not so irresistible that I can keep this. I have so many mixed feelings inside."

"Are there any good ones in the mix?"

Asa nodded.

"Then there's some hope for me. Keep it."

"I will," she told him finally on a soft breath.

Zain relaxed, not realizing how much stress her indecision had put him through. He glanced left, then right.

"What are you looking for?"

"A place that's not crawling with parents and kids. I've got this irresistible urge to kiss you."

"Oh" was all she said.

Playing it her way, keeping in mind her wish to keep their relationship secret, Zain did something he hadn't done in a long time. He grabbed her hand and pulling her with him raced down the block, through a tiny park with white picket fences and specks of color that blurred as they passed. They ran past an old fashioned gas station and sped the two blocks to her house. Taking the steps almost at once, Zain pulled her into his arms.

Their breathing, harsh, and breathless, blended as Zain leaned forward. Suddenly the kind of kiss he'd wanted to give her a mere second ago changed. Instead of claiming her lips, a demand of what he wanted from her, Zain laid a whisper of kiss on her lips. A whisper of a promise of more. Much more.

He leaned back to study her beautiful round face. Much more, later. "Get whatever you need. Grammy Dee's waiting for us."

He noted the disappointed twitch on her face and found it irresistible.

CHAPTER 9

"I win again!" "Are you sure you've never played Booray before?" Zain asked her.

"Never!"

"Stop looking at my sweet angel like that." Grammy Dee swatted at Zain. "If she says she hasn't, then she hasn't."

"Now, Grammy, that sounded too much like sweet angel over here can do no wrong."

"You got that right. She's putting up with you, isn't she?"

"And it's one of the hardest things I've had to do in my life," Asa nodded, finding herself easily joining in the teasing.

"I get it. Two against one. Bad mouthing me right in front of my face." Zain stood and moved away from the little square table where they had been playing cards. "Somehow, some way, you've developed this low opinion of me and my loving grandmother is backing you up."

"What are you gonna do?" Grammy asked.

"Nothing much." His eyes connected and held onto Asa's.

"Nothing much of no good is what it looks like. Watch out, sweet angel," Grammy Dee warned as Zain slowly made his way around the table.

"I'm not worried, Grammy. He may have some strength, but I've got the brains in this relationship." Relationship. They had a relationship. Asa found that she liked that. She wanted it. She was enjoying her day of discovering a new Zain Darby, nice, sweet, irresistibly romantic, and funny. Asa wanted to laugh at him now as he crept closer to her. Zain looked like some strange dark villain from one of those silent movies, eyebrows twitching, fingers moving as if they were itching to grab her. Asa wasn't a bit worried. What was he going to do in front of his grandmother?

Apparently a lot. As soon as he was close enough, he grabbed her by the waist and plopped her onto the sofa behind them, cushioning her fall with his body. Then he did something she didn't expect. So quick that Asa didn't know how he did it, he was above, his hands moving at her waist to tickle her. Zain Darby was tickling her unmercifully.

"Stop it. Oh, Zain, I c-c-can't stand this!"

"You're not doing much standing."

"Grammy, help me!"

Grammy stood and swatted at her grandson once again. "You get off my sweet angel, boy!"

"That's how you use those brains of yours?" Zain taunted, his fingers moving from her sides to the sensitive skin under her neck to that little spot behind her knees. How did he know the most ticklish parts of her body? "You gotta do better than that, Asa," he teased as she tried to breathe between the giggles taking over her body.

"He's got you there, angel. These bones of mine are too old to help you. You kids work it out." Grammy turned, Asa's only hope deserting her. "I'll be in the kitchen."

"She left me," Asa gasped out between a huge guffaw and a giggle.

"Yeah, she left her sweet angel all alone, with me." Zain was now concentrating on her rib cage, the barrier of her t-shirt little protection.

"Come on, Zain, you don't believe in torture, do you?"

"This is not torture, you're laughing."

An uncontrollable burst of giggles flew out of her mouth. Zain's hands had crept under her shirt. This was too much.

"What'd I tell ya?"

"I—will—hold—my—breath—until—you—stop." Asa gulped in a breath and held it. A second later she released it on a sigh of incredible emotion. A giant wave of feelings passed through her body, pushing the laughter, the guffaws and the giggles completely away. Zain's fingers were no longer running up and down her rib cage. They were gliding smoothly, softly on her skin. His warm hands gently grazed, spreading heady emotions of wonderment, wanting and ooooh-how-do-you-do-the-things-that-you-do-to-me through her entire being.

The atmosphere had changed. A simple shift in touch had converted the moment from playful to steamy. His hands stopped. They lay flat against her sensitive skin. He lay over her, closer, much closer than before. They were still, both listening to the other's rapid breathing, their foreheads rested against each other. Zain's fingertips moved against her skin once more, only a fraction of an inch as each second went by. They stretched until the very tips of his fingers grazed her breasts. That barely-there touch sent a pulsating wave of longing through her breasts, concentrating at her nipples that were straining and throbbing for more.

"Asa." Zain's dark eyes questioned.

Hers couldn't do anything but honestly tell him exactly what she wanted because in one smooth move, both warm, gentle palms skimmed over her breasts, then back again as his head lowered to pull her into him.

"It's mighty quiet in there." Grammy Dee's voice blasted into the room from the kitchen.

Asa pulled back, her head pressing into the sofa. Zain followed her down. Didn't he hear Grammy's voice? She turned her head trying to talk, trying to remind Zain that they weren't alone. His hot kiss landed on her check continued down her neck.

"Zain, stop," Asa hissed. Her breathing was heavy, rushed. "Quick, get up. Grammy's in the kitchen, remember?"

Zain was slow to move, his eyes not once leaving her face as he inched back.

"You know what they say when it gets quiet," Grammy called from the kitchen.

"No, what do they say?" Asa yelled, straightening her clothes, patting her hair, desperately trying to look normal. How was she going to do that when she didn't feel like herself. How could she even attempt it when Zain looked at her with those hot eyes of his.

"Stop that," Asa told him in a husky whisper.

"What?"

"Stop looking at me like that."

"Don't think that I can help it."

"They say," Grammy Dee continued, seemingly oblivious to the tension in the tiny living room, "that's when the trouble starts."

Trouble? The kind of situation that Grammy had interrupted was going to get her in trouble. And the look he was sending her way? Double trouble. None of it mattered because she was not going to hop into bed with Zain Darby, no matter how unexpectedly, deliciously stormy he made her feel.

Grammy placed a tray on the table. "Some goodies."

Laid out before them was a tray full of homemade treats. Asa saw brownies, cookies, and Rice Krispie treats, the real ones, not the sugar free pretenders she ate once in awhile.

Sugar free. Diabetic. Snack! All three important thoughts flashed in her head. Asa eyes zoomed to her watch. He had done it to her again, made her forget, or almost forget her snack time. Never before in her life had she had so much trouble sticking to her schedule.

"It's only three-fifteen. You haven't missed your scheduled break time," Zain announced, a smile on his lips, the heat still in his eyes.

"Good." Asa gave him a half smile, still hoping he'd look someplace else.

"Break for what?" Grammy wanted to know.

"For a snack." Zain told her.

"We have enough here. I was in the baking mood this morning and Rose was nice enough to help me. What do you want, sweet angel?"

Asa glanced at the choices. She could afford to treat herself. A little real sugar now and then wouldn't harm her as long as she didn't overdo it. Thoughts of overdoing it brought Zain's soft touches to mind. Those had her breathless, excited. Asa was sure her blood sugar bordered on low. Zain's caresses had probably burned all the carbs in her body, leaving none for the insulin she'd taken this morning. Yeah, she needed one of those brownies. Asa reached over for a mid-size piece and took a bite.

"I've noticed that you don't eat many sweets, but I was right in figuring you for a brownie, girl." Zain's eyes, the same color as the deep, dark treat were promising the same satisfaction that her taste buds were experiencing. "Would you like another, maybe share one with me?"

"They're delicious, but I've had more than enough. For now." Did she really say that? The double meaning was clear. She hoped Zain didn't get it, or would be nice enough to ignore it. He could be nice, he'd proved it. His steady gaze told her otherwise. He got what she said and wasn't going to ignore it. "I think I'll get myself some water."

"I'll help." When she stood and stared he added, "Show you where the glasses are."

"Kids," Grammy laughed, holding her head in her hands. "Get me a glass of milk," she tilted her head toward the kitchen, "while you're there helping sweet angel find that water."

"Sure thing." Zain followed her into the small kitchen.

He had his arms around her pulling her toward him until all of him surrounded all of her, taking up from where they'd left off minutes before. His lips sought, found and pulled her in. Zain's thumbs inched under her shirt, her bra, where he grazed her nipples with the soft pads. Asa couldn't breathe. The feelings were too intense. She had to breathe. She took her mouth away from his. Somehow she got away from him, those melting brown eyes. She went to the fridge, the counter, the cabinet. She collected bottled water, milk and glasses, the entire time forcing air in and out, deep, long slow breaths.

He was behind her. "Asa, you *are* a sweet angel." He kissed the side of her neck as he'd done once, before inhaling deeply. "And I'm glad."

"About what."

"That you realize that we already have a relationship."

"A *brand new* relationship."

"True, it's brand new." Zain moved to the other side of her neck, inhaling, laying soft kisses on her skin. "That's why I have to be with you. I have to know more about you, Asa."

Asa moved away from him, his kisses, his touch, so that she could gather the scattered words in her head to ask the question that had been clear a moment before. "What is it you need to know, Zain?"

He followed her across the kitchen, taking three giant steps to reach her. "You, all of you. I need to know, to have all of you, Asa Taylor." His hands softly landed on her shoulders. "You have to realize that." His voice was soft, sexy, another side of him. The seductive Zain Darby. And he was good.

"No!" was all Asa could say with so much of him surrounding her.

"No?" His eyes held shock. If Asa's body weren't experiencing so many waves of emotion, she would have laughed at the unexpected, probably never before seen, look of surprise on Zain Darby's face.

"You can't tell me you didn't feel the connection between us. It's still here. This is no ordinary wanting."

"I realize that."

"And?"

"No. I mean—you can't have all of me. It's too much, too soon."

Zain's hands fell to his side. A look that couldn't be described as anything more than frustration skipped across his face. His expression turned thoughtful just before he spun away from her.

Grammy Dee stood in the doorway. "It's quieter than when I walked in. Something's up." It was a statement of fact, not meant to question or pull an explanation from either of them. Grammy glanced at the back of Zain's head, then winked at her. "Think you could get your poor old grandmother that milk, Zain?"

He turned at the sound of his name. "You're not poor—"

"—but I'm old, so you have to do what I say."

Zain gave his grandmother a weak smile. Asa watched as he walked toward her. Her hand still held the half gallon of skim milk. He took one of the glasses from the counter and reached for the milk, his thumb caressing her hand in the same circular motion he'd used on her nipples. They reacted instantly, hardening, straining for his touch. Asa clenched her teeth and turned to fill her glass with the bottled water she had taken from the fridge.

"We're gonna have to get going, Grammy," Asa heard Zain tell his grandmother.

"You're leaving already?"

Grammy voiced the exact question that had popped into her head. Asa wanted a few more minutes with Grammy, hoping her presence would ease some of the tension between them.

"I'll be back tomorrow. Remember Easter dinner with Miss Rose."

"That's right. Did you invite sweet angel?"

"Not yet."

"What are you waiting for? Ask her. She's standing right here."

Zain turned to her, really looking at her for the first time since Grammy Dee had walked into the kitchen. "Asa, come have Easter dinner with us."

"I'd love to, but I can't. I'm visiting my parents, and my aunt and uncle in Pensacola. They live on the beach."

"Florida?"

"That's where Pensacola is."

"You're driving on the highway by yourself? When were you going to tell me this."

"Before you got to know all of me, I'm sure," Asa said, just loud enough for him to hear. "Not that I couldn't handle driving on the highway myself, but I won't be alone."

"Good."

"Brent's coming with me."

"Thomas!" Zain spat Brent's last name out like it was a dirty word.

"And Lisa."

"Good, all right then."

Asa didn't know whether to be amazed, amused, or annoyed at the quick change in Zain with that added news. Zain seemed to have a strange jealousy towards her cousin.

"Maybe you should go with angel," Grammy suggested, "I'll be fine with…" Grammy paused, her brow wrinkled in concentration.

"Rose, Miss Rose," Zain reminded her. Zain shared a concerned look with Asa. This was the first time Asa had witnessed any indication of the disease Grammy suffered from.

"No, Grammy. I promised to spend Easter Sunday with you, and that's how it's gonna be. We've got the rest of the day together, right Asa?" his eyes questioned.

"Exactly." Asa relaxed for the first time since Zain's tickle attack. His uncertainty helped her to rise from the waves of emotion traveling between them. The last thirty minutes had not been the easiest of her life and had ended with the possibility of Zain meeting her parents.

Asa gave Grammy a big hug. "Don't let that boy push you where you don't wanna go," she whispered to her, that lapse a minute ago seeming almost as if it hadn't happened.

They were out the building and in Zain's car driving toward the river before he spoke again.

"So, what you're telling me is that we won't be making love anytime soon."

"Is this how you normally reintroduce a topic?" Silly question, Asa knew, because this was a side of Zain she was used to. Putting what she already knew of him together with the parts she was learning was making Zain Darby an irresistible package.

"Usually."

"Just jump right in as if there were no interruptions."

"If it works."

"What you really mean is that it works if it confuses the other person, catches them off guard."

"You know me too well."

"Not all of you."

"Which is exactly the problem. Stop stalling, Asa. Answer the question."

"You are persistent," she quietly answered, then firmly told him, "No, we won't be making love anytime soon."

Asa heard him swear softly under his breath. She found herself flattered, but knew better than to show it. Zain Darby, the god of all men, wanted her that badly.

"When?"

"When can we make love?" she squealed not knowing why she was surprised by his one track mind.

"We weren't suddenly talking about something new." His tone was soft, seductive, careful, yet firm. Everything she'd come to know about him so far.

"No."

"All right then." They stopped at a red light. One of his hands left the steering wheel to claim the one that lay on her lap. "Believe it or not, I hadn't expected to have this conversation with you today. And I didn't expect a few kisses to bring us so far so fast."

"Neither did I."

"Which leads us to when?" His full attention went back to the driving when the light changed. "Can you give me a projected date? Two months? A week? Two days?" he ended on a hopeful note.

Asa didn't know whether to be insulted or amused. She decided on a little of both. "Zain, this is not a business deal. A relationship doesn't work like that."

"I wish it did," he muttered, parking in front of her house. A silence filled the car. Neither one rushed to fill it. This conversation, the moment of quiet, all seemed natural.

"That's not very romantic."

"I can give you romance."

"I know you can, but that won't change anything. There's too much about each other we don't know. One thing you should understand now is that I am not a bed hopper."

"I never said you were. Asa, I've got enough sense to know that. It's a part of your personality that I admire. One that's bound to frustrate me."

"There's nothing I can do about that," Asa told him point blank.

"Maybe."

"No maybe about it." Asa knew she had to stand firm. "I don't feel comfortable moving any faster."

"I realize that. I understand that you have to do what feels right for you. I'm just hoping I won't die a slow death waiting for you." He leaned toward her, gently pressing his mouth against hers. He pulled back a fraction of an inch before saying, "When I do make love to you, Asa Taylor, our relationship will be no secret. I will not be able to keep my hands off you."

He kissed her deeply. Asa wrapped her arms around his neck in agreement, knowing that he was right.

Zain pulled away first, his look silently communicating the power between them. "Are you going to invite me in?"

"Not a good idea."

"I'll come back for you in an hour."

"No, I'll meet you."

"So, you actually drive that thing once in awhile." He glanced in the direction of her driveway where her little blue Volkswagon bug sat, then back to her.

She nodded. "I'm even taking it to Pensacola."

"Is it ready for the trip?" He took one of her hands in his own. "Did you get an oil change?" He claimed the other. "Transmission checked?" He leaned forward pressing his forehead to hers. "Tune up?" He breathed against her mouth.

"Quadruple yes," Asa whispered. His words could have been erotic suggestions the way they flowed out of his mouth.

"Good." He leaned back but his eyes roamed her entire face. "You are simply beautiful."

"I can say the same for you."

Zain went on as if he hadn't heard her compliment. "I don't know what it is exactly." One of his brown fingers found its way to the side of her face. His thumb moved behind her ear, his warm palm against her cheek. His other hand followed, caressing the other side of her face. "These full lips and brown eyes can be so sweet, but then they can be soooo sassy." His pinky traced her eyebrows as he spoke. "Your nose is simply perfect." A finger traced the bridge of her nose. "Maybe, its the shape of your face. Putting it all together, bringing out your..."

At his pause Asa heard herself fill in the dreaded word. "Cuteness?"

"Sweet angel, that's the last word I'm thinking right now. Sexy, sensual, temptingly seductive. Those are the words that hit me when I look at you."

He gave her one last kiss. "I'd walk you to the door but I think you'd better get inside while I can still let you do that by yourself."

"Good idea."

"Asa."

She had gotten as far as opening the car door. "Yes."

"What do you feel like eating? Seafood, steak, barbeque?"

"Seafood sounds good." Asa agreed with his first choice not remembering the others.

"Then meet me at Joe's by the lake. Unless you want me to come back for you."

"No," she quickly answered. "I'll meet you there."

Asa went into her house and straight to the bathroom where she could take a good look at herself in the mirror. Her heart-shaped face and round cheeks looked exactly the same. Where had Zain gotten sexy from? If that was what he saw she wouldn't contradict him. Asa felt exhilarated and scared at the same time. She and Zain Darby. Amazing. Then again she and Zain Darby, was she falling for him too fast?

"Only as much as you let yourself," she told her reflection, comforting herself with that advice although it tilted on the edge of being false. As much as Zain pushed and she gave way, was more like it.

Asa showered quickly, trying not to concentrate on her body's intense degree of memory as she washed. While she could ignore the sudden heaviness of her navel and the tingling sensation of the skin covering her rib cage, Asa could not avoid noticing the firm, pointed brown tips of her breasts aching for more of Zain's touch.

Out of the shower she quickly snapped a bra on to hide the evidence. Asa went to her closet to find the peach-colored sun dress she'd bought the other day. She slipped on a pair of brown sandals, then eyed her toenails. They needed a good polish.

She found a nice shade of brown and applied it to her toenails. While they dried, Asa tackled her hair. She pulled it out of the bun she wore daily and let it fall down to her neck. Although her thick mass of hair curled naturally Asa never wore it down. The moisture in the air and the trips across the river always made it frizzy. Last time she had gotten her ends trimmed her hair dresser had recommended something that would control the frizz. Asa figured this was a good time to try it.

Toes dried, hair done, Asa went to Brent's side of the house to look at herself in the mirrored wall in his living room.

"You are gorgeous." Lisa echoed the exact words that were running through her head.

"Yes, you are," Brent said, walking through the door behind his girlfriend. "Where are you going?" he asked in that I'm-older-than-you-and-need-to-know way of his.

"On a date."

"And we were coming to see if you wanted to eat with us. Brent seemed to think that you'd be here all alone."

"It was my turn to cook," he said by way of explanation.

"I know, but I figured you'd be out with Lisa. Which was fine with me."

"Didn't I tell you Asa would be okay?"

"Perfectly okay, it seems." Brent looked none too pleased.

Asa wasn't going to let that stop her. She was her own person and didn't need a keeper.

"That's exactly right. You two go on with your plans. I'll be leaving in a minute myself."

"Who are you going out with?" He was standing right in front of her now.

"Nobody you need to worry about. Lisa, take him away." Asa nudged her cousin away.

"You're going out to eat, right? It's almost your dinner time."

"Yes, I am," she laughed.

Lisa grabbed him by the arm and pulled him toward the door but her efforts didn't prevent Brent from cautioning, "Don't get so caught up that you forget to take your shot." He was finally at the door, almost on the porch. "And don't forget about your bedtime snack!" he turned back to remind her.

"Won't." Asa would take Brent's reminders to heart. Zain Darby on too many occasions had made her forget about taking care of herself.

Asa closed Brent's front door in a hurry, not wanting to be late meeting Zain. Her reflection in the mirrored wall stopped her. She really was gorgeous. No wonder Brent was worried. Her hair hung down curly but soft and frizz-free. The look released a carefree feeling inside her, and the sun dress, lightweight and more form fitting than most of her office wear, made Asa feel like a whole new person.

She clicked off the lights as she went through both houses, then she stopped at her own front door, remembering that she wanted to check her sugar before leaving. Instead Asa decided to take her small quick take monitor and check it at the restaurant. She peeked inside her purse. Satisfied that both the monitor and insulin were inside, she locked the door behind her.

Asa took the Crescent City Connection, exited at West End and drove down Ponchartrain Boulevard to get to Joe's Crab Shack. She'd heard of the place but had never been there. If she remembered correctly, people actually danced on the tables. Asa couldn't picture Zain in his business suit dancing on any tables. Now the jean-clad Zain, that was another thing.

From a distance Asa's eyes zoomed in on the sign: Eat At Joe's. She parked. Since she had made it across the river so quickly, Asa decided to check her sugar before going in.

She pricked her finger, applied a drop of blood to the strip she inserted into the machine and waited for it to beep, indicating that it was finished. Twenty seconds was all it took. Twenty seconds later the monitor beeped at the same time a loud thump sounded in her ear. Asa jumped, throwing the small monitor toward the passenger seat.

"Asa." That was Zain's voice. "Open up."

"One minute," she told him, holding a finger up. Asa stretched to find the monitor. The strip was amazingly still sticking out at the bottom the way it was supposed to. The small drop of blood had scattered. There was nothing she could do about that. Asa glanced at the reading, 102, turned it off and pitched it into her purse.

"What was that all about?" Zain asked as she came out of the car.

"I dropped something."

"I could see that—," he paused, his eyes lingering on her face, her hair then traveling down and up again, "—that I'm in trouble." He took both her hands, gently pulling her out of the car, then slamming the door shut with his hip leaning back against it. Before she knew it Asa was standing between his hard thighs, her upper body pressed against his as he kissed her. Asa's nipples were quick to react to the heat of his body. "Thank god I had the sense to pick this restaurant. A little dancing on the tables might help alleviate the sudden, intense amount of energy that hit me the moment you got out of the car."

CHAPTER 10

They didn't dance on the tables, she suddenly realized. "Asa, pay attention to the road and a little bit of what I've been saying."

"What *did* you say?" Asa turned to her annoyed cousin.

"That's it! Pull over! I'm driving!"

Asa slowed the car, pulling onto the shoulder, gladly giving up the driver's seat to Brent. She was much too full of Zain to give her entire attention to something as mundane as the highway. A moment later she was in the passenger seat. The car door slammed. Brent let out a grunt as he snapped on his seatbelt, the sound reminding Asa to do the same to hers.

"Now you have one thing to concentrate on, the sound of my voice." Brent smoothly pulled back onto the highway heading east to Pensacola. "Where did you go last night?"

"Joe's Crab Shack."

"That place where they dance on the tables?"

"We didn't dance," Asa said, twirling one of her tight curls.

"But you ate?"

"Of course," Asa answered, remembering the huge seafood platter they had shared, the perfectly seasoned crab balls, Zain splitting the last one by swooping toward her mouth and biting it in two after she had claimed it for herself. Funny how it didn't bother her that time. Maybe she was getting used to Zain swooping down at her. It couldn't have had anything to do with having more than enough carbs to replace what he had stolen.

"No drinking?"

That question had Asa turning toward her cousin. "Of course not. Not only do I have you to remind me of the dangers of drinking while taking insulin every day of my life, I'm also reminded every time I go to the pharmacy for a refill. It's there in black and white."

"I know you do. But I see you drink those fake martinis so often at the Dry Dock, I thought maybe…"

"I have no interest in drinking, Brent. The pretend martinis are just—fun. Something my roommate and I started in college because neither one of us drank. Besides, I found myself high on him most of the night."

"Him who?"

"I wish I could tell you."

"I don't like this, Asa."

"I know you don't," she told him without an ounce of apology.

They were quiet after that, traveling the next few miles nursing their own thoughts. Brent's mind was probably on Lisa, Asa guessed. Brent's girlfriend couldn't come with them at the last minute. Lisa's sister, who hadn't been in town in five years, had come in as a surprise for the family, Lisa had explained at the sunrise service they'd all attended early this Easter Sunday morning.

Brent, being the person he was, had understood but disappointment had been written all over his face. While Asa could understand his grumpy mood she also couldn't help how happy she felt. It had only been two days since she had allowed Zain to talk her into letting their relationship grow and already she felt like a different person.

"Want an apple to go with that smile?" Brent asked, not mentioning that it was her snack time, which she was more than certain that it was.

"Sure." Asa glanced at the clock. It was actually two minutes into her snack time. "I packed some grapes myself, in little Ziploc bags exactly like someone I know. But an apple sounds good."

"Mini-cooler, backseat."

Asa reached back for the cooler. Besides a few apples, there was a pack of small juices and crackers. Brent would be Brent, Asa realized, and didn't have the heart to remind him that she knew how to take care of herself. She handed an apple to him and inspected her own. "Let's see, not too small, not too big, fourteen point five carbohydrates I'll bet. I'll be missing half a carb."

"You can have some of mine," Brent grinned.

"Much better, cuz." That grin was what Asa was shooting for.

"I know I've been grumpy for about the last eighty miles."

"More like a hundred, but I understand. I was looking forward to Lisa coming myself. I like her."

"You do? I know, you can't help but like her, she's amazing."

"My cousin's in love."

"I think so. This thing between us has gotten so serious so fast."

"Admit it, Brent. This thing's been going on since Christmas."

"If I'm going to confess to anything I'd better tell you it's been going on for more than a year. Starting on the exact day Lisa started working at Execute."

"You've been interested in her that long? What stopped you from—. Oh, I know. Me."

"No, Asa, It's not like that," Brent said dividing his attention between the highway and her.

"Right."

"The truth is you were only part of the reason. My work, my ability to talk coherently in front of her. It was all easier to let it ride."

"But you got there eventually."

"And we're moving on a fast track."

Asa knew about that firsthand. Zain wanted to move at the speed of a hurricane with a hundred mile an hour winds.

"I wanted Lisa to meet Mom and Dad."

"They're going to love her," Asa told him, pulling her mind from hurricane Zain.

"What about you? This mystery guy."

With those few words Hurricane Zain was instantly there again. "Every member of our family would be," Asa paused to find the right word, "surprised. Even you."

"Sounds like you went out with somebody like 'Zain the Pain.'"

Asa couldn't stop the gasp that flew out of her mouth.

"That's not what you did."

"I never said it was."

"What was that sound then?"

"I coughed."

"You better be careful, Asa."

"You worry too much." Asa admitted to nothing, taking a bite out of her apple to keep herself from saying another word. At about noon Brent pulled up to the beach house near the coast. Their parents lived next door to each other, a dream the sisters saw come true two years ago, their retirement homes.

Asa and Brent went up the stairs of his parents' home calling out, "Auntie Reenie, Uncle Boyd. Mom, hey Dad," acting like a couple of kids. Asa couldn't wait to see her aunt and uncle.

The reunion was always the same. Great big hugs from her aunt and uncle, all four of them talking at the same time, until Uncle Boyd said, "Cool it, one at a time."

They did a five-minute catch up session, then Aunt Reenie interrupted to nudge her toward her parents.

Some of the joy of the moment left her. She hadn't finished telling her aunt and uncle about yesterday's Easter egg hunt. But she knew her obligation and turned to speak to them. "Hello Mother, Father. I didn't see you there." Asa gave them each a peck on the cheek. She knew her greeting was stilted and polite, but she couldn't help it. It had been practiced and perfected throughout her childhood when they would take the time to visit. Aunt Reenie and Uncle Boyd were her true, deep down family. Her parents were nothing more than visiting relatives.

"It's good to see you, Asa." Her mother held her eyes much longer than usual.

"You look good there, girl," her father said, getting out more words than was customary for him.

"It's your hair, you're wearing it down—for a change," Ann Marie Taylor commented.

"Yes, Mother, I am."

"And it's beautiful, isn't it, Ann Marie?" Auntie Reenie rushed in to say.

"You look too good for any of those crazy young men out there nowadays," Uncle Boyd announced.

"I wouldn't know about that," Brent told no one in particular.

Ann Marie's eyes widened, "What does that mean?"

"Probably nothing," Auntie Reenie said, giving Brent and Uncle Boyd a warning look. She didn't need to cast one her way. Asa was not into sharing confidences with her mother.

Brent, his mind probably on Lisa, had obviously missed the warning signal and Aunt Reenie's attempt at saving her, answered Ann Marie's question. "There's this mystery guy Asa's going out with."

"You went out with a man? Is that the reason you couldn't drive over on Saturday and have a longer stay with your family?"

"No," Asa answered.

At the same time, Brent, realizing his mistake, blurted out, "Of course not, we had an obligation at church."

The joyful reunion was quickly turning sour. It was all her mother's fault.

"Don't cover for her, Brent."

"Ann Marie, Brent wouldn't do that," Aunt Reenie told her sister, attempting once again to be the peacemaker.

"He'd do that, and almost anything, for her."

"I don't lie, Auntie," Brent defended himself.

This was getting out of control. The problem, if there was one, was between her parents and her. "Mother, you shouldn't talk to Brent that way."

"Asa's right," Uncle Boyd interjected in a burst of cheer. "Let's eat. We've got—"

"Maybe you don't lie, but you're pretty good at smoothing things over for your cousin."

"You're going about this the wrong way, sister girl," Auntie Reenie warned her sister.

Asa turned to each of the four people who'd had a hand in either bringing her into this world or helping her learn to live in it. Auntie Reenie and Uncle Boyd grimaced apologetically; her mother stood silent for the moment, a sour expression on her face; her father as usual said nothing, a hard look plastered on his face. Asa's thumbs were pressed against the corners of her eyes, hands in prayer. Something was about to happen, something big. She could feel it. Asa begged for divine intervention before asking, "What's going on?"

"We're worried about you."

Asa blinked hard and opened her eyes wide to see if that was really her mother talking.

"Your father and I," she continued, "your aunt and uncle."

"Don't put us in this," Uncle Boyd warned.

The expression on Ann Marie's face seemed to sour more, if that were possible. "In that case, your father and I want you to come live with us."

Asa laughed. She couldn't stop. Her mother and father, with whom she had an almost nonexistent relationship wanted her to come live with them.

"What's so funny about that?" Ann Marie asked.

Could she have possibly heard a touch of hurt in her mother's voice? Asa opened her eyes. The laughter died as they traveled to each member of her family. Brent, Auntie Reenie, and Uncle Boyd all wore the same worried, endearing faces she'd known in times of hurt, confusion, or something as simple as a cut that needed to be bandaged. Her mother…Asa could never tell what the expression she wore meant. And her father simply stood there beside her mother, rigid and expressionless as ever.

Asa walked toward them. "Why the sudden concern?"

"Sudden? We've always been concerned about you."

"Really, Mother? When? On my many parentless birthdays, report card conferences, mother-daughter days, graduations?"

"We were there for your college graduation."

"The official end of my childhood," Asa softly declared, carefully modulating her voice to remain steady, calm, respectful, as her aunt and uncle taught her. "How about the day I passed out in Aunt Reenie's backyard? Not my own, because I didn't have one. Where were you that day?" Asa didn't wait for an answer. "How about the many clinic visits, the first time the nurse drew my blood with that huge needle that terrified me, still terrifies me, and the countless times after."

"We were there in spirit," her mother had the nerve to say.

"Well, these people were there in the flesh." Asa pointed to her aunt, uncle and cousin, feeling her control slip, her voice escalating.

"Asa, watch what you say here," her aunt warned behind her.

But tears were running down her eyes and she wasn't thinking about being respectful anymore. "I care about them, they care about me. We have a history together. What do I have with you?"

Her parents stood there as one solid wall. She repeated softly, slowly this time, "What do I have with you?" She hadn't yelled but her tone let everyone know that she held no respect for the people who bore her.

"Do not ever talk to your mother that way again, Asa girl." Her father's voice was deep and forceful. The voice of a man who led. Despite being an adult of twenty-three Asa felt a tremor pass through her body. Her father rarely spoke to her and had never reprimanded her. He'd never had to the few times she saw him. She had always been as terrified of him as she was of those blood-sucking needles. Still, she forced herself past that to ask, "Why, when she's never been a mother to me?"

Her father took two steps toward her. Two precise, military steps. Asa took twice as many back, landing in a chair behind her. Her father stood firm and solid before her, moving in closer than he'd been to her as long as she could remember.

"Melvin," Uncle Boyd warned.

"This is my daughter, Boyd. I have a right," he said without moving.

"Mine too, so watch how you say, what you need to say."

Asa watched as something passed between the two older men. Was there some big secret they were trying to tell her. Wild thoughts flashed through her head, unthinkingly she let one out. "You're not my real father?"

"Don't be ridiculous, of course he's your father. This is real life, Asa, not television. This is about something else," her mother quietly intervened staring at her for a long time before turning back to her father. "It's okay, Melvin. Let it be."

"You're crying. She needs to know."

Asa looked closely at her mother. She was crying. She had never seen her mother do that. Asa was almost afraid to hear what her father had to say.

"I'll be okay." Ann Marie insisted.

"Like you have been lately when you think I'm sleeping."

Was this the same man she's known all her life having an *actual* conversation with her mother? Asa's eyes moved back and forth between them. She had never heard her father say so much at one time. "What's going on? Tell me, whatever it is, I want to know!"

"Let's leave them alone to discuss this," Aunt Reenie suggested, shooing Uncle Boyd and Brent out of the room.

"Don't go anywhere," Asa begged, suddenly afraid, needing them there.

"We'll stay, if you want us," Brent spoke for the three of them.

Asa's father cleared his throat with two short neat grunts. "Your mother's been taking care of you for as long as you've been in this world."

"But—"

"Listen," he roared.

Asa closed her mouth, intrigued, anxious, and afraid of what she would hear.

"The decision to send you away was not an easy one. Your mother cried for weeks before you left, a whole year after, and for every important milestone she missed. She didn't want to let you go."

"But she did," Asa whispered, needing to say that.

"Because she wanted to do what was best for you. To give you a stable environment. We moved to a place, a new city, every six months. She knew that wasn't good for you. But she's seen every one of your plays, birthday parties, graduations. Reenie and Boyd taped every moment and sent them to us."

Although this news was surprising, it wasn't enough. The feeling of desertion still hurt too much. "You could have stayed in one place."

"Blame me for that, not your mother."

"Well, I blame both of you."

"Then blame us for that college degree that you have."

"Melvin, don't." Her mother was at her side, staring up at the man who was her father.

"She should know that there was no way we were going to let her stay away from her aunt and uncle for four years to go to LSU, traveling back and forth on the highway to Baton Rouge. Not with that disease she has."

"What about my diabetes? And what does that have to do with LSU?"

No one said a word. Her father finally spoke again. "Your mother didn't want you to go out of the city, away from your aunt and uncle."

Asa was confused. "So?"

"So she did what she could to make it happen. She spent a whole summer interviewing people to be your roommate. To hire someone to look after you."

"You did what?" Asa was on her feet walking around the room just like Zain when he had something on his mind. Zain. She would think about him, not the crazy things coming out of her father's mouth.

"Asa," her mother was saying, "we did it to protect you. Karen was a nurse. She wanted to go back to school, so we paid her tuition in exchange for her services. "

"And I actually thought Karen was my friend. Was I too ignorant to take care of myself? Was that it?"

"No, of course not."

"Asa, calm down." Brent stood beside her.

"I can't calm down. Did you hear what they said?" Realization dawned. "You knew. You knew, then you took over where Karen left off."

"No, Asa, that's wrong."

"But you watched over me, watched me check my sugar, count my carbs, take my shots as if I needed a guardian, a protector. I can take care of myself," Asa told everyone in the room. "I don't need anyone of you to do that for me." Her voice was steady and calm the entire time, rising only at the end.

Asa marched into the kitchen. She opened the fridge and pulled out a carton of orange juice. A glass appeared before her. At first, she thought she was imagining things until her aunt spoke.

"Here, I'll pour it for you."

The sound of liquid pouring was strange and distant. Asa took the glass and drained it quickly.

"How long were you low?"

"Just toward the end. It's my lunchtime." Her speech was slow, slurred.

"I know, let's eat. Then we can talk about all this."

"I'll eat because I have to, but I don't want to talk about anything, Auntie Reenie. I resent having a friend for hire."

"I know."

"And you knew all about this, too."

Her aunt nodded. "It was the only way your parents would let you go. And you wanted to go away so badly."

"I remember. I'll forgive you and Uncle Boyd and eventually Brent. I don't know about my parents yet."

"You'll forgive us all."

Asa went into the dinning room with her aunt. The rest of the family moved to the table as soon as she sat. No one was happy.

Asa ate, counting her carbs as she went along. Her body language, her expression dared anyone to give one suggestion or word of advice on her meal. The hurt ran deep. She couldn't look at any member of her family for long.

Asa stood. She cleaned her plate in the kitchen and came back to announce, "No, Mother, I won't be living with you, ever. As a matter of fact, I think I'll be moving sometime soon. After all, Brent, I'm sure, would like some privacy and the opportunity to live his life without the burden of his cousin to look after."

"Asa, you are not a burden." Brent was up and at her side in an instant.

"Brent, I can't talk to you about this right now. If you're coming with me, I'm leaving now. Goodbye, everyone."

Asa was out the door, down the stairs and in the driver's seat before she knew it. Brent followed her outside. "Happy Easter," Asa muttered as they pulled away.

CHAPTER 11

Zain couldn't believe that he was going to do this. He was a man who was rarely unsure of himself, and had always taken control of almost every situation. But he was also a man who knew when he needed expert advice. That's exactly what he was seeking now. Who better to go to but a woman.

"What's wrong with Asa?" Zain asked Lisa, having no idea what was going on with the woman he had dreamed about in his bed, in the shower, on his boat Easter Sunday evening, even driving to work this morning. Asleep or awake Zain could not keep his mind off her, and he didn't know what to do about her. Asa hadn't been herself this morning, had even acted strange on the phone last night. She had reluctantly played their new game of shared secrets by revealing that she was tired after *he* had admitted to thinking about her all day long.

Today, Asa had said barely two words, almost completely ignoring him. Zain understood and respected her wish to keep their new relationship quiet, but this went beyond that. After three hours of being ignored, Zain had decided to confront her. But then she wasn't at her desk. Break time, he had remembered.

"Boss, hello there, boss. Mr. Darby?"

"Yeah, Lisa, what do you say about Asa?"

"I don't know, boss, she did look a little off today. Maybe something happened this weekend when she visited her parents."

"Didn't you go, too?"

"No, I had to bail out at the last minute. Brent went with her, though. He's so sweet. I'm sure he took good care of her."

Zain's eyes narrowed at his receptionist. Could she really be that gullible? Thomas and Asa must still have something going on and were stringing them both along. Nobody strung him anywhere. Now Zain had an explanation for her strange behavior. "I'm sure he did," he muttered before storming away to find Asa. She had a few things to answer to, and she was going to do it now.

Zain spotted Asa swaying down the hallway. She could barely stand. He slowed to watch her. She was at it again, drunk, that had to be it. Was alcohol the real explanation for her attitude? But when did she find the time? Asa didn't come in drunk and had finished almost every assignment he had given her today, perfect as always. But then again, he didn't have his eye on her every second this morning.

"Now what?" he muttered when Thomas showed up, just as she tripped on her own two feet. He was holding her to his side. Zain's hands should have been around her. And where was he taking her? To the restroom. The ladies' restroom. "Hey, hey you, Thomas!"

Thomas whispered something to Asa, she peered at him, said something to Thomas and they both went into the bathroom. "What the hell is going on?" Zain was at the door. It was locked. He banged on it once, no more. They knew it was him. Zain waited a full ten minutes listening to the whispers on the other side of the door, not caring if anyone saw him standing there.

They came out cautiously scanning the hallway. Neither of them noticed him off to the right. Thomas was talking.

"I know you don't want me to ask, but I can't help myself. Are you going to be okay?"

Asa smiled that sweet angel smile at Thomas and nodded. She backed up right into Zain.

"Ms. Taylor, I will see you in my office."

"Mr. Darby, I can explain," Thomas interjected.

"You can, and you will because I'll see you in my office right along with Ms. Taylor in no less than two minutes!"

Zain left the two of them there to return to his office. Controlling his movements, slowing his stride, he reminded himself that he was the man in charge. He swung open the door and went straight to his desk chair. If he was in charge then why was this woman, with her drinking problem, too involved ex-boyfriend, brilliant mind, beautiful smile, sweet personality making him crazy? There was knock at the door.

Both Asa and Thomas stood in the open doorway. Zain nodded them in, motioning for Thomas to close the door. He wanted to shoot all the anger and jealously he was feeling directly at them. But he was a professional business man. His suspicion of something between them not something he would address in the workplace. His workplace. His business. "Sit," he ordered.

They sat and so did he.

"Let me explain, Mr. Darby."

"No, Brent, let me handle this."

Zain had pulled himself together. His eyes fell on Asa as she spoke. His mind automatically continued to catalog her virtues. Full lips waiting for his kiss, firm hot nipples dying for—

"Mr. Darby."

He was listening now.

"I was simply on my fifteen minute break. I tripped and Brent insisted on seeing if I was okay."

"By walking with you into the ladies' room. Did he stand by and watch you use it too?"

"That's a ridiculous question."

"But important." Zain's eyes bore into hers, communicating just how important. She was his. Satisfied she understood, he went on. "Thomas was only helping, you said. I'm supposed to believe that."

"That's exactly what I was trying to do." Thomas looked from him to Asa, confusion written all over his face.

"Brent!" Asa hissed.

"Thomas, you've said enough," Zain told him sternly.

Understanding dawned. The younger man stood. "I don't think you need me here. I'll leave the two of you to discuss this without me." He went to the door. "Asa, I hope you know what you're doing," he told her before closing it behind him.

Zain forced himself to stay exactly where he was. He wanted to move, to pace up and down the office. But that would show how nervous he was. Why did this women make him feel this way? Nervous or not he dove right in. "Why would you need Thomas's help?"

She was wearing that calm face that made him crazy.

"I tripped, Mr. Darby."

And the cool-as-a-cucumber voice was back.

"I'm okay, thanks for asking."

He wouldn't let her see that the voice annoyed him and the crack amused him. This was his Asa. The one he was getting to know.

"It was a small incident *at work*," she emphasized. "I don't think it is necessary to discuss it right now."

Asa looked him straight in the eye as she said this, daring him to go back on his promise to keep their working relationship separate from their personal one. Zain had had no idea it would be this hard.

"True, but this tripping and falling all over the place could affect your work."

"It won't," she said before walking out of his office. The sweet woman he spent time with all day Saturday, who'd dyed Easter eggs, hid plastic ones, and played games with little children was hidden under the cool woman who'd just left his office. The woman who'd allowed him to kiss her and feel her excitement at his touch was being worn away by alcohol. The cool act had to be her cover.

Zain felt helpless. Drinking changed her behavior, that was certain. He felt better knowing that he would be attending another Al-Anon meeting. Maybe he could get some insight on what he found out today.

Zain stayed in his office thinking and brooding, tempted to call Lance to get some feedback, some direction on this urge Zain had to make Asa a permanent part of his life. Urge, no, that wasn't the word. An urge can be controlled, eliminated. This couldn't even be called a desire.

This new overwhelming feeling was a need. Zain needed Asa in his life. It was as simple as that. Which meant he needed to set the record straight with Thomas.

He left his office in a rush, forgetting to grab his suit jacket, flying past Asa until he turned back to study her beautiful face surrounded by tight curls instead of the bun she usually wore. Maybe she kept it down for him, because he'd told her how much he liked it. He hoped so.

"Yes, Mr. Darby?" she asked.

He walked back to her desk and sat on the edge. "I'll be out for lunch." His finger caught a curly strand to gently pull and watch as it sprung back to its original curl.

Asa gave him a nod to show that she had heard, for now ignoring his very unbusinesslike behavior. He hurried off, controlling an itch to remove that cool-as-a-cucumber expression from her face with a long, slow kiss.

"Thomas," Zain called when he spotted his competition. He was talking to Lisa at her desk. "I need to see you. We'll have lunch."

"Sorry, Mr. Darby, I was planning on eating with Lisa." Thomas eyed him warily.

"That's right, boss. We were waiting for my relief," Lisa chimed in, barely able to take her eyes off Thomas.

What was with this lanky, quiet genius?

"Can we do this after lunch?"

"No, Thomas, we can't. Say your good-byes, I'll see you on the first floor." Zain went to the elevators, giving him no room for excuses.

Zain paced the lobby of the large office building. He didn't have long to wait. Thomas was in the next elevator car.

"This way." Zain led him out of the building. Out of nowhere a jolt of nervousness hit him. Nervous? Him? Wrong description. Anxiety. That was it. Anxiety to get this out in the open.

They walked the few blocks to a small restaurant that catered to workers in the CBD. They sat, settling at a table all without saying a thing to each other. Thomas looked none too happy. Zain was far from being in a joyful mood himself. The waitress took their drink orders, gave them menus and still not a word had passed between them.

"I got a feeling that I should have ordered something harder than Coke."

Zain shook his head slightly, his eyes zeroing in on Thomas. Alcohol. *Was* Thomas an enabler or as helpful as those women at the church implied.

"No, you won't need that. I brought you down here to discuss something."

"Something new? Shoot." Thomas relaxed, seeming to warm up to the idea.

That's how Zain would handle it. He could throw a new project at his troublesome employee, get him to let down his guard, then hit him for the information he needed and warn him off Asa. They talked business and ate lunch. Thomas rattled on, excited about the nonexistent project, throwing one probable approach after another at him. His ideas would create a unique software program. Zain was impressed. Thomas's enthusiasm reminded Zain of his reasons for hiring the man nearly two years ago. Innovative, that was the word. Involved with Asa, he hoped not.

"I've got a concern," Zain said as Thomas paused to drink some of the Coke that had remained untouched during the meal.

"Nothing to worry about. I can set up the—"

"Not the project. I'm concerned about Asa. I'd like to discuss her problem."

Thomas stared at him, his manner defensive. "What about it?"

"You seem to know a lot about her situation, a lot about her in general."

"Does this have to do with work?" His head bobbed up and down, the curls bouncing. "I've dealt with Asa and her problem for years and I can assure you that in no way will it ever affect her work."

"It hasn't."

"Asa takes pride in doing a good job."

"I can agree with you there, but I find her problem has a tendency to alter her personality."

"Sometimes she gets a little down, but Mr. Darby, Asa always bounces back."

"My question is—and I don't want you to think of us as employee/employer right now, you seem to be there for Asa, but I wonder, are you there for her too much?"

Thomas had just put the glass of coke to his mouth. He slammed it down. "Did Asa put you up to this?"

"No, why?"

"Sounds exactly like something she would say."

"Well, are you?"

"Maybe. But that's what you do when you care for somebody."

"What about Lisa?"

"Now Lisa, that's a whole 'nother kind of caring. That's all-out-love."

Zain finally relaxed. They had come to some kind of understanding. "Could be I know what you mean," Zain told him, an image of Asa appearing before him.

"Can we keep this conversation about Asa to ourselves?"

"Certainly." Zain did not have to be told that Asa would not like being discussed this way.

"I don't know exactly what's happening between the two of you. But I'm telling you now, watch your step. Asa's special."

CHAPTER 12

Asa covered the computer monitor and keyboard. Today had been rough, but had gotten better when she had taken a step toward forgiving Brent. Allowing herself to do that much eased a little of the anger inside of her. Still, hurt feelings and preoccupation with her family's deception had resulted in Asa unintentionally ignoring Zain. Somewhere in the back of her mind, Asa had realized that he was not pleased. That realization had come with his bulldozing attitude earlier today. That had been completely unnecessary, but then again, completely Zain. Asa could even say his attitude showed he cared.

She needed to talk to him but he hadn't been back since leaving for lunch. And the way he'd left pushed her family problems to the back of her head, his powerful touch leaving tingling waves behind that triggered memories of his kisses. Just as those thoughts entered her mind he came rushing in, moving past her without a glance.

"Zain, wait a minute?"

"Zain?" He spun on his heels. "It's Zain now, Miss Taylor?" He slowly studied the alcove. "Funny this still looks like work." He glanced at his watch. "Ah, but it's three minutes past official working hours. Does that make a difference?" he asked, slowly advancing toward her.

How could she have ignored him all morning? The storm she had always felt when he touched her was there in his chocolate eyes, there almost visible on the smooth brown skin of his face. Hurricane Zain, she thought again.

It would hit her if he released the control Asa could see on his face. "I guess it does."

"Then this working and personal relationship rule can be bent."

He made it a statement, not a question, leading Asa to answer carefully. "Occasionally." His milk chocolate eyes had zoned in on her lips, watching, anxiously anticipating her answer.

"Then come with me." His arm hooked her waist and pulled her with him. "I have something to tell you."

They were inside his office with the door closed. The lights were out. This was the same room in which they had spent hours in meetings, conferring, and dictating. Now, it was different. Somehow soft and intimate. Not because the room was dark. Fading light gently filtered in through the windows behind Zain's desk. The lack of the bright over-head lights that neither one of them moved to turn on, the closeness of Zain, and the realization that she'd missed him, changed the entire atmosphere. Asa had been, if not exactly with him, around him most of the day, had spend an entire day with him not long ago, and still she missed him as if she hadn't seen him since forever.

Zain stood with his back to the door.

"Asa." That was all. Then he kissed her.

A teasing storm of caresses erupted inside the soft corners of her mouth. Intimate, that's what it was. His lips moved, parted and became a part of her own. A slight probing led to all-out possession, his tongue demanding, hers responding. Intimate couldn't begin to describe this rush of feelings swirling inside of her.

The kiss ended, but not the storm. He was nuzzling her neck. Asa felt the deep breaths he took as he inhaled, his finger wrapping around the edge of her curls. He pulled back to stare down at her. "Beautiful. I love your hair down."

"Is that the only reason you kissed me?"

"One of many. Before I'm tempted to come back for more. Tell me, what did you want?"

Asa almost laughed out loud. She'd forgotten. She concentrated, slowly backtracking her thoughts to the moment he walked in. "I wanted to talk to you. About today."

"And you will. Later. I've got a meeting to go to."

"Oh." She was a bit surprised to hear that. "Do you need me to come?"

"Not at all."

Asa didn't like the sound of that.

"It's personal."

Personal? She really didn't like the sound of that. What was more personal than the soul-moving storm of a kiss they had just shared. Asa stopped herself from becoming upset. They had just begun this relationship. She couldn't demand too much too soon. One thing was certain, they needed to set some more specific guidelines on the working/personal situation.

"I can come by later, after the meeting."

Asa nodded.

Zain teased her with a few kisses that felt like tiny raindrops before the promise of a downpour. He opened the door to his office, trailing a pleased humming noise behind him.

Asa calmed the storm inside of her before making her way out of Zain's office. There Brent sat in her chair at her desk, waiting for her.

"Mr. Darbry passed a minute ago."

"Oh?"

"You were both in there quite a while."

"Yes."

"Asa, I know you don't want me to get into your business—"

"Then please, don't." The irritation she was feeling leaked out. She didn't want to fight with Brent.

"I can't help it, Asa, I'll hate myself if I don't."

"Then go on!" Asa's thumbs pressed against the corners of her eyes, her fingers pointed upward, making a silent plea to the heavens above for patience.

"Sending a request up above for my lips to lock shut?"

"For my patience to grow when dealing with my overly protective family members."

"I'll make it quick. Be careful."

"You said that before."

"Then be extra careful."

"Brent, my cousin," a hand landed on each of his shoulders. "I can assure you that I am going into this relationship with my eyes wide open."

"It's already a relationship?"

"Brent, please!"

"All right, okay." He held his hands up. "You handle this *relationship* your own way." His voice lowered. "Just know that I'm here for you."

"As always." Asa kissed him on his cheek.

"I'll be keeping my eye on Zain Darby."

"Not too close, cousin. For some reason he seems worried about you."

Brent stood. "Too bad. One thing I've noticed is that he is very concerned about you."

"What does that mean?"

"Nothing." Brent's eyes shifted nervously. "Nothing more than I should put two and two together and realized that Mr. Darby was your mystery man. Zain Darby at an Easter egg hunt, that was suspicious enough, then your mystery date, and the comment on the way to Pensacola," he paused, "my own eyes seeing you pulled willingly into his office. It all added up to me stepping forward to tell you to—"

"'Be extra careful,' I know, and as I said before, I know what I'm doing." Asa gathered her purse and briefcase, and went into the lunchroom to get her bag. Brent was right behind her.

"I'll be ready to leave in ten minutes." Lisa stopped him long enough for Asa to wave good-bye and make a getaway.

Brent caught up with her at the elevator. "I did have a reason for waiting at your desk. I won't be catching the ferry with you today."

"Date with Lisa?" Asa pressed the lighted button to signal for the elevator.

"Yep, don't make dinner for me."

Asa stepped into the elevator. "Be careful, now," she teased as the doors closed between them. Brent's heart was in the right place and he was still trying to back off a bit. He'd had enough sense not to mention the low blood sugar she'd had earlier. They were becoming ridiculously regular, belying her assertion that she could take care of herself. She could, but never before had she had so much to contend with; Zain and her overpowering attraction to him, her parents sudden interest in her life, her discovery of her four years of protected independence in college. It was upsetting her entire system.

But to be honest, that last episode *was* her fault. Asa couldn't blame it on Zain as she'd done before. And she knew she would have been okay without Brent's intervention, but he was there and Asa leaned on him because she was feeling a depression that had evolved from the restlessness and anger she had awaken with this morning. Asa had used her treadmill to burn some of it off before leaving for work. She had eaten her regular breakfast, not taking into consideration the effect of the extra exercise. Her body was regulated, used to her evening workouts, but the extra jog she took this morning had burned a lot of the carbs she had eaten, leaving little for the insulin she took this morning, resulting in another low. Asa knew she was supposed to have extra carbs with extra exercise. She had to get her act together if she was going to prove that she could be a completely independent woman.

During the ferry ride home Brent's worries faded to the back of her head. Even the thought of her family's deception that had occupied her mind most of the day had changed from a stabbing pain in her heart to a dull ache. The change had happened, Asa realized, after Zain had held her in his arms. Talk about kissing your worries away. If she had known that was all it would take to ease her frustrations and hurt, Asa would have tried the remedy immediately. On second thought, she wouldn't have. Their relationship was too new, and Asa was too concerned about broaching a personal matter in the workplace. She was determined to stick to their agreement of keeping work and personal matters separate. The rule had lasted until the end of their first workday together as a couple. She sighed deep and long leaning against the rail. Her eyes were fixed on the view, for once in her life seeing but not really appreciating it.

The ferry docked. She slowly exited with the other passengers. Asa went right past the Dry Dock Cafe. She thought about stopping for a few minutes but didn't feel like it. What she felt—Asa stopped in the middle of the block. What she felt like doing right this minute was anything with Zain. Well, almost anything, she amended as she remembered the kisses she had shared with him and the stormy feelings that always took over. Feelings that could easily progress in the directions Zain had already told her he was more than ready to go, had already demanded a time frame for.

Asa shook her head. How could she, a twenty-three year old virgin, hold up against such an incredible, demanding god among men. At the moment none of that mattered. The need to see him, to be with him, that's what mattered.

Her feet took her home faster than she would have thought possible. Asa made her way to the back of the house, wishing that Zain had ridden the ferry with her, wondering for the first time what this meeting could be about. Why hadn't he said more? Should she really expect him to say more at this stage in their relationship? Asa hadn't revealed any of her problems to him. Not even when he'd asked her to share a secret last night. Guilt rose to the surface as she remembered admitting being tired after he confessed to missing her. Her response showed exactly how upset she had been. Asa decided to do better because she wanted to know more about the dynamic boss/man in her life. Maybe she would even find out what this personal meeting he had gone to was all about.

The house was quiet. Asa liked it that way. It gave her time to think and cook. As she grilled a trio of chicken breasts, Asa forced her mind to think back on her child-hood days before living with Auntie Reenie, Uncle Boyd and Brent. Funny, she had no memories before that. Asa had always assumed that she was simply too young to remember, but other people had memories before the age of five. The chicken sizzled on the stove top grill. Asa flipped the pieces over absently planning to save the leftovers for lunch one day. As she concentrated, a picture in her mind formed, hazy, then suddenly sharp and clear as a mirror image. It was she, a much younger version of herself, younger than five she was sure, sitting in the middle of a white wooden bed, surrounded by painted flowers on every wall. Her mother, Ann Marie, sat next to her reading out of a huge book. Where had that come from? Asa had wanted to remember something but she hadn't thought she would come up with something so quick and so clear. The picture was etched in her brain now, along with feelings she'd never associated with her mother before, peace, comfort, and belonging. Why had it stayed hidden for so long?

She absently put a pot of water on the stove to boil. Now that her mind was opened, other long ago scenes flooded her mind: her mother coloring with her on the floor, making cookies, comforting her because she had to leave her painted flowered room to move to a new house. A hug, a kiss, and a promise from her mother that they would make new flowers in her new room stopped the tears. This was all so amazing. And they had made new flowers, Asa remembered. Her father, of all people, had helped. No less than three different rooms flashed in her mind, all with painted flower walls. An image of her father painting a fat pink petal was the last before the memories faded.

The water was boiling and the chicken needed to be turned over. Asa flipped the chicken and added pasta to the pot, stunned by what her mind had revealed to her. Why did she remember this now, after all these years? The entire revelation shook her up. Asa completed the meal, then methodically checked her sugar, drew up her insulin, took her shot and ate without remembering much of what she was doing. The past still filled her mind. Maybe her parents really did care about her.

The phone rang. She picked it up, forgetting to say hello.

"Asa."

Zain's voice. She let out a breath, clearing her mind. She had thought enough about the past, been angry enough about things that happened years ago. This man represented her future, maybe no more than her immediate future, but she wanted to think about him right now and nothing else.

"Asa? Are you okay?"

"I'm fine…"

"Zain," he finished for her.

"I know who you are."

"Simply checking. I didn't want you mistaking me for Mr. Darby."

"And you aren't?"

"Not when Mr. Darby isn't allowed to so much as smile at you when I have so many other more enjoyable things in mind."

"Zain."

"Exactly who I am and more than happy to be."

"Where are you?"

"On my way over. Am I still welcomed?"

"Yes," she answered, hanging up after a soft good-bye.

No sooner had she put the phone down than the doorbell rang. Must be Brent, she thought. "Probably left his keys," she muttered loudly, then let out an unexpected squeak as Zain's handsome face appeared behind the curtained window. She pressed her forehead against the cool glass. Did he look that good all day? Anger was a horrible thing if it had kept her from noticing.

She stepped back to open the door. Zain stepped inside, closing it behind him without making a sound. The coolness on her forehead was replaced by gentle warmth as Zain leaned his forehead against hers.

"You've started talking to yourself?"

"How'd you get here so fast?"

Neither answered. They had spoken at the same time, their words and breath colliding. Zain's arms went to her waist, traveled up her back only to move down, a second's pause, down once again, caressing her bottom with gentle, possessive hands as he inched her closer.

Asa wanted to speak. She wanted to say wait, then again, don't wait, as a wave of Zain's power hit her full force. She rode the wave, moved with and against his hard, male body. His hands cupped her bottom, firmly lifting her against his hardness, shifting her one way, then another, positioning her to feel, no, to ride, and crash into the energy he created. Too much. This wave was too high, too intense.

"Please stop," she whispered in a voice that begged him to do anything but. Yet his hand, his body, froze immediately. He held her still.

"Asa?" he breathed in her ear. His voice was heavy with longing. It asked. Asa answered.

"Please don't stop."

His hands pulled her against him once again. Every bit of him was a hard and thunderous wall of sensations. The lower half of their bodies sought a union Asa had never experienced before. She closed her eyes tight, savoring the feel of his hardness probing, circling the pulsating area between her thighs. She wanted more.

Asa could feel Zain moving differently. What was he doing? The rhythm had changed. His body was still pressed against her, yet he was moving her back then downward. Asa didn't speak. She was feeling too much to protest. Instead a moan flowed out of her mouth as easy and natural as any sound she had ever made.

She opened her eyes to find Zain's milk chocolate ones boring into hers. They were hot and—they were hot. Somehow she had been positioned on top of him. They were on the sofa, Asa realized.

"Shall we continue?" he asked.

Asa answered without words, her lower body pressing into his and at the same time brushing his mouth with her own.

Zain was quick to respond to her nonverbal answer, his hands moving to slowly raise her skirt until it bunched up across her hips. His fingers moved under the elastic of her panties to caress her bottom. Finally, skin-to-skin contact. A part of Asa's brain related to her tactical senses that this was only one of the many sensations she would experience. Asa's body of it's own accord moved even closer, pressing harder against him, the waves inside her pounding, the blood rushing where it had never rushed before.

"Asa." Zain's hands were on her hips. "Asa, wait, be still." He let out a long, hissing sound.

Zain held her hips, freezing the movement. She was now motionless, but only because Zain held her that way. She couldn't stand this sudden stillness when the waves inside her were pushing to be set free.

He began to rain soft kisses on her neck. She was enjoying this but—"Zain, please!" Then, "Oh, yes, please!" One of his hands found its way under her panties and into the mist of curls and pounding waves. His fingers moved, gently separating her, delving into her moistness. That's where the wave of sensations built, rising through and above her, pulling one word, one thought from her.

"Z-a-i-n!"

Asa's head lay against his chest. His heart beat loudly in her ear. Asa had never felt so relaxed, so wonderful, so satisfied. This was all more than she expected, more than she had planned to deal with. His fingers moved, still inside her panties. A new surge of feeling rose beneath his touch. Asa nuzzled his neck, gasping as Zain's finger found its way inside her, stopping at the natural barrier he had discovered with this new touch.

"Exactly what I thought. You're a virgin."

Asa shivered slightly at the feel of a part of him inside her before lifting herself, rising slightly above him to ask if he had problem with that when he whispered, "My sweet, virgin angel. Do you know how much I want to be inside of you?" His fingers moved slowly out, then in again. Asa's body reacted with a swell of something more, something bigger then what she had just experienced. Then the doorbell rang.

CHAPTER 13

Asa sat up. Zain's finger carefully eased from within her. He gently cupped her before slowly reclaiming his hand. Their different reactions highlighted his experience and her lack of it. He enjoyed her innocence until Asa quickly shifted, leaving an empty feeling inside and out at the loss of her warm body. Then there was a shy glance she cast his way, a nervousness surrounding her that Zain attributed to the newness of what they shared. The guilt. No! That could not have been guilt that flashed across her face before she turned to the door when the bell rang once again. Just the thought that she would feel guilty was more painful than the fact that he was hard, ready and wanting his sweet, virgin angel back in his arms.

Someone leaned on the bell good and long. "Asa, open up."

It was Thomas's voice. Zain stood, wanting to growl at him to go away and leave them to what they had started before the doorbell rang, before Asa turned shy and nervous and—please let him be wrong—guilty.

Instead, the look of nervousness on her face, her head twisting from him to the door, prompted him to say, "Point me in the direction of the bathroom and I'll let you get rid of Thomas. I don't think either of us wants anyone to see me in this condition."

They both looked down. His pants were heavy with his swollen hardness wanting nothing more than to be surrounded by her just as his probing finger had had the pleasure of experiencing.

"Asa! Open up!" Thomas yelled, beginning to sound panicky.

"Sounds impatient," Zain said calmly for Asa's sake, wanting to open the door himself and give Thomas a good—naw, that wouldn't be nice, Asa wouldn't thank him for it.

Asa nodded.

"The bathroom?" he asked.

"Straight back before the kitchen," she whispered as if she were worried about Thomas hearing her.

He couldn't resist laying a kiss on her lips before walking toward the back of the house.

"What took you so long?" Zain heard Thomas ask, his voice carrying straight through the house reaching as far as the bathroom. He wanted to hear every word, his only reason for leaving being that he didn't want Asa to be embarrassed.

Zain heard the words "forgot" and "keys" as he went into the bathroom. He lowered the toilet seat and sat. Thoughts of Thomas and the fact that this was the second time he'd heard mention of a key in connection with Asa and her house sent a tormented knot into his stomach. Jealousy gripped him, killing his arousal in an instant. Good. Zain stood. He wasn't one to hide in bathrooms anyway.

Zain walked out of the tiny room, closing the door behind him. He stopped in the narrow hall, not moving because they were coming his way. Thomas was in the lead, walking through Asa's house as if he'd done it many times before.

"I realized something that made me rethink my advice to you earlier," Thomas was saying.

Zain leaned back, not wanting to be seen. He didn't want to interrupt Thomas's tirade. They had stopped in the dark room just before the hallway. Asa was blocking his path. Still shooting for secrecy, he supposed.

"And?" Asa questioned.

"And I realize that I have to do something about it."

"We've been over this. It's my life."

"True, but I can't stand by and keep my mouth shut, let you do this to yourself. I know *why* you're making this choice. It's all tied to that mess on Easter."

What mess? Zain wondered, not all that concerned about that bit of information. Asa had already agreed to give him a chance, to show her who he really was before Easter. Zain was simply trying to follow the argument. He was missing something, he realized, but one thing rang clear. Thomas did not like the idea of Zain and Asa as a couple.

"Now how do you figure that, Brent?" Asa said with a calm coolness that chilled even Zain's bones.

"You're angry because you want to do everything on your own. I won't let you go that way. You are going to have to get used to that fact that I love you and I'm going to be a part of your life forever."

The knot in Zain's stomach grew, spreading, twisting his insides, amplifying the pounding in his chest. If Zain hadn't realized he was jealous, he would have thought he was coming down with something. He had heard enough. This had to be a good time for an entrance. Zain was tired of hearing Thomas's voice anyway and ready to fire him this instant. But that wouldn't be professional. He deleted that option before joining them.

"Good evening, Thomas," Zain said casually walking toward them to wrap an arm around Asa.

"Mr. Darby," was all the younger man said as Zain coldly stared at him.

"Brent," Asa's voice broke the strained silence. "Get what you need. If we have to do this it'll have to be later."

"We definitely will." He rushed past them.

Zain watched as Thomas went into the room that had to be the kitchen and directly to a closed door.

"Where is Thomas going?" Zain forced himself to ask with a calmness he didn't feel. He had to remember that he had no hold on her, not yet anyway.

"To his side of the house."

Surprise at this answer caused a dozen questions to pop into his head. Before he could ask any of them someone called from the front of the house, "Asa? Brent?"

"Back here," Asa answered Lisa's call.

Lisa stopped cold as she eyed them standing so close together, his arm around Asa, who he was pleased to notice, hadn't moved an inch from him.

"So, it's finally gotten like that?" Lisa folded her arms.

"So much for keeping our relationship low profile," Zain told Asa.

"When has it ever been?" Lisa said matter-of-factly. "Where's Brent?"

"Next door."

"And mad as a crab just before it hits a boiling pot of water."

Asa nodded. "Talk to him."

"All I can do is try. Which is what I did before he came charging in here. We were eating at that Dry Dock when he went nuts." Lisa disappeared behind the same door Thomas had gone through.

"All right, Asa, what's the deal with Thomas?" Zain demanded as soon as Lisa had gone.

"The last person I want to talk about is Brent. Can we do that later?"

Zain stared at her long and hard. She seemed very upset, not cool and calm as usual.

"We'll save it, but I need to get one thing clear. Does he live here?"

"No, he lives next door. This *is* a double."

"That usually means you live in separate houses. This one has a connecting door."

"I know." She turned sideways deep in thought. "I've been thinking that it's not such a good idea."

Good, Zain thought, nodding in agreement.

"Come on, give me a hand. I know what I should have done a long time ago."

Asa grabbed Zain's hand, pulling him into the kitchen. She dug inside a drawer. He looked over her shoulder, his eyes catching her scent as he inhaled. She swished around, kite string, a screwdriver which she handed to him, tacks, pens, and pencils before pulling the drawer completely out and raising her hand triumphantly a few seconds later.

"A lock." Zain was liking this idea more and more.

"Help me put it on."

It was one of those hinge locks that could be easily screwed into place. "We don't need a screwdriver for this."

"I realize that," Asa said, taking the tool from him and throwing it back into the open drawer. Her fingers brushed against his. An excited wave, a taste of what they'd shared before Thomas's interruption, passed between them.

"We've got a lot to talk about." Asa handed him the lock.

Zain gladly screwed the eye of the lock into one side then twisted the other half into the door. That done, he clicked it into place. It was a satisfying sound.

Zain thought he saw a touch of sadness in her eyes, but the next instant her lips lightly pressed against his. "Thanks."

"You're welcome." Zain pulled Asa into another kiss when she would have backed away.

She did pull back a second later. "This is what we need to talk about."

"I prefer to use a variety of options when attempting to communicate."

"I've noticed. Why don't you have a seat. The kitchen's as good a place as any to have this discussion."

"How about the room behind us."

"That's my bedroom, and right now the forbidden zone."

It was obvious that Asa, wasn't interested in sharing any more hot anything. Zain sat at the table, resigned to a night of frustration. At least this time it would be eased with the memory of what it felt like to have Asa in his arms, the feel of her body against his and the pulsating tremors he'd felt against his hand as he made her scream his name. On second thought it wouldn't help.

Frustration was his destination tonight.

"Uh," he unknowingly grunted aloud.

"It's chicken and pasta," he heard her say. She moved to dish out some food. Somehow he had agreed to eat. He might as well satisfy one of his appetites tonight. He hadn't had time to eat earlier, coming over right after the Al-Anon meeting. Important details flooded his mind. His worry that he'd find Asa drunk or drinking because of her strange behavior today. One fact he was sure of: There was absolutely no alcohol on her breath.

Asa placed the pasta-laden plate into a small microwave. Zain glanced around the room for evidence of alcoholic beverages, his frustrations and the things he would love to do to his sweet angel's virgin body thrown to the back of his mind. He scanned the open shelves, nothing. But then again, why would she keep the stuff out in the open. She probably had a stash somewhere. The fridge. Maybe she had some beer or wine there.

"Mind if I have something to drink?"

"Sure." Asa opened the fridge, leaning forward to reach for something inside. Zain's hands itched. The lovely shape of the bottom he had molded, caressed and held shifted left, then right before she stood to offer something. "Bottled water, diet soft drinks or the regular stuff. Sorry if you were looking for something stronger. I never keep anything harder than that in the house."

Was that because she drank it as soon as she bought it, binging, or that she only drank when she was out. Probably both.

"Zain," she was looking at him strangely, "which one?"

"Water's fine."

Asa handed him a clear bottle of water and closed the door with her hip. Zain had forgotten to look inside. At the meeting tonight he had heard the experience of others regarding their attempts control their loved one's addiction. Zain realized he couldn't control Asa's problem. He would have better luck attempting to control his reaction to the distracting picture Asa had made a minute ago. Asa, was the only one who could control her addiction. Still, he felt a need to learn her habits in connection with this disease. This preoccupation with her body had to come second.

"Zain."

Asa was giving him that strange look again. The microwave gave a beep. Zain stood. "I think I'll have a coke instead."

"Help yourself," she offered, setting the hot plate of food on the table in front of him.

Zain went to the fridge wishing Asa would stop giving him that "what's-wrong-with-you look." It was worse than that calm and cool expression she wore at work.

Zain quickly scanned the contents. Tons of diet drinks, sugar-free jello, carrots, broccoli, grapes, a bag of apples, fat free milk, and those tiny little juice boxes. All the signs of a person concerned with having a healthy diet. Zain grabbed a juice box and tossed it up in the air. "You didn't offer me one of these."

"I didn't take you for a juice box kind of guy."

"You'd be surprised to discover the kind of guy I really am."

"I'm working on that, remember?"

Zain jabbed the straw into the little box and emptied it in one swallow. "And how is it progressing?" He threw the box into a nearby trash can, then moved to stand directly in front of her. "Would you care to elaborate?" Zain had meant only to ask that question, having resigned himself to a night of talking. But she was looking at him with those beautiful eyes, her round angel face and curly hair a perfect combination that deleted his reasoning. His hands went to her waist, intending to pull her closer. Instead, they were making their way down. Asa grabbed them both before they got to their destination.

"Don't," was all she said.

Zain gave her a quick kiss on the forehead, put both hands in his pockets and let out a frustrated breath. "My food's getting cold," he said to fill in the silence and change the subject. He sat at the table.

"Please eat, then." Asa sat at the table across from Zain and studied him a second before going on as if their conversation hadn't been interrupted. "I *can* elaborate, you know."

"Go on," he paused, the fork halfway to his mouth. "I'm listening."

"You stopped when I asked you to."

Zain started to choke. Huge, hacking coughs that shook his entire body in an attempt to force an entire pasta twist out of his windpipe. Asa was banging on his back, shaking him more than the choking. She handed him a bottle of water when he finally stopped. He took a huge swallow and glared at her.

"What did you expect? That I'd force you?" From the expression on her face it was obvious that she'd thought exactly that. "I suggest you keep your mind open while you're getting to know me."

When she said nothing, simply stared at him with a surprised look on her face Zain went on. "Unbelievable!" He kept his seat as both of his arms flew on either side of him in one frustrated move. "What kind of man do you think I am?"

"Zain, I didn't mean to insult you. It's just that you're so…male."

"Is that a negative assessment?" He leaned forward to ask.

"You don't understand. You're so there, so all over. You can't be ignored."

From his point of view there was nothing wrong with that. For him, Asa was everywhere. Inside his brain, his dreams, his bed. All she had to do was smile that sweet angel smile and he was done for. "And?" he asked not fully understanding.

"You surround me and give off these feelings of—"

"Sexual desire." His voice had lowered. "That's exactly what it is. It is exactly what exploded between us before Thomas came banging on your front door." He leaned across the table resting his forehead against hers. "Admit it. It's what makes you want me. It's one of the reasons I want you, too."

"One?"

"We'll get to the others when you know me better."

His sweet angel actually gulped before answering. "I can deal with that."

"And understand this. Mutual desire means mutual consent. I will never force you to do anything you don't want to do." Zain stepped back a bit and with a thumb raised her chin high. "Do you understand what I mean?"

"Does any of this have anything to do with my virginal status?"

"Not beyond the fact that it makes me want you more. You are in control, Asa. You set the pace. When you're ready, I'll be with you every step of the way."

"No more talk about timelines then."

"No." He was going to say more but how do you tell a woman not to make you suffer too long after you've promised to wait until *she* is ready.

Asa kissed him softly. "I'm glad there's more of you to know." She took his plate to warm once again.

Having her say that to him was worth holding back.

Zain left a half hour later, full, frustrated, but happy. Their relationship was growing, bursting out of the secret pen Asa had tried to establish. No more than twenty minutes after he left her, Zain walked into his condo. He went straight to the phone.

"I need a secret," he said as soon as Asa's hello flowed into his ear. Zain was hoping their discussion, their new start would ease Asa into trusting him enough to reveal her biggest secret.

"I've got one for you." Her voice was serious. Zain waited but didn't have to for long. "I'm a horrible daughter," she said in a rush.

This was the last thing he expected to hear. "Why would you say that? Your parents didn't raise you, right? You can't be a horrible daughter if they were never parents."

There was silence on the other end and a barely audible sniff. "But at one time they were. I just didn't remember or I decided to forget. I don't know."

This was more than a secret. Asa needed to talk, Zain could tell. "Tell me about it."

There were a few more sniffs, then she must have pulled herself together because she went right into a summary of her visit to Florida. She told him of her parents' request that she live with them, then about the discovery of the room-mate for hire.

Zain understood the anger and resentment. He would have felt it too. A sadness crept into Asa's voice as she told about the unexpected memories of her mother and father when she was little. "I feel so guilty. How could I have forgotten?"

"Maybe you wanted to. It might have been because they sent you away." Zain felt a growing warmth inside. Asa was confiding something important to him. This was not the secret he wanted, but this sharing proved that they had taken an even bigger step forward than he'd realized.

"No, I didn't want to be sent away. I was only five."

"Of course not. What five-year-old wants to be separated from their parents?"

"I didn't mean to, but I've been so ugly to them for so long. Maybe there are other times, other things they've done for me that I've blocked out."

"Possibly."

"Still, that doesn't excuse them from hiring a guard dog."

"No, it doesn't, but, Asa, did they give you a reason for that?" Was she battling alcohol even then? That would be reason enough for parents to pay for someone to watch over their child. That could be. There was such a thing as a teenage alcoholic. This was his opportunity to get her disease out in the open. Suddenly, a loud banging came through the phone line.

"That's Brent," Asa said before he could ask.

"Tell Thomas he's not welcome. You're all mine."

"That sounds pretty possessive."

"It is," he admitted. Then going all out he added, "I am." Zain paused before asking, "You don't like that?"

Asa didn't say anything for a long time. "I think I actually do like it. As long as you don't turn crazy on me."

Next Zain could hear Thomas's voice. "I'll call you back," she promised before hanging up.

Zain waited impatiently five, then ten, then a torturous fifteen minutes. The long narrow hand on the clock had agonizingly inched toward twenty minutes when the phone finally rang.

"Asa!"

"I need a secret," she said quietly.

The banging had stopped and he could hear nothing but his sweet angel Asa. Zain's face split into a grin. "I've got one for you, but first tell me about Thomas. How did he take being locked out?"

"He's dealing with it."

"Good." Zain let out a breath. He didn't want to have to interfere with the way Asa was handling Thomas, but would have crossed the river in a flash to convince him what a good idea that lock was.

"Your secret?" Asa prompted.

"I've got a boat."

"Oh?"

She sounded disappointed. No more than she deserved for that lousy confession of being tired that she had given him the night before. But Zain wouldn't leave it at that. There was more.

"Yesterday when I went sailing on the lake, this vivid image of you standing beside me sharing the whispering breeze and the open natural beauty around me grew in my mind."

"Oh!" This time there was no trace of disappointment in her voice.

"You were there. Even when you're not with me, Asa, you're with me. That's my secret. The image of your beautiful face can be brought to my mind in an instant. Unfortunately it's not enough."

She sighed his name, "Zain."

"I'm going to visualize you here with me tonight, Asa, until I can see you, touch you, feel you tomorrow."

"I have a feeling I'll be doing the same."

"Have a few sweet, hot dreams about me, then."

"I don't think I can do anything else."

Zain disconnected. There was a thin layer of sweat on his forehead. He closed his eyes. There was Asa behind his lids. Beautiful, sexy, wanting him. Sleep would be a long time coming.

CHAPTER 14

Zain strolled into the office at exactly 7:30 A.M. He stopped at her desk and leaned forward, firm arms supporting his weight, eyes catching hers. "I need to see you in my office, Ms. Taylor."

Asa quietly followed him inside, closing the door behind her. Then she rushed him. There was no other description for the way Asa threw herself at him. Zain caught her by the waist and held her to him. They shared a good morning kiss, the night of separation too many hours apart. His lips slowly left hers, coming back a few times to linger before softly accusing, "You almost knocked me backwards."

"You're strong, the god of all men. You can handle it."

"What's that supposed to mean?"

Asa hadn't told him about her initial image of him. Deciding to save it for another secret session, she changed the subject. "A simple morning kiss from one small woman is not going to knock you to your knees."

"You underestimate yourself, sweet angel Asa." He blew into her ear. "I've had myself a whole week's worth of kisses. That in itself is enough to reduce a man to nothing."

"It has been a week. I can't believe it's Friday already." The speed with which the last few days had passed gave her a lightheaded feeling. Their relationship seemed to have accelerated. Asa realized now that it had been a ridiculous idea to try to confine the love she felt for this man to mere out-of-office encounters. Her feelings were much, much too strong. Love.

Yes, Asa had to admit that it was love.

She hadn't told him, didn't actually realize it until last night, after their secret sharing conversation. Those secrets were becoming more and more personal. Not to mention gently seductive and intimate. The ability to divulge vivid dreams, to discuss their concerns and to anticipate making love was natural and free. How could the fact that she loved this man do anything but explode in her mind?

"What do you want to do tonight, sweet angel Asa? I'm open to any suggestions."

A few suggestive ideas sprang to mind but Asa directed her comments in another direction. "That's right. This is the weekend. No slave driving timekeeper of a boss to worry about the next day."

"'Zain the Pain', you mean?"

Asa laughed and nuzzled his neck. "That's right, you know all about that nickname."

"There is little I don't know."

The phone rang. Zain reached for it with one hand, using the other to keep her next to him. "Think about what you want to do this weekend," he whispered before turning his attention to the phone.

"Grammy Dee?" Zain sounded surprised. Asa listened to his side of the conversation. It was strange for Grammy to call so early in the morning. "Is something wrong?" He paused, his hand tense on her waist. "Not a thing, huh?" Zain's finger walked a path up her side. "Hold on a minute."

"Visiting Grammy Dee should be one of the things on our 'to do' list." He kissed her lips before releasing her, ending their morning greeting. Zain seemed to easily shift into work mode. "Those files on the Ramsey account need to be updated." He kissed her once more.

Well, not quite so easily. Asa moved away from him as Zain went on talking to his grandmother, his expression one of confidence in her feelings for him and her ability to do the job he had assigned.

"Our list," Asa whispered as she sat at her desk. They had a mutual list. That felt wonderful.

Asa's morning flew by with Zain passing through once in awhile. As it had been all week, he concentrated almost completely on whatever program glitch, problem or client he was dealing with at the moment. But not so much that he didn't let her know that he knew she was there, and not simply as his assistant and secretary. Zain would sit on the edge of her desk to say hello but left more than that brief message as his deep stare communicated some of the thoughts reflected in his eyes. A slow heart-melting smile, like the kind he gave her when he hadn't seen her in a while, a few minutes, a few hours, however long, was proof that he missed her when she wasn't around. Before a dictation session, Zain would stand so close Asa could feel the heat of his body. His long fingers would gently pull a curl and watch it bounce before getting to the business at hand.

Asa was amazed at his self-control. She wished she had it. Each time Zain came anywhere near her she wanted to pull him to her, rush him as she had done this morning. She peered at the clock, mid-morning. It was snack time. Asa saved the changes to the file she had been working on and dug into her purse for the grapes she had stashed there.

Zain popped his head out of his office. "Break time?" He glanced at his watch. "Ten on the nose." He came to sit on the edge of her desk. "Got some for me?"

Zain had been teasing her all week about being so rude. If she ate in front of him, Zain thought that he should at least be offered some. "Invite me inside your office and I might have something for you."

He stood immediately. He had a bit too much anticipation on his face. "I'm only offering—"

"—any offering from you, my sweet angel Asa, is welcomed," he interrupted.

When he said things like that the words were not only heard and understood but seeped into her skin dissolving into her blood stream to flow straight to her heart. Blood pounding and her heart swelling, Asa suppressed a grin as she pulled another container from her purse. "Will sweet, juicy white grapes do?"

Zain leaned toward her, his forehead resting against hers. "Will they be offered by your fingers."

"That might be a possibility."

"While my head rests in your lap?"

The image was promising.

"Excuse me?" a voice interrupted behind them.

Zain growled, though low enough so that only Asa heard him before turning around to grumble, "What can I do for you, Thomas?"

"I came to speak to Asa."

Zain took a small step back then folded his arms. "Go on."

"Privately."

"Then do that on your own time, not Execute's."

This was quickly getting out of hand. The all-powerful Zain had suddenly appeared while the overprotective Brent was rising. "Zain," Asa quietly interrupted to remind him, "this is my own time. And last I checked I get to decide how I use it, not Execute."

"That might be true, but Thomas can say what he needs to say right here and now."

Brent turned to her, a bit of sadness in his eyes, obviously thinking she would automatically side with Zain. Asa hadn't said two words to her cousin all week long. Partly because he hadn't spoken to her since she installed the lock between their houses.

"Give me a minute or two," Asa told Zain, not completely giving in to either of them.

Zain nodded but looked as if he wanted to say more. He went back into his office without another word. His steady stare directed at her cousin said it all. Asa hated the tension between her favorite cousin and the first man in her life she had come to love. Just saying that, the first man in her life that she loved, gave her a thrill. Brent wasn't going to spoil it for her. He looked at the grapes on her desk.

"At least you're remembering to have your snacks," were the first words out of his mouth.

"Falling back on old habits?"

"Hard not to. Sorry."

"You don't have to be. I'm only looking for you to tone things down a bit."

"Yeah. That's hard."

"I already know that. Change isn't easy." This was going better than she thought it would. "I'm glad you're talking to me again."

"I've been trying to for days. That lock, Mr. Darby, and your new earlier morning hours have made that impossible. Are you trying to knock all your family out of your life?"

"Brent, you didn't say that." This wasn't going so well after all, Asa realized.

"It's true. First your mom and dad, me, and I know for a fact that you haven't spoken to the aunt and uncle you claim to love so much."

"That doesn't mean I don't love them. When was the last time you spoke to them?"

Brent ignored this, saying, "I don't like what's happening to you, Asa."

They'd been through all of this already. "Tell me exactly what's happening to me."

"You're changing."

"Yes, I am, but for the better. I'm not knocking anyone out of my life. I'm only trying to stand up to life, on my own two feet."

"Which involves locking me out."

Asa nodded in agreement. "I'm sorry if I hurt your feelings, Brent. I love you but it was a step I needed to take."

"I was only protecting you."

"From the man I'm falling in love with."

"Don't tell me that, Asa." Brent's hands were waving wildly around. "You can't. He'll hurt you."

"You don't know that."

"Minutes roll by very quickly." Zain stood at the open office door. He had removed his jacket and rolled up his sleeves. He looked ready for battle.

"I've had enough of this. I'll see you later."

"How about lunch?" Zain suggested. "All three of us. We can get this all out in the open."

"I like that idea." Asa turned to her cousin. "Brent?"

"Okay."

"Bring Lisa along."

"Not a good idea, Mr. Darby. This is between the three of us."

"A love triangle?"

"I guess you can call it that," Brent agreed.

"Of course not!" Asa answered at the same time.

"Exactly why we need to clear the air. See you at twelve, Thomas. Asa, I'd like a word with you."

Asa turned from one to the other. They were both the most important men in her life and they were both walking away from her. She wanted to follow Brent, let him know she wanted him in her life just not protecting it or controlling it—but she'd said all that already. Brent couldn't be told, he had to be shown. That lock was a symbol of her independence. She couldn't move backwards.

"Sweet angel Asa."

She turned toward Zain's deep seductive tone. Asa didn't know if he was her future, but he was definitely her present. No man made her feel what Zain Darby made her feel.

"Bring the grapes," he suggested before disappearing inside.

"My break's almost over," Asa announced, closing the door behind her.

"I might be able to find a way to get you a few extra minutes."

It was strange yet unsurprising that Asa went straight to the sofa in the corner of the office with Zain comfortably settling himself with his head on her lap. Almost as if they hadn't been interrupted by Brent earlier.

Zain closed his eyes as Asa fed him a grape, giving herself one, then alternating until they were all gone. Not a word passed between them from the moment she sat and for a full five minutes after.

Zain's eyes suddenly opened. "I've got a secret." He sat up.

"You're a few hours early with that, aren't you?"

He stood towering above her. "This one can't wait. I've got to get it out. I've never dealt with this before."

"Okay," Asa said, nervously wondering what he would say, hoping he'd express his feeling even though she hadn't done much expressing of her own.

"I'm jealous of Thomas."

Asa almost laughed out loud, but pulled it back deep into her stomach at the serious expression plastered on his face.

"I know."

"And?"

"You have no reason to be."

"Maybe, but it's there. I'm getting to the point where I can barely look at him without—"

"Don't."

"Don't what? Be jealous?"

"Yes. Zain, we have something together, don't we?"

"I thought so."

"Brent has nothing to do with it."

"He's too much a part of your life."

"True, for now. He will always be in some way."

"I don't know if I can deal with that."

"At least you're honest." Asa had meant it when she told Brent that she was not knocking her family out of her life. She had room for Zain and her family. "I'm sorry you feel that way."

"Is that all you can say, Asa?"

"Right now, yes. We can discuss this further at lunch with Brent. My relationship with him should not affect ours."

He continued to stand above her for a long moment before finally nodding as if he understood. The frown on his face said the opposite. "I'd better get back to work." He grazed her lips and turned to his desk.

Asa went back to work, for the first time this week unsure of where they were going. Their relationship was moving exactly like the zig-zag that formed the first letter of his name.

Nothing with Zain seemed to be straight and easy for long.

Zain twirled the pen around and around between his fingers. This was the work he had been doing for the last hour. He had paced and fidgeted. He had never been so unnerved. One woman was doing this to him. One woman he wanted all to himself. He wanted no other man to have any claims on her. Her problems, her time, he didn't want to share any of it. But to feel it and to say it were two different things. Zain was sure he would come off sounding like some caveman. What modern day woman would appreciate a man saying that about her, "Me man, you woman. Stay away or me pound you with club!"

Or even worse, Zeus, as Asa had called him this morning, taking any woman he wanted simply because he wanted her. But Zain didn't want just any woman. He wanted Asa. Either image would do nothing to make him look good in her eyes. He could only be himself.

Zain threw the pen down and strode to the door. He took a huge breath before opening it. She was at the computer, probably decoding more of the Stewart files that had come in yesterday. Grammy Dee was right; she was an angel, his angel.

Zain went to sit in his usual spot on the corner of her desk. He gently kissed her on the cheek. When she turned toward him, he claimed her lips, pulling away almost immediately. "I've got a meeting with the geniuses."

"I know."

Zain was across the room when she called, "Please stay out of it with Brent."

"I'll try."

She silently nodded, looking as if she didn't believe him. Which was probably because he didn't believe himself either.

The object of his frustration came into view a second later. Thomas stood at the receptionist's desk drooling all over Lisa. Zain was ecstatic and disgusted at the same time. Thomas obviously had an interest in Lisa, but where did that leave Asa? Zain's thinking was idiotic because he wanted Asa. This falling in love thing was making him stupid.

Zain digested the *love* word, let it seep into his system and conscious mind. A blur of color suddenly shot past him. Thomas, he realized.

He was headed for Asa. It couldn't be anything good. Zain went after him, pausing a second to take a quick glance behind him. A middle-aged couple was entering Execute's offices headed toward the receptionist's desk. Zain caught up to Thomas before he reached Asa's alcove office, his hand landing on the younger man's shoulder. "What are you up to, Thomas?"

Thomas didn't turn around but clearly said, "Let me go, Mr. Darby. I've got to warn Asa. She doesn't want to see them."

"Who?"

"Her parents," Thomas faced him to say.

"The couple at the desk?"

"She's had enough surprises from them." Brent had moved from under his grasp and had already turned to continue with his warning mission.

"Maybe."

That stopped him. "What do you mean, maybe?"

A hard look Zain had never seen before entered Thomas's eyes. How could a man whose mind he respected, with whom he had had such a good working relationship, get so messed up? He wanted to delete the last few weeks and reinstall them, making necessary changes. Zain would interview Asa himself, decide not to hire her, instead, take her away with him where they could be alone. Crazy, but not such a bad idea.

"Wait a minute!" Thomas looked at him suspiciously. "What do you know about it?"

"Everything. Asa told me what happened on Easter Sunday. It'll be good for her to see them."

"How do you know what's good for her? You hardly know her!"

Hardly knew her! Something inside Zain snapped. He knew his sweet angel, her taste, her smell. He knew her, more than knew her. "I love her."

Thomas spun around, his eyes boring into Zain.

"What is all this noise?" Asa's voice reached them before her face came into view around the corner.

Zain was astounded at what he'd let slip out. He had only hinted before at what he felt for Asa. He hadn't told her, hadn't said a word to Lance, his best friend. Then why had he let his competition in on the news? Love wasn't making him stupid, he just was.

Thomas's eyes were on him. "You know, I almost believe you." Brent grabbed one of Asa's arms and pulled her back toward her alcove office. "Your parents are here. Lisa's stalling them. You don't want to see them. I can distract them while you get away."

"Not a good idea." Zain attached himself to her other arm. "You need to face them, talk to them straight and simple. Let some of that hurt inside of you out."

"Mind your business, Darby," Brent hissed in a heated whisper.

"This is my business, Thomas," Zain said in a calm, steely tone.

"Will you both let go of me!"

Zain had been concentrating so thoroughly on Thomas he had almost forgotten Asa was there. He dropped his hand, but only after Thomas had taken his own off Asa.

"The only thing I'm sure of is that this is *my* business, and *I'll* decide what I'm going to do."

She said it in that calm professional voice of hers. Asa was looking at both of them as if she would gladly pitch them both out the nearest window.

"Asa?" a woman's voice called. The couple had entered Asa's domain. The woman, who looked a bit worried and anxious, was a beautiful older version of her daughter. The man stood solid and stiff with no expression on his face. They stood close together, the woman's hand holding her husband's, tightly by the looks of it. Remembering what Asa had said about her parents, Zain was surprised by this aura of nervousness, and the open display of support by her father.

Asa didn't move, remaining where she was between Zain and Thomas. Her arms folded, she greeted her parents. "Hello, Mother, Father."

Couldn't she see how nervous they were? No, Zain realized as she calmly waited for her parents to respond.

"Is that how you greet—"

The older woman raised a hand. Asa's father clamped his lip shut. "I believe Asa has company. We'd better visit another time."

"Asa!" Zain softly demanded his eyes and voice begging her to stop them from leaving, to use this opportunity for a new beginning.

"Asa," Brent's plea was for her to do just the opposite, Zain was sure.

"No, don't go." Asa called them back. "This is my boss, Zain Darby and of course, Brent."

"Nice to meet you. You have a wonderful daughter here." Zain shook their hands while Brent merely gave them a weak smile.

"We were in town and hoped that you'd be free for lunch."

"Asa," Zain encouraged, spreading a hand before him.

"Asa," Thomas called in a warning voice.

Asa looked from one to the other then whispered, "I'm getting tired of hearing my name. I suddenly have a great need to get away from both of you." Zain was annoyed at being put in the same boat as Thomas, but pleased to hear Asa tell her parents with a ring of sincerity in her voice, "I'd like that."

The couple visibly relaxed, and still it amazed Zain that Asa hadn't noticed. "You two," she directed, pointing to Zain and Thomas, "need to keep that lunch appointment to straighten some things out before I see either of you again."

"Nice meeting you," Asa's mother said before turning to leave. Her father stopped long enough to shake his hand.

"Should you talk that way to your boss?" Zain heard Asa's mother ask as they walked down the hall.

Zain found himself alone with Thomas, valued-employee-turned-enemy. "Lunch?" he asked only because Asa would want him to.

"I don't think so."

"Then you're not interested in talking this out?"

"Not with you, sir. I only work for you." He took a few steps then turned to say, "Just know that I value Asa, her feelings and her happiness more than I do this job. Hurt her and I'll have to hurt you."

Thomas gulped at the end of his little speech. Zain was impressed. That took guts. New respect grew for him. Thomas had always shown his brains; maybe he had a little brawn in there, too. Still, Zain had to make his position clear. "Neither Asa's feelings nor your job are in danger as long as you stay out of our business."

"Right!" Thomas stormed away.

That would have been a perfect ending to their discussion if Zain hadn't had to follow him to get a late start on the project Thomas was in charge of presenting. The one Zain had invented a week ago. He could be professional. He wouldn't allow his relationship with Asa to affect his work. Zain put on his best irritated-boss frown, thinking to make Thomas nervous. Maybe he'd live up to the name 'Zain the Pain.'

CHAPTER 15

Asa stepped into the elevator coming back from lunch feeling closer to her parents then ever before. They had not suddenly become her confidantes, but for the first time in as long as Asa could remember, they simply had sat down and talked without the usual awkwardness. She thought that maybe recalling those special memories with her parents had melted some of the tension away. The elevator door opened. The two people who had shared the ride up with her stepped out. Her exit was blocked.

"So, how did it go?"

Zain stepped inside and pressed the first floor button.

Her eyes traveled from his firm brown finger, up his well-dressed arm and landed on the handsome face. Zain, she was surprised to discover, was genuinely concerned about her relationship with her parents. They had nothing to do with him, yet he had encouraged her to go with them. And now he stood anxiously waiting to hear the results.

"It was a good start."

"I'm glad." He hugged her. It was a hug of reassurance, of congratulations that could have easily turned intimate, but the elevator doors opened to reveal Brent and Lisa.

"Hi Boss, Asa," Lisa greeted as she walked inside, literally pulling Brent with her. He turned hard eyes on them.

Asa felt Zain's nod of acknowledgment. Having never received such a look from her cousin, Asa decided to ignore Brent's hostility. "Hey, Lisa, have a good lunch?"

"I ate. Brent stared at his food. I thought he was trying to blacken that fish with the heat from his eyes," she joked.

He was upset. Brent never ate when he was upset. Good thing he didn't have diabetes. He would have to eat no matter how he felt. Zain gave her hand a squeeze, somehow sensing that Brent's attitude was worrying her even when she tried to hide it.

"I guess the two of you didn't take my suggestion," Asa said to no one in particular.

"I tried," Zain muttered.

"Didn't feel the need," Brent answered.

A young woman walked quickly to the open elevator but paused before entering. "I'll take the next one," she said, backing away.

"I don't blame her," Lisa said as the doors closed. No one commented.

The tension in such a small space was overpowering. Lisa caught Asa's eye and rolled her own in exasperation.

"The need is obvious," Asa told Brent.

"The only thing obvious is the way this man is taking over your life."

"That's enough, Thomas." Zain growled.

"Brent, that was horrible," Lisa exclaimed at almost the same time.

"Now I'm the bad guy? What I said is nowhere near enough, and stay out of this, Lisa."

Asa was both surprised and appalled at her gentle cousin's behavior. "Brent, it might be better if we don't talk about this now."

"I think that we should."

The elevator doors opened and they all filed out. Zain still held her hand as they headed to his office. Brent followed. Lisa wasn't far behind.

"How did things go with your parents? Did they chew you up and spit you out as usual?"

Asa stopped at her desk and turned to face her cousin. He had always helped her deflect her parents' attacks. At least what she thought were attacks. Asa wasn't so sure anymore. He might be angry now, but Asa knew Brent would be happy for her. "No, they didn't. As a matter of fact we actually talked."

"You did?" Brent's light brown face turned red, his eyebrows moved up and down, the curls on his head jumping in sync with them. "So, Mr. Darby's advice was sound. You might think you don't need me now, Asa, but you will," his face turned sad, "when all this is finished." He directed a look at Zain and once more at her before leaving.

"Sorry boss, Asa, I'll talk to him."

Without conscious thought Asa's head lowered, her thumbs went to the corners of her eyes. Her fingers were not pointed upward for guidance. She gripped them together tightly seeking tolerance. Asa threw her hands up in the air. "I can't believe all this fallout from seeking a little independence!"

"Anything worth anything is not easy." Zain kissed her on the forehead.

"True." Asa sat at her desk.

Zain stooped before her. "Tell me exactly what it is with Thomas that makes him so…" Zain paused as if searching for the right word. That was unusual in itself. "There's only

one word I can think of to describe it and I have already
admitted to feeling it too."

"What word?"

"Possessive."

"You've never elaborated on that." Asa smiled, relieved
to find something else to dwell on. "As far as Brent's
concerned, his problem comes from years of protectiveness."

"How many?"

"Practically all my life. We grew up together. He was my
buddy, my pal."

"I'm beginning to understand."

"I hope so. Zain, please don't let his attitude jeopardize
his position here."

"He cares more about you than his job, Asa."

"I'm not surprised, but I don't want to be the reason for
him losing it." Asa paused. "I've got a secret for you."

"Now? You're early, and bold. This will be a face to face
sharing."

"You did it earlier. I can handle it." "Brent's jealous of
you."

"The feeling's mutual then."

"Looks like it."

They were both quiet for a while. Zain's hand was in
hers. Asa found herself amazed at what she'd learned about
him. The real Zain Darby had been slowly revealed to her as
the week progressed. This was not the same man who'd
appeared to be so full of himself when they first met.

"I've got it!" Zain pulled her up, dragging her into his
office. He rummaged inside his desk a few minutes before
holding up a brochure.

Asa read, "Computer Software Convention. This thing starts tomorrow."

"I know. I'd registered to attend, but then Lance went and got married on me. I didn't want to leave Execute for an entire week."

"But you're willing to now?"

"The geniuses can handle things while I'm gone. Lance will be back before us."

"You'd even trust Brent?"

"Thomas is a good man, our problems have nothing to do with work. They are of a more personal nature." His milk chocolate eyes connected with hers. She read wanting there, giving, and a pool of hot promises.

"I understand." The words floated out of her mouth in a soft breath.

"And to alleviate those problems the best course of action is to remove ourselves from his presence. At least until he gets used to the idea of us."

Asa was warming up to Zain's plan. Her thoughts were bursting through the wave of sensation brought on by his mesmerizing voice and eyes. "Brent doesn't stay mad long. He'll get over it, before we even come back."

"If he knows what's good for him."

"Zain." Asa said lightly not having the heart to put much emphasis on that admonishment. Zain was being very understanding.

"The only reason he's gotten away with so much is because I value his ability and you seemed to have this liking for him. I'm also still trying to show you what a nice guy I am."

"Thank you for your gracious understanding," Asa teased, needing to steady some of the waves that had begun to rise within her. His voice and look had started that. Was this really a good idea?

"So, how about it? We leave tomorrow morning, stay the week in Alabama, lounge around the beaches, enjoy Mobile Bay, maybe go fishing or sailing."

"How about attending the convention?"

"Of course."

"This is a working trip, right?" Asa knew she had to set some parameters now.

"Aren't you my assistant?"

"For now."

"You aren't still thinking of leaving?"

"That depends on what happens on this trip."

"Is that a warning?"

"I'm not ready to move this relationship to the next level."

"I thought we'd discussed this already. I'm only ready when you are." As he spoke, Zain closed the small distance between them. Asa leaned into the soft kisses he pressed on her lips. His head moved back, barely. "Well?"

"I would love to go to Alabama with you to lounge around the beaches, to fish and sail on the bay."

"And go to the convention."

"That, too."

"You have to realize, Asa, that I want your body." His hand landed on her side, moved up her rib cage and down again. "But only as much of it as you're willing to share. Right now I'm more interested in getting to know you. I enjoy being together and working with you. You have a sharp mind and a wonderful personality, sweet angel Asa. Now that I've found a woman with so much, I can't imagine my life, personal or business, without you."

One second he was standing in front of her, the next he was behind his desk. Asa turned to face him. His words stunned her, gave her hope for the possibility of a future with him, melting Brent's warning right out of her mind.

"Why don't you take the rest of the day off. Pack, do whatever you need to do. Later tonight we could visit Grammy Dee, maybe go out to dinner."

"I can do that. What about you?"

"I've got a few things to wrap up around here, delegate some duties, and I've a meeting later on."

"I can stay." Asa's blood was pumping in waves, her heart swelling. He looked just the same, as if he hadn't said those sweet, wonderful things to her. She didn't know how to act.

"No, go. I can handle this myself. I'll come to pick you up at about six-thirty."

Asa nodded. That would still be within her dinner hour. As soon as he saw her nod, Zain's mind, she could tell, went into hyper drive. He was jotting down something on a pad before him. His entire concentration was focused on trying to reschedule a whole week's worth of work. Asa walked up behind him and placed a kiss on the back of his neck. "See you tonight," she whispered, afraid to break his concentration.

He froze, then spun his chair around. Asa was in his lap, confronted with the most intense feeling of possession she had ever experienced with him before. It scared her. Should she back out of this idea of going to a week-long convention with him? Completely alone with him. His area of concentration moved to her lips. Lips that he marked as his.

"Tonight," was all he said before releasing her. Zain went back to work almost immediately but called out as she reached the door, "And all next week."

Asa kept going: to her office to collect her purse, the lounge to get her uneaten lunch, snack and insulin. She kept moving until she was on the ferry headed home. She had wanted to stand in the doorway of Zain's office. She had wanted to hear him say, not only tonight and all next week, but forever. Asa wanted to say the same to him herself. She wanted forever with Zain. She wanted it so bad, but would it be fair to him? Would Zain want a woman with a disease that would be a part of her for a lifetime? One without a cure.

Diabetes was one big pain. Yes, it could be controlled, but it also controlled her life. When she ate, what she ate, if she could do this or that at a certain time. It also gave the people in her life license to control her under the guise of protecting her.

Zain wouldn't want her forever. But now, maybe just for now.

The ferry docked and Asa walked home, refusing to think anymore about the future, willing herself to enjoy simply being with Zain.

Asa packed business wear, lounging wear, and an interesting sheer baby blue piece of lingerie her friend Evelyn had bought for her as a good-bye present after Stewart Enterprises had been sold.

"Live a little," her ex-co-worker had told her.

"Maybe I will, Evelyn," Asa said aloud, carefully placing the nightie into the suitcase.

She had an afternoon snack of sugar free vanilla wafers and milk, straightened her house, and was about to spend a relaxing half hour in the tub when the doorbell rang.

Brent was at the front door. She loved her cousin, but he was wearing her patience thin. Asa was going to ignore him, but he was wearing an expression she'd never seen before. Nothing like the angry glare he'd given her earlier. Asa could take that knowing he would just have to get over his anger. Now he was worried, but it even went beyond that. There was a deep sadness surrounding him, an inconsolable aura. Could something have happened to her aunt and uncle? Unthinkable! Or her mom and dad? No, not when they were beginning to communicate. "Brent, what's wrong!" Asa heard herself screech before she could open the door.

"Everything!" He pushed the door closed behind him and headed straight to the back of her house looking, searching for something.

"What's going on? Was there an accident? A fire? Did someone get hurt?"

He finally stopped in the middle of her bedroom, finding what he was looking for. "So it's true."

"What?"

"You're going." He pointed to the suitcase. "You're going away with Darby."

"I'm going to a computer software convention, yes."

"I don't care if Lisa doesn't talk to me for a month. I'm going to say what I need to say."

"Has anyone or anything ever stopped you?" Asa asked, calmly resigning herself to hearing, then ignoring, everything he said.

"You can't do this."

"I can and I will."

Brent went into the kitchen and landed in the exact chair Zain had sat in a week ago. The memory made her smile.

"You're loving this, huh? This crazy idea of going away with him makes you happy?"

"Yes, it does."

"It doesn't do the same for me. This is just another battle in this independence war of yours."

"It doesn't have to be a war, Brent."

"But it is. And it's bigger than you think."

"Brent, I'm a person with diabetes and will be for the rest of my life. I can't depend on you for the rest of yours."

"But you need someone there for you at all times. Someone who understands and can help you when you need it. Zain Darby can't be that person."

"How do you know that?"

"I know him. I've worked for him long enough."

"Maybe you don't. At least not as well as you think."

"Have you talked to him about your disease?"

"Not directly, but he knows about it. It's in my file."

"That means when you have a low sugar he knows what you need."

"He doesn't need to know, I do. Besides I won't have a low. I'll check my sugar more often. I will be okay."

"What if it happens in the middle of the night? What if you pass out?"

"I won't." But Asa remembered once when she had. Brent had been there. She didn't remember a thing that happened beyond her cousin hovering over her with juice, crackers, and a shaky expression on his face. "That happened once in my life. It won't happen again."

"So you can tell the future." If possible, he seemed even sadder. "You're in denial. You are going to get hurt both physically and emotionally."

Asa knew that Brent loved her, that he was only telling her this to protect her. Well, Asa was tired of being protected. "The only hurt I'm feeling right now is from you constantly implying that I can't take care of myself."

"Of course you can."

"Then let me."

"I have been."

"By telling me that I can't go to a computer convention with my boss?"

"By advising you to stay away from danger. This situation is full of danger. Since you can't seem to understand that, I plan on staying here until Mr. Darby makes an appearance."

"Why?'

"To let him in on all the details you've left out."

"You don't have any right to do that."

"That's what you think. Look, Asa, if Zain Darby knew everything he needs to know about you he would drop you in an instant. Mr. Darby runs a smooth company, without flaws. I didn't want to say this but you are so hardheaded."

Brent took a breath and went on. "He could not possibly be serious about someone with any type of flaw. Zain Darby lives and breathes perfection."

Asa was dismayed and hurt. For the first time Brent's words made her want to cry. Not because he'd said them, but because she was afraid that he was right. "Brent, get out of my house!"

He gave her an intense stare. "Okay, I'll wait outside."

Asa followed him, closing the door behind him. Tears welled in her eyes. She had the most irritating, stubborn, overprotective cousin alive. Why did he have to voice her deepest fears? No, she wouldn't let him ruin it all. Asa had already realized that a possibility of a future with Zain was slim, but not impossible.

Zain wasn't due for at least another hour. She would take her bath, call him on his cell phone and tell him to meet her at the Dry Dock. Brent had done enough. They did not need anymore input from him.

Less than an hour later, after sneaking out of her own backyard, Asa sat at the bar drinking her water cocktail, laughing and joking with Ernie, trying not to crumble inside as she waited for Zain to join her.

Zain walked out of the Al-Anon meeting with a crowd of people. People with the same concerns as he. Tonight many of them had shared success stories. He had heard good, positive advice and encouragement. Not that this last week hadn't been promising. Zain hadn't detected a sign of alcohol use or abuse from Asa. Having her all to himself for another week would certainly help to keep her on track.

Zain waved good-bye as he got into the car. He checked the voice mail on his phone for messages. One was from Grammy Dee. "When are you coming and what have you done with my sweet angel?"

Zain smiled until he heard the message from Asa. "Something came up. Meet me at the Dry Dock." That was it. That was all she said and she had used that cool, calm professional voice he hated. Something was wrong.

The Dry Dock, Ernie the enabling bartender, and the fact that he was in Metairie, a suburb at least thirty minutes away, instantly ate at him. What could have set her off? Thomas. It had to be him. Zain had been too tolerant of his interference, too much of a nice guy. That was going to stop, especially if he was driving Asa to drink.

Zain made it to the Dry Dock in record time. He parked right in front of the restaurant bar, almost tripping on the huge anchor chains used to decorate the base of the poles outside the building. He paused outside the door. He could see Asa sitting on a stool, slumped against the bar. She looked beyond wasted. Ernie the enabler was handing her a small glass of something with orange juice in it. No martinis this time. What was it? A screwdriver or maybe a fuzzy navel? Asa's shaking hand could barely hold the glass. But that wasn't stopping Ernie. He held it to her mouth so that she could continue on her self-destructive path.

Zain was enraged. He yanked the door open, flinging it wildly. Before he let a word out, Zain caught Ernie's suggestion.

"Asa, baby. I think you might need another—"

"J-u-u-u-i-c-e!" Asa finished for him, her speech slurred and heavy.

"Don't give her another drop!"

Ernie narrowed his eyes at him.

"Z-z-z-zain." Asa sat up. "I've been w-a-a-a-iting for you."

"I see that."

Her eyes were fixed on him. They slowly focused, becoming clearer as the seconds passed. She pulled herself up. "Are you mad at someone?" she carefully asked.

"Yeah!"

"Who?"

"Him!" Zain jerked a thumb at Ernie.

Ernie ignored him, talking to Asa once more. "Asa, honey, how about another one to be on the safe side. Ann's fixing you some food."

Asa's head moved up and down in a jerky semblance of a nod.

"No!" Zain yelled. People at the bar turned to stare at him. He didn't care. Zain knew he couldn't stop her binges; only she could do that. But he was here now and he would do what he could to stop her from hurting herself any further.

"I need some juice," she told him.

"Sure, but no alcohol."

Ernie looked at him as if he had gone crazy. Zain watched as the bartender filled the glass again from a can that was clearly labeled as orange juice.

Asa drank it. She sat holding the empty glass in her hand for longer than Zain was comfortable with. Would she demand more? This time more juice with alcohol. But she didn't.

"Thanks Ernie," she whispered, pushing the glass toward him. She stood and dug into the pocket of her jeans, unwrapped a peppermint and popped it into her mouth.

"It's a little late for that, don't you think?"

"No," Asa said, her eyes finally turning to his again.

"It can't hurt," Ernie put in.

"Another word and I'll show you what can," Zain warned before telling Asa, "come on, let's go." He took her arm, leading her to the door.

"Asa, do you *want* to go with this crazy man here?"

"Yes." She gave the enabler a grateful grimace.

"What about your food?" Ernie asked, giving Zain a hard stare.

A confused look crossed her face. "Oh, I forgot about all that."

"You should have fed her before this happened," Zain muttered throwing some money on the bar.

"Hey, she was waiting for you. I'm still trying to figure out why, though."

Asa mumbled something that sounded like, "I know why," then threw over her shoulder, "Thanks, Ernie, I'll see you sometime soon."

Not if he could help it. For a drunk, Asa was suddenly full of energy. She seemed more like herself. Asa eased away from him, walking out the door without him and going straight past his car.

"Wait." Zain caught up to her with no problem. "What's wrong?"

"That was rude." Asa continued to walk, heading in the direction of her house.

"Rude?"

"You shouldn't have treated Ernie that way."

"Why not? Look at what he allowed you to do."

"Allowed me?" Asa stopped in the middle of the block, her voice cool and calm. "Ernie has no control over what happens to my body." She walked on.

So, she'd finally brought it up. *Good*, Zain thought. He would take advantage of this opening by hitting her with words she needed to hear. First he had to catch up to her again. Zain stopped her a half a block from her house. "What about you? Don't you have control?"

"In a way."

"You can do better than that."

"Then I'll tell you I do. Does that make you happy?"

"I hope what you're saying is true. You need inner strength. You need to control this disease. *You* are the one who has to be in control every hour, every minute of the day."

"I know that."

"You had a funny way of showing that tonight."

Asa let out a long tired sigh. "Look, a lot's happened today, between my parents, you, and Brent—." ""What are you trying to say?"

"That I want to go home and rest."

Zain studied her face. She did look tired. Strange enough, that was all. The drunkenness, and slurred speech seemed to have disappeared.

"Fine. I'll pick you up at seven tomorrow. We're driving in. It's only a few hours."

"Yes, that's fine."

Zain's chest lowered as he released a pent-up breath he hadn't known he had been holding. Her consent meant more to him than he realized. Asa didn't seem too enthusiastic about going. But at least she hadn't tried to back out of it. The alcohol was the cause of her personality change. He would bet a million on that.

He took her hand and leaned in close to lay a kiss on her forehead. "I'll see you home."

"No, I can make it."

"Are you sure?"

"Positive."

Zain watched Asa walk to the middle of the block, up the steps and into her house. When she was safely inside, he noticed a tall figure standing on the porch. It was Thomas, and he was waving at him. Zain didn't want to be anywhere near the man. The way he felt right now, he would end up breaking something on Thomas' skinny body.

CHAPTER 16

Why was she even here? Why was she doing this? Asa didn't know for sure. The only thing she was sure of was that despite Zain's negative summary of her disease last night she still wanted to be with him. Brent's warning had been confirmed, and her hope for a future with Zain crushed.

Asa could hardly believe that a little less than twenty-four hours ago she had been in this man's arms indulging in the new feelings she was experiencing with him, planning and anticipating a week-long trip with him, only to have it all turn on her.

"You ready to talk to me yet?" Zain asked out of the blue.

"Of course I am." Nervous about what he wanted to talk about, Asa answered in her controlled office voice.

"I'll wait."

They had already been on the road for more than an hour, and had driven in almost complete silence. Asa wanted to keep it that way for a while. She quietly ate her morning snack, a juicy purple plum, and took in the scenery. Later they stopped at a gas station and were on their way again almost immediately.

"You ready to talk to me yet?" he asked again.

"Of course I am," she answered in exactly the same tone.

Zain tilted his head her way without saying a word. She wondered what that meant. What was he thinking?

Five miles later Zain's right hand had somehow moved to her side of the car. It lay innocently enough next to her. but Asa knew there was nothing innocent about any of Zain's actions. If he wanted to feign innocence, she could do a bit of faking herself. She ignored his hand, or at least tried to. Two miles later a soft swirling touch at her knee triggered tiny pounding waves that built and exploded to the many parts of her body pulsating in anticipation of his touch. Zain's hand moved past her knee, finger-walking to the hem of her dress, then back down to her knee. The barely there touches continued, his fingers moving under her skirt, higher and higher until they brushed against her upper thigh. The entire time his eyes stayed on the road and Zain's face was a picture of concentration.

Asa refused to react, sitting as still as a grain of sand waiting to be pushed and pulled by a thunderous wave. She attempted to regulate her breathing barely holding on to her attempt at faking him out. She wanted to stop him but then again, didn't. Not meaning to, not consciously even considering it, ever so slowly she parted her legs, leaving herself open to him. Zain's fingers found their way up the tender skin of her inner thigh. A flash of a touch breezed against her panties. She gasped. Another. Asa let out a tiny breath-catching moan, grabbed his hand and flung it back to his side of the car.

A few minutes later he asked, "You ready to talk to me yet?"

"Of course I am," Asa answered without a gasp or a moan but also without the cool careful controlled voice she'd used before.

"Good."

Zain didn't say a word about what had just happened. Instead, he talked about work and what to expect at the convention. He went that way for the next half hour, without a personal word passing between them. Was this a preview of what would happen in the near future? Would Zain make her fall in love with him, make love to her, then forget about her just as easily as he had softened her with the power of his touch before moving on to discuss upcoming business without a qualm? That didn't sound like the Zain she had begun to know. But what did? Who was Zain Darby really?

Asa added nothing to the one-sided conversation. Her silence didn't stop him. He knew he had gotten her attention, overconfident man that he was.

Zain was thankful that they were almost there. He continued to drive down the narrow two-lane highway talking nonstop. He had to. If he didn't he'd do something stupid, like pull over to the side of the road to finish what he had started, or yell at her for getting drunk last night. Zain had only been trying to knock away that office facade of hers. But his attempt backfired, and now he was stuck in a car, a small, closed environment, right after releasing that burst of desire. He had no alternative but to talk about work. And what else could Asa do besides listen? Zain wasn't even sure she was doing that. If nothing else, the sound of his own voice was therapy for him.

"This is it! We're here," he said aloud. Then whispered, "Finally," under his breath.

Zain drove down the long drive. Spread out on each side were the wide open gardens of the Grand Marriot Resort where the convention was being held this year. There were several buildings and a parking area to the left. More gardens and a curving path to the right where he could see glimpses of smaller buildings. Probably the cottages where they would be staying. They were close enough to the convention area yet farther away from the other conventioneers for privacy's sake. He had worked fast and hard to snag a cottage. Now he wondered if they would need the privacy.

Zain turned into the circular drive. He hopped out and handed his car keys to the waiting attendant. Another attendant had already opened Asa's door by the time he came around.

"You can check on your reservation, sir. We'll only move the car if it's necessary."

They went into the lobby. Zain collected the key cards as Asa looked around the lobby. He watched her select a few brochures at the hospitality desk and peer into the gift shop. He wondered if she was searching for a local bar or night spot to feed her addiction. No, he had to think positive. One slip didn't mean she would fall again. He had to be supportive. She was worth it.

"Excuse me, sir."

Zain turned back to the desk clerk. "Yes?"

"The cottages are on the other side of the grounds in the opposite direction of the convention center. This map will help you find the way."

Zain nodded his thanks and turned to find Asa gone. It took him less than a minute to find her. But the instant fright he felt when she wasn't in sight sent a fear he had never before felt through him. Asa was inside the gift shop. She was fingering two small block letters, the kind used to make necklaces or key chains.

"Do you want another key chain?"

"I'm still trying to fit the first one you gave me into my life."

Whoa, Zain hadn't expected that. "I hope that you do. Come on, let's get settled."

Asa dropped the letter "A" then the letter "Z" back into the tiny cubes they had been sorted into.

The trip was improving already. The cottage they were assigned gave them more than enough room. One large living area and two bedrooms.

"I didn't know we would be staying in a suite."

"Not a suite exactly, a cottage."

"Same thing." Asa peered into both bedrooms.

"We each have our own bathroom."

"I noticed," Asa said as she walked back to the larger bedroom. "I'll take this one."

She was obviously still a little upset with him. Zain went back for the rest of the luggage. He found Asa sitting on the edge of the king-size bed. "Soft enough for you?"

"More than soft enough."

Zain placed her luggage next to the bed. He was at a loss as to what to say or do next, a completely intolerable feeling. Asa hadn't been very receptive to his bold move in the car. Zain honestly didn't know much about how to deal with women in connection with a serious relationship, but had enough common sense to know when to tone it down. "Registration and check-in for the convention have already begun. The general session starts at ten."

"That's what you said in the car." She stood lifting the suitcase onto the bed before he could help.

So she had been listening. Zain felt reassured by that. "Do you want to walk over?"

"I'll be there in a minute." Asa was rummaging inside the open suitcase for something. "If you don't mind, of course, Mr. Darby."

"Asa." When he had her attention, Zain took the three steps that divided them and closed the distracting suitcase, "This is more than a business trip."

"It's supposed to be."

"This is about us."

"Should there be an 'us'? Can there be an 'us' when *my disease*," Asa said the word as if it pained her, "stands in the way."

"We are already an 'us.' And as far as your disease goes, we all have some personal problem to deal with. My only concern is your ability to control it."

"I don't know if I can live up to your ideal. My goal is to control it as much as I possibly can."

"What's that supposed to mean?"

"That I can only do my best."

"That's all I can expect. So, what's the problem?"

"You."

"Me!" With both hands Zain pointed to himself in amazement. How could he be the problem? He was trying to be there for her, to help her live with it. This was what he got for falling in love. It couldn't be easy for him, like Lance. He had to fall in love with a woman full of problems. Not just any kind of problem; alcoholism was a lifetime struggle. Zain paced up and down in front of her. He understood all that; he already knew that she was worth it. What more did she want? He was going to Al-Anon meetings, for god's sake. Of course she didn't know that. He stopped in front of her, shoving his hands into his front pockets. How could she say that *he* was the problem?

Zain took a step back. "Explain yourself," he said.

"Your attitude."

"My attitude!"

"Yes." Asa stood before him, her arms folded. She was serious.

An anger he'd never experienced before began to build up inside him. It was foreign but strong and created a pain in his heart. He—was—hurt, Zain sensed, not taking the realization very well. "Then let me tell you this, Ms. Taylor. I don't like your attitude about my attitude. This trip has been officially reclassified as all business!"

"Then leave my room, Mr. Darby. As a matter of fact I think I need more privacy. I want my own room."

Zain was already at the door, "Too bad. There's not a room left in the entire resort!" Zain was out of the cottage and down the path that started outside the door. He didn't head toward the convention building, instead marching in the opposite direction. He needed a drink. A hollow laugh escaped his lips at the irony of that thought. Zain was surprised when the path led him straight to the pool. It was as huge as his anger. He wondered if it was as deep as the hurt he was experiencing for the first time in his life. No woman had ever affected him this way. Zain peeled off his suit jacket and flung it over his shoulder. He took a slow walk along the perimeter of the pool. No one was there. Late April was still too cool for people to enjoy the pool, he supposed.

Zain circled past a bar and poolside restaurant, both closed of course. It was much too early for that drink he craved. To the right of the pool was a short flight of steps. Zain discovered a hot tub, and much further down, a ping-pong table. There were also a playground and a net set up for volleyball beyond that. His eyes swung back to the hot tub. He and Asa obviously wouldn't be spending any time relaxing in the warm spray. That didn't stop him from imagining Asa in a two piece inviting him to join her. Her problem with his attitude popped that fantasy right out of his head.

Behind the hot tub he found another building. It housed a health club and spa. Zain felt like using the equipment to work off some steam, but he wasn't dressed for that. Instead, he completed his walk taking the long way back to the convention center building.

Zain discovered a marina where over a dozen sailboats were docked. He admired the scene a few minutes, wishing he had access to his boat. A few hours on the lake would do him good. But he didn't have his boat and this wasn't Lake Pontchartrain. Mobile Bay stretched out before him. He took a deep breath, pulling in the scent of water and sand. It calmed him somehow.

Zain followed the cobblestone path along the bay, passing the various buildings that made up the resort. He noticed none of it, not the extensive gardens, the beautiful lattice rail, the putting grounds, the bridge and pier designed for fishing. He felt only the warm spring breeze that blew across his face and the calming effect the water had on him.

By the time he reached the convention building his anger had softened and his earlier resolve strengthened. Asa was worth fighting alcoholism for. Nothing would get in his way of helping her. Even her attitude about his attitude. She would have to get used to it because he wasn't going to change what he knew was good for her. He wanted Asa. As Zain had told her, he was possessive. Neither alcohol nor Thomas would interfere with winning the woman he wanted in his life forever.

Zain stopped at the glass doors of the convention hall. Yes, forever. Each time that thought hit him, his heart seemed to beat louder and stronger. Zain slipped his arms into his suit jacket and walked inside. There he heard the murmurs of voices, the rich smell of fresh brewed coffee, and the sight of people milling in the hall. It was the standard convention scene. Zain picked up his packet and name tag, then went into the general session that had already begun. It was well after ten. Zain gritted his teeth. He hated being late for anything.

He settled in the back row. The speaker was a dynamic man he knew well. In the computer software business they were not exactly competitors since their businesses more or less complemented each other. Zain focused on software designed to protect private, sensitive material, whereas James Lin designed specified software for office materials that would require protection. They both had ventured out on their own at about the same time, each becoming successful in his own right. Zain had joked that James was merely a paler version of himself, a private joke James never took offense at, having been born a racial mix of Asian and African-American.

Zain's attention drifted from the podium and scanned the room for Asa. He hoped their argument hadn't sent her on a binge. No, she wouldn't do that. Not while understanding that this trip was all business. Asa was here somewhere, on the job, effective as usual. He finally spotted her in the very front row almost directly diagonal from where he sat. She was avidly listening to James and taking notes.

For the next quarter of an hour Zain ignored James, watching Asa instead, the way her head tilted to the side as she listened. Once in awhile she would touch the tip of the pen to the side of her mouth, a habit he'd never noticed before. He wanted to be that pen, his mouth nibbling at the corner of her own, traveling across until he had access to her entire mouth. Then he would pull her lower lip inside, gently sucking until she opened up for him.

There was a thunderous sound of applause as over three hundred people stood to show their enthusiasm and praise.

James had that effect on people. Zain stood and joined in the applause.

He made his way to the front of the room. There he found a small crowd surrounding James. Asa was one in the crowd. She was throwing questions at him, jotting down answers and smiling. Not more competition. The distasteful idea flashed across his mind. Zain had no room for that kind of development.

"Zain Darby!" James called out to him. "Excuse me, please," he told the people surrounding him. "I thought you couldn't drag yourself away from Execute's door?"

"I decided to come at the last minute."

"Where's Lance?"

"Still on his honeymoon."

"That must be some honeymooning he's doing. The wedding was absolutely something."

Zain shrugged his shoulders. "As weddings go, I guess." Zain wouldn't need all that. Only sweet angel Asa, a preacher, a few family members as witnesses, and definitely Grammy Dee.

The crowd around James had dispersed. Asa was the only person there, standing in the same spot studying her notes. That was Asa, still on the job.

"James, I want you to meet one of Execute's newest employees." Zain directed James to Asa standing behind them. "Asa Taylor, meet James Lin."

"I should have known you were one of Zain's people. The questions you asked were beyond ordinary." James shook her hand in greeting, holding on a bit longer than he needed to, Zain thought.

"No more than general curiosity," Asa said, using her office tone.

"Ms. Taylor's pen didn't pause once the entire time I was up there." James pointed to the podium.

"Ms. Taylor is a hard worker."

"Would you hire any other kind?"

"No."

James laughed. "Look, I'll see you around. I have a few mini-sessions to conduct. The ones I got stuck with because a certain someone wasn't supposed to be here."

"You'll be brilliant as always. Catch you later, James."

"Mr. Darby?"

Zain clamped his teeth together and shoved his hands into his pocket, forcing himself not to give in to the urge to caress her until that voice floated away, never to be used again. His hand tingled with the desire to brush a finger across her ears as he held her head still to…Even if he gave into the urge, there were too many people around. Instead he offered her a hard stare. "Yes, Ms. Taylor."

"I have a problem with this schedule."

"Oh?"

"According to the program, we have two forty-five minute sessions before lunch."

Zain nodded, not saying a word because if he opened his mouth he would have kissed that tone right out of her.

"That means lunch won't be served until one o'clock."

"And that interferes with your precious schedule."

"Yes, it does," she responded, slower and more rigid than before.

Knowing from his Al-Anon meetings that he couldn't be with her every second, that he couldn't control her every action, he quickly gave in. "Do what you need to keep to your schedule, Ms. Taylor, but make sure you are here with me every other moment."

"Of course. I have one more question."

"Go on."

"Exactly when does my work day end?"

That question would have never come up if Zain had kept his big mouth shut. The argument would have been over, he would have smoothed things out and right now they could have been discussing the use of the hot tub or a sail on the bay. "At four-thirty, as usual." Zain knew that was ridiculous since an earlier glance showed that the sessions were over at three.

"Four-thirty?" she had the nerve to question.

"We'll need to review notes, do dictation, make a list of new contacts, that kind of thing."

She nodded.

"Let's head to the next session."

She nodded again, walking beside him but so far away. He had to think of something to save this trip.

CHAPTER 17

Asa left Zain in the middle of the second session. The speaker had been on the verge of introducing many of the new wonders in technology. The more advanced the technology, the smaller the product, Asa noticed as the presenter held up a pen. She didn't stay long enough to find out what it was used for, desperately needing to get away from Zain.

He had offered her a seat next to the wall and then proceeded to sit as close to her as possible. She couldn't breathe. Correction. She couldn't breathe anything but Zain. His scent, and that cologne that mixed perfectly with him. It was making her crazy, and dissolving her anger.

Asa pushed the glass door wide. She pulled fresh air into her lungs. It was as if he were still beside her. Zain's scent was etched inside her olfactory nerves. She shook her head in annoyance. The click of her heels on the path gave her some satisfaction.

Zain Darby. The nerve of him to give her such a hard time, then use her sense of smell against her to melt away her anger and frustration. It wasn't fair. It wasn't right. As a matter of fact, this whole idea of them as a couple was inconceivable. She was in love with him, but she could not be with him. Brent was right. Zain Darby needed someone perfect. Living with this disease made her imperfect. She couldn't even be a good assistant. Why? Because she had to keep to her schedule.

"Stupid disease!" Asa yell as she entered her room. Adding a childish action to an equally childish outburst, she flung a shoe across the room. "Stupid pancreas!" She threw the other as she cursed the organ that had so long ago stopped providing her body with insulin. Asa had never before allowed the fact that she had diabetes get to her like this. Not even as a child when she had to learn to prick her finger four times a day, take injections twice a day when other kids flinched at taking one every few years, not even sitting through a Christmas party watching candy canes and all sorts of sweets get passed around when she couldn't have any. Aunt Reenie had always said she was an amazing child. What was she now?

Asa sat on the edge of the bed and cried for herself, for her struggling battle for independence, and most of all, for the loss of her first love. She cried until she felt the ususal dizziness that preceeded a low blood sugar. She dried her eyes, not even having time to cry.

Asa went to the miniature fridge in her room. She took out a small can of apple juice and drained it, feeling better almost instantly. She called room service and ordered a turkey sandwich and a vegetable plate. Asa sat in the middle of the king-sized bed feeling lonely as she ate a handful of grapes from the fruit she had brought along as she waited for the rest of her lunch to arrive. She should have left the session sooner, but she hadn't wanted to leave until it was absolutely necessary.

Grapes eaten, Asa checked her sugar on the glucose monitor. It read eighty-eight. She must have been very low. Asa couldn't allow herself to be pushed into stretching the limits of her schedule. The last thing she wanted to do was pass out in front of Zain. That, she couldn't control. That, he wouldn't understand.

Asa picked up her phone. She had promised to call Brent at lunch and every night. It was the only way she could get him to back down from approaching Zain this morning. Asa had gave him the hotel and room number. She dared not mention the low-blood sugar she had just experienced. She didn't need to. She's taken care of it herself. There wasn't much more to say. Her relationship with Brent at the moment was still very shaky. Her relationship with Zain seemed to be over before it had really begun.

There was a knock at the door. Asa grabbed the remnants from her blood sugar testing, the sharp needle lancet, alcohol swab and the case and put them all under the covers, not wanting any evidence of her imperfection to be visible to Zain. But it wasn't Zain, a waiter brought in her lunch. She was starving. One benefit, if you could call it a benefit, of having diabetes was that food tasted like ambrosia when your sugar was low. Any food tasted like heaven. Even the sadness she felt in her heart didn't take away from the explosion of flavors in her mouth.

Having finished her meal, Asa noticed that it was barely one o'clock. Everyone else would be sitting down to eat. The next session didn't begin until two-fifteen. She couldn't stay inside these walls feeling sorry for herself. She couldn't imagine giving in to another crying binge. That wasn't like her.

Asa threw on a pair of jeans and a pair of tennis shoes. She decided to explore the grounds. Nature would take her mind off everything for a while. Key card in her pocket, a juice and snack in her purse for later, Asa followed the concrete path outside the cottage. Soon she went past a huge pool. A few brave souls were swimming today. There was also some business at the pool bar. Asa wondered what they would think if she ordered one of her special martinis. She was surprised to find a small restaurant as well. Asa tucked that information away for future reference. It would be a good place to grab a quick bite instead of depending on room service.

As she walked Asa noticed the wide variety of plant life on the resort. There was a variety of ferns, and flowers. She discovered marigolds, azaleas, and even noticed a few crab apple trees. There were a few others that she recognized but many more she couldn't name.

Then she reached the bay. It was beautiful. The sunlight reflecting off the smooth surface of the water produced a calmness deep inside of her. The beauty of nature all around her made her problems seem small and petty. Asa had never been one to give in to a problem. Her pancreas didn't work like everyone else's, so what? If Zain Darby couldn't live with someone who wasn't as perfect as he, then too bad for Zain Darby. Asa Taylor was too good for him.

So what if he made her insides churn into waves that took over her entire body? So what if she loved him with all her heart? So what? she whispered softly to herself.

Asa walked slowly along the bay. It wasn't the Mississippi, this wasn't New Orleans, but the bay helped her to collect her thoughts, to make a very hard decision. She would stay for the convention, but then she would resign, just as she should have before he convinced her to stay on at Execute. She would tell Zain, Mr. Darby, she corrected, when they returned to New Orleans.

Asa went back to the cottage to change into the clothes she'd had on earlier to meet Zain, no, she reminded herself again, Mr. Darby, at the two-fifteen session. James Lin, the man Zain introduced her to was at the door. "We missed you at lunch."

Before Asa could open her mouth to respond, Zain's voice interjected, "Ms. Taylor has a rigid schedule that keeps her away at times."

Asa stared at him in disbelief. It was one thing to have little tolerance for her schedule but another altogether to ridicule her about it in front of someone else. Asa was beginning to think that he was just as bad as Mr. Stewart.

"Isn't that right?" he had the nerve to add.

"Whatever kept you away," James Lin threw in, probably sensing the growing tension in the air, "deprived us of some interesting conversation."

Asa gratefully turned to him "I'm not sure that's true, but then again you could be right, Mr. Lin."

"James," he laughed. "You've got an original there, Zain."

Zain nodded as James walked away. He leaned in close to Asa. "That I do," he whispered in her ear. His nose brushed against her cheek quick and hot, leaving a touch of wanting, moving across her face to graze her other cheek with the same searing touch before whispering once again, "That I do."

That had nothing to do with the computer software business. He was in complete violation of their agreement but Asa couldn't respond to it. She sat in the first seat she spotted, straight and tall, resenting the turmoil her body was in from such a light devastating touch combined with a few choice words from one Zain Darby.

Zain paused. Asa's pen stopped a second later, waiting for him to continue. They had been in their suite for the last half hour. He had dictated half a dozen notes and letters. He couldn't think of anything else to say. His mind had never been so empty. Did falling in love make you lose your brains and good sense too? He let out a huge breath. The evenings were supposed to be their free time together. "I think that's it," Zain reluctantly told her.

"No more dictation?"

"No." He paused, his brain waking up to plant an idea in his head. "But I want you to type these notes, save them on file so I can review them when we get back to New Orleans."

"Now?"

"I've brought my own personal laptop. You can use that."

Asa nodded, took her notes and the case that held his laptop straight to her room. So much for being near her. At least he knew she wasn't drowning in martinis, nor had she indulged at lunch. He hadn't detected any on her breath when he couldn't resist getting close to her before that last session. There hadn't even been a sign of the peppermints she used for cover. The fractional softening in her eyes when he leaned into her was all that he could detect. But that didn't last long.

Zain went into his room to change out of the suit and into something more comfortable. He twisted his neck from side to side, the cracking noise the only sound in his room. Zain threw the suit jacket onto a chair and slowly unbuttoned the white dress shirt he had on underneath. He slipped it off, adding both his pants and shirt to the pile. It felt good to be out of all those clothes. Being in that suit all day had been uncomfortable. He felt like jumping into that huge pool he had seen earlier.

Wearing only briefs, Zain stood over the air conditioning unit allowing the cool air to breeze across his heated body. There was a knock, then Asa's voice.

"Do you want—" She froze.

Zain couldn't have planned it better himself. The official office tone converted into a squeal similar to the one she had given in the car. Zain stood unaffected, unmoving.

"Um—" The pen she was holding went to the corner of her mouth as it had done before, bringing to mind the image of him taking that pen's place, taking Asa into a world of careful, hot lovemaking. Unaffected? He had to take that back. Asa was staring down at the evidence proving that he was more than a little affected.

"Yes, Ms. Taylor?"

"Um—this can wait till later."

"Later when?" He walked across the room to stand before her. "Later when I'm dressed, or later when I'm not so…" They both looked down, "desperate to have you in my arms," he finished. He laid a gentle kiss on her forehead, the tip of her nose. He claimed her top lip, then her full bottom lip before pulling all that was his sweet angel inside.

"Zain," she sighed.

"No, Mr. Darby?" he breathed into her ear.

"Zain, we can't do this."

Zain froze, counted to three. Closed his eyes to count again but couldn't get to ten if his life depended on it. "I know." Zain went to his suitcase, pulled out a pair of jeans, and slipped them on, having great difficulty with the zipper.

"I didn't know you were changing," Asa explained nervously as he struggled with the zipper.

"I know."

"I wouldn't have come in, but it felt so much like the office. I knocked and walked right in as usual. I didn't even think about the possibility of—"

"Asa, I know."

"Is that all you can say?"

"At this moment when you're rattling on about things I already know, yes!"

"You promised—"

"I remember," Zain quietly cut her off. "It's after four-thirty. You're officially off duty. Go do whatever you want," he growled.

Asa went into her room, changed and left the suite as quickly as she could. If she thought she was in over her head before, Asa was sure she was drowning now. She was never in doubt that Zain wanted her, that he wanted to go to bed with her. But she herself had never wanted so badly to give in to making love to him, despite knowing he didn't love her, that he loathed her imperfection. Could this be her last chance? No, even if it was, Asa couldn't. She had higher standards than giving in to a man who didn't love her. Wanting and loving were two different things.

Asa suddenly stopped. She'd had no idea where she was going. She found herself at a duck pond and watched the happy birds glide across the water her mood and theirs completely opposite. She watched them for a long time. "You don't have any problems, do you, guys?" One or two ducks quacked in reply. "Some nice water to swim in, friends, plenty of food."

Asa dug into her purse and pulled out a pack of crackers. "Cheese on cheese?" she offered. "I hope you guys like this." Asa crumbled the crackers and threw them to the ducks. They swam closer loudly quacking their thanks.

"Trying to bribe the ducks? Think they have some software secrets?"

Asa turned to find Zain's friend James Lin behind her. "That would be a fruitless effort. Ducks don't carry that kind of knowledge, they have no worries."

"Maybe during hunting season."

They laughed. Asa stood as they watched the ducks eat the last of the crackers. As the last crumb was snatched from the water's surface Asa felt James's attention shift her way. The flattering observation was a lift to her spirits.

"Watching these guys is making me hungry. Would you like to join me for tea in the lobby?"

"Tea?"

"Coffee, tea, sweet treats?"

"No, thank you. I'll stay a while with these guys."

James left. Asa sat on the grass trying very hard not to think about Zain, his smooth solid chest, and bulging briefs. Briefs that were too brief to hold in the raw male power that was Zain, Zeus, god of all men. That thought slipped into her head.

Suddenly, Asa wanted some coffee. She wanted to sit down and enjoy a simple cup of coffee with a nice man who didn't make her want him, who didn't act like the god of all men.

❋

Zain went into the lobby. He had just come back from an interesting walk. After Asa left the suite he had dressed and stomped the grounds, trying to burn off the sexual tension Asa had caused with her surprised stare, innocent response, and sweet eyes. When he calmed down, Zain walked to the entrance of the resort, crossed the two-lane highway and visited the golf course. On the way back a huge oak caught his attention. How he had missed it before Zain had no idea. It was beautiful and strange because part of it was lying on its side, but still growing upward. An old man who was working nearby told him the story of the oak.

It was called 'The Leaning Oak.' Many a wedding was held there, the old gardener had told him.

Wedding! His and Asa's. It could be right here. Right before this magnificent specimen of nature's strength. It had been knocked down by a hurricane but refused to give up and die, instead had grown roots and was shooting upward from its leaning position. He and Asa could stand tall against the disease that led to her craving of alcohol. Zain could replace that craving in her life. But now the easy relationship they had been building was crumbling right before his eyes. He decided to rebuild it. But first, he had to find her.

Zain looked in the bar. He was relieved to see no sign of her there. On the other side of the lobby he noticed two long lines of people. A buffet? It was a bit early for dinner. He stopped at the desk in the lobby. "Is something special going on back there?"

"It's tea time, sir."

"Tea?"

"You can have complimentary coffee and desserts if tea is not to your liking, sir."

Zain smiled a thank you. Asa wasn't much on sweets, but maybe he would find her there. He maneuvered himself around the line and made his way through to the restaurant. There she was, bringing a cup of something to her mouth and sipping it slowly. She licked her lips. Zain gritted his teeth. Then she laughed. Zain's eyes darted sideways. She was laughing with James.

Zain ground his teeth in frustrated jealousy. He forced the feeling back into his gut and attempted to muster some control before walking up to them.

"Are you sure you don't want a dessert? A brownie? A cookie?" James was saying.

The nerve of him asking her if she wanted a brownie.

"No thank you," Asa answered.

"You can get me a cup of coffee, James. If you're getting up, of course."

"Zain—" James paused, looking from him to Asa, who was avoiding looking at Zain at all. Zain almost laughed out loud as sudden understanding reached his friend's eyes. "We were enjoying tea time. Join us."

"Thanks."

"I'll get that coffee for you while I grab a few of those peanut butter cookies that are calling my name."

"With that sweet tooth, you should have a huge gut."

"Never, my friend, never."

Zain sank into the deep, soft chair next to Asa.

"Why did you do that?"

"Do what?"

"Chase James away."

"I didn't."

"It doesn't take much, Zain. You've got a look that could scare the devil away."

"Not you, I hope."

"No, there are other issues that do the job just as well."

"Such as?"

"There are too many to name."

"Try a few."

"Look, I didn't want to tell you this until we got back to New Orleans, but maybe it's best that you know now."

"This doesn't sound like something I'm going to like."

"This relationship we have, personal and business, is too confusing."

"Asa."

"No, don't talk. I've been fooling myself. I'll stay for the convention, but that's it. It's over. I don't want to have any contact with you when we get back to New Orleans."

"They not only had peanut butter but oatmeal raisin, too," James announced as he came back to the table with a plate of cookies and a cup of coffee.

"No thanks," Asa said, her tone even cooler than her office voice. She stood. "I have to go now. Thanks for the company, James."

Zain sat stunned. He had been racking his brains trying to find a way to propose to her, and she had left him flat.

CHAPTER 18

Asa closed the door to the cottage behind her. Today had been horrible, and it was only the second day of the conference. How was she supposed to get through three more days of this? The high points of her time here had been her conversations with Brent. Last night before bed and again at lunch. They seemed to have come to some sort of understanding. He was finally accepting the independence she had been fighting for, showing only gratitude and a touch of concern when they talked. The only bright spot in this storm of a trip.

Asa went to her room. She had left the last session of the day early, having forgotten her afternoon snack in the room. There it sat in the middle of the bed. Leaving had gotten her a dirty look from Zain. Not to mention the intolerable one he gave her when she left for lunch. His reaction assured Asa that her decision to call it quits was her best course of action.

She grabbed the can of vanilla-flavored beverage made especially for people with diabetes and exchanged it for a cold one in the small fridge in her room. She accidently knocked the diet Coke bottle in which she'd disposed of her used syringes. Since she was little, Asa had been drilled on the importance of disposing of syringes properly. At home a bleach bottle served her needs; an empty soft drink bottle was perfect for traveling.

Asa kept it in the fridge. She didn't leave it out in the open because she felt funny about the maid coming across it. There was no telling what she might think. Asa put the bottle back into the fridge and took a huge swallow of the cold liquid. It slid down her throat, cooling her entire body as it spread. Asa stopped for a breath and swallowed the rest, pressing the can against her face.

"Ms. Taylor."

She jumped in surprise, tossing the can inside and slamming the door of the fridge. A second later she wondered, *What am I trying to hide?*

What is she trying to hide? Zain wondered, his entire body rigid with suppressed desire, unfulfilled desire, raving testosterone, dying to touch, to feel, to have any connection with his sweet angel, to be that can of whatever she'd thrown into the refrigerator.

"How can I help you, Mr. Darby?"

They stared at each other, Asa wishing she had shut the door to her room so that he couldn't stand there staring at her, Zain wishing that he could do more than stare at her.

"You're still on office time. I've got some letters to dictate."

Zain dictated a personal letter to each presenter, six in all since there were two in each session. The notes he dictated were extensively detailed and completely ludicrous. Asa didn't comment, simply recorded it all as she reminded herself over and over again that his handsome face, sweet kisses and devastating nearness were not what she wanted.

The power he barely held in check as he paced up and down the small confines of the living area was not something she dared to tap into. The room grew quiet as Zain's voice paused mid-sentence. Asa felt his eyes on her and glanced up to find them burning, pleading. She nervously touched the tip of the pen to the corner of her mouth, a habit she didn't have until this convention.

"Scratch that last part and end with the thought before that. And please keep the pen out of your mouth!" he almost shouted.

Asa slowly removed the pen. "If you're finished, Mr. Darby, I can get started typing these."

He nodded.

Asa moved toward her room.

"I hope you don't mind working a little overtime," he said in a way that told Asa he didn't care if she minded.

"Not at all," Asa told him as coldly as she could.

"I hope it doesn't interfere with your precious schedule."

"Of course not." Asa went into her room, closing the door behind her.

The tapping of the keys and the monotonous business of typing seemed to calm her. By the next hour Asa was done. Using the portable printer, she printed, filed and labeled the letters and notes Zain had dictated with time to spare. She was still within thirty minutes of her regular dinner time.

Asa tested her sugar. It was a whopping two-hundred eighty-nine. She was surprised. She had never had so many low blood sugars as she'd had this last month and had attributed it to Zain coming into her life. Now her sugar was way too high. Strange. Maybe she could blame that on Zain too.

Asa went to the fridge to get her insulin. With the ease that came from years of practice she accurately filled the syringe, adding an extra unit to help bring her sugar down to a more normal level. She put the syringe into her purse, gathered the files she'd completed and geared herself up to facing Zain again. But she didn't have to. The living area was empty. Asa didn't waste time lingering. She put the files on a table where he could find them and was out the door in the next second. Asa headed to the resort hotel restaurant, where she planned to enjoy a nice solitary meal.

Zain stepped out of the shower. It wasn't a cold one. A cold shower would do him no good. His need for Asa went beyond physical gratification. When she was out of his sight, when she wasn't near him, Zain felt empty. He had hated it when she left him at noon to follow that strict little routine of hers, and was downright rude when she had done it again this afternoon.

That's why he'd dictated all those stupid letters he wasn't going to mail. He simply wanted to be near her, even if she was rigid and cold. Zain could eventually melt that away, he knew. And all that talk about leaving Execute and him. She couldn't mean it. Zain was dying inside, constantly fighting a vision of his work and his life without Asa.

He dressed and headed straight to her door. He would start the melting process now, apologize for his behavior, tell her exactly how he felt. Propose, if it looked like it wouldn't scare her away any faster than everything else he had already done.

Zain knocked and waited a full five seconds before knocking again. "Asa," he called. Maybe she was working and concentrating so hard she couldn't hear him. "Asa!" he called even louder, knocking a little harder.

What if she'd broken down and spent the last hour drinking from some secret stash and had passed out from

having too much too fast? People died from that kind of
overindulgence.

Blood rushing to his head, his heart beating so fast he felt
as if it would stop from the strain. Zain yelled her name,
pushing the door open. The room was empty. No empty gin
bottles or Asa on the floor. Relief was quick and calming. Zain
strode to the bathroom and opened the door with hesitation.
She wasn't in there either.

She wouldn't have left without finishing the work he had
given her, Zain realized. He went back to the living area where
he found his laptop, printer and a neat stack of files. Zain
picked up the files, feeling a strange sense of loss because Asa
hadn't told him good-bye. This was probably what he would
feel if she actually did say good-bye to him forever. But today
wasn't forever. She'd probably left to keep to that precious
schedule of hers. How could someone so rigid and so sweet
fall into the trap of alcoholism? It just didn't fit. A sense of
inconsistency struck him as it had on occasion when dealing
with Asa. Zain had always attributed the contradiction to the
feelings he had for her. Could there be more to it?

He trailed back into her room and sat at the edge of her
bed. Her scent still lingered in the room. Zain flipped
through the files in his hand, glancing at the perfect work. He
stood and headed back out the door, cursing himself for being
so lovesick that he sat in her room trying to milk what he
could from a place she had been. He slapped the files against
his leg in annoyance. They spilled all over the floor.

Cursing softly under his breath, Zain bent to gather the
scattered papers beside the dresser, under the bed, in the little
crack of the fridge that wasn't completely closed. Zain placed

his arm against the door, meaning to push it closed. Still stooping, he slipped on a sheet he had missed and fell backwards, knocking the refrigerator door open and landing on his butt. Something flew out, hit him in the chest and rolled to a stop between his legs.

Zain was surprised to find an empty diet Coke bottle lying in his lap. He pushed the door closed and stood picking up the bottle. It rattled. Zain lifted it to have a look inside. His eyes widened in disbelief. Syringes! Asa had a bottle of syringes in her fridge. His mind didn't want to interpret what this meant. His feet took a few steps back. His legs hit a chair and he automatically fell into it. There was only one explanation. Asa wasn't just an alcoholic, she was a drug addict too.

After dinner Asa was feeling amazingly better. She was either fooling herself or handling her first brush with real love amazingly well. Though she had to admit that more than a touch of sadness hung around her, overall she was handling it well because she kept reminding herself that Zain was the one with the character flaw. Her heart would forget him. Eventually. He was too much for her anyway.

Asa left the main lobby, not knowing where to go. The last place she wanted to be was the cottage. Zain might be there, and this feeling of control she felt was better kept in place if she stayed away from him as often as she could.

Asa drifted away from the bay, following the path toward the entrance of the resort. A few steps took her to a wooden swing hung beneath a huge canopy of oak leaves offering peace and tranquility. She pushed the swing into motion. The movement lulled her into an even deeper contentment. Asa sat in the swing for a long time, just thinking. She thought about the people who were important in her life. Her aunt and uncle, Brent, the hope of a new relationship with her parents, and most of all Zain.

Her parents and Zain, were there some similarities there? With her parents there seemed to be a lack of communication. She and Zain talked finally bringing up the issue of her disease, but did they ever have a real get-everything-out-in-the-open discussion without her worrying about his reaction to knowing all there was to know about her? All they had experienced were those quick flashes of arguments that resolved nothing. Was it too late to do something about it?

Asa was scared to find out but even more afraid not to give it one more try. Tonight, she committed to herself, she would do something about it, but first she would finish her walk. "Coward," she whispered to herself before leaving the comfort of the swing to continue further down the path. A huge tree caught her attention. It was different; she could tell even from a distance that it was no ordinary tree.

The huge oak wasn't tall and stately like some of the many trees Asa had seen in New Orleans's own City Park, where oaks dominated the area. This one was lying on its side. A huge branch had somehow broken off and proceeded to grow right where it landed. Asa was surprised to see the healthy green leaves spread a wide canopy, evidence of a thriving tree.

"Amazing, isn't it?" a deep gravely voice asked behind her.

Startled, Asa turned to find a much older gentleman standing behind her. "Don't tell the others," he whispered, "but this one's my favorite."

Asa relaxed, smiling at the older man as he gently patted the tree's unusual trunk. "It looks special."

"Yes, it is. There's only one word to describe it: persistent."

"Is that right?" Asa asked, warming up to a conversation with the friendly man. It would delay her confrontation with Zain.

"Yes, indeed, miss. This tree is over three hundred years old, and you'd think that after living for so long it would just give up and die when trouble came its way."

"What kind of trouble?"

"A hurricane back in 1949. It knocked this branch of the tree nearly clean off, but this baby didn't give up and die. No way. The roots started to grow from where those terrible hurricane winds threw it. When people thought it was a goner, this mighty oak proved them wrong and lived, growing upward from this very spot. Been here ever since."

"What a wonderful story," Asa whispered in awe, impressed by the will of this beautiful product of nature. If she hadn't already decided to have everything out with Zain, the tree's determination would have inspired her. "This tree deserves a name, does it have one?"

"It's called 'The Leaning Oak.'"

"Perfect."

"It's been the perfect place for people to hold weddings. Many people want to start their lives together near something of nature that wouldn't give up. Want their marriages to be made of the same stuff."

"I can understand that." Asa herself had always thought that she was made of such strong stuff. Now she couldn't believe that she had been ready to run.

"You know, just yesterday I told this story to a nice young man. Never told it two days in a row before."

"I feel special then. Thank you for sharing it with me." Asa shook his hand. "I have a thing or two to share with someone myself."

Asa turned and sprinted down the path, her purse bouncing at her side. She slowed as she neared the cottage she and Zain shared. The story had given her the boost of courage she needed. If she was going to be an independent woman, then she needed to express her independent thoughts. And right now she thought she and Zain would have it out once and for all.

Asa opened the door. The suite was dark, not completely because the sun had just begun to set. He wasn't here. The realization deflated her burst of courageous energy. Not bothering to put on any lights, Asa went straight to her room. She threw her purse on the bed, sitting on it to untie the laces of her tennis shoes.

"You've been gone for quite some time." Zain's voice came at her from the corner of the room.

"What?" Asa squealed. She stood. "What are you doing sitting in my room in the dark, scaring me like that?"

"Don't you mean, what have I discovered in your room that would make you nervous, even scared of being found out?"

Asa frowned at him in the dusty light, having no idea what he was talking about. She wouldn't guess, she wouldn't make assumptions that she knew what he was thinking and feeling in regards to her disease; she'd done that before without any positive results. And she wouldn't be cautious about what had to be said. Zain had yet to know all the specific details, precautions and the possible reactions her body had to the insulin she needed every day of her life. She would risk breaking away a little of what they had to build something stronger between them. Honest communication was the key.

Zain had been sitting there for hours. Waiting. His thoughts a collage of evidence, suspicions—assumptions. He didn't know what to think. Was his confusion, his need for a logical explanation that had nothing to do with drugs proof that he was in denial? Did the love he feel for Asa force him to grasp at any other possibility despite the proof in his hand?

Asa's face held the look of innocence. The same innocence that didn't connect with the evidence that proved she was an alcoholic weeks ago. Now he had proof of a drug addition too; something wasn't right here.

"Zain, what on earth are you talking about?"

At least she didn't use that cool office voice on him. "This!" was all he could say as he stood switching on the lamp at his side. He held the bottle high, shaking its contents, hoping and praying that she had some good explanation.

"What about it?" she calmly asked.

Zain's insides turned cold, his worst fears confirmed. Alcohol was one thing, though a drug, it was at least a legal one. But the drugs Asa were into were illegal. Zain didn't even want to think about the kinds of people and places she would have had to encounter to get them.

Cocaine, heroine, crack, everything surrounding them were dangerous, lethal, certain death. But she wasn't dead yet.

He would help her, convince her to go into a rehab center. Asa was an amazing person. If she kicked these bad habits, an even more wonderful woman could emerge.

"What about it, Zain?" Asa repeated.

Zain took a step toward her. To get started on the right track he had to get her to admit that there was a problem. "You tell me about it." She didn't move an inch. He crept closer. She stood her ground, holding her head high. She looked determined. Determined to do what? Cover up, maybe even justify her addictions? Zain wouldn't allow that.

"It saved my life."

"How?"

"What kind of question is that?" She looked genuinely confused.

"I'm trying to understand all this, Asa. You said you couldn't survive without it—without drugs."

"Without…" Asa paused. A strange look crossed her face. "Oh, no, Zain. You couldn't—you don't. You can't believe I've been using *drugs!*"

"What else should I believe? Maybe I should have these tested to see exactly what it is you've been injecting into your body that has supposedly saved your life." The syringes rattled in the bottle as he raised it high above his head.

"Zain, listen."

"No, I don't think I could stand to hear what you're about to say. What I should do, for your own sake, is check your purse."

Asa took the purse off her shoulder and calmly handed it to him. "Go on."

That should have let him know that he was barking up the wrong tree. But he was beyond interpreting anything. He dumped it on the bed, scattering keys, a small wallet, a checkbook, peppermints, a juice box, and a used syringe. He waved it at her, holding it in one hand while shaking the diet Coke bottle in the other.

"You even take it with you when you're on the go! Asa, why?" Zain didn't give her a chance to answer. *It was all true.* He had so many questions, so many solutions, so many thoughts slamming into his head as he tried to figure out a way to help her. He was desperate and determined to do what he could for her, so much that he had worked himself into a state of frustration, firing questions at her without waiting for answers. "Where is it? We'll dump it together, and start all over. We could have a good life together, Asa. You're a beautiful woman. Don't let your life go like this." Zain stopped.

There were tears running down her face. He threw the bottle and the syringe to the floor and pulled her into his arms. "Don't cry sweet angel Asa. I'm here for you." Zain held her tight. The tears shook her entire body. Zain didn't know what to do. He lifted her into his arms and sat with her in his lap, in the same chair he had waited in for hours. Her head rested on his chest.

"Don't cry, Angel. We can beat this," Zain told her over and over again. As quietly as the crying began it stopped.

She sat up pushing both hands against his chest. "Zain."

"Yes, Asa, I'm here for you."

"There's something you don't understand. I don't know how but—"

Asa's hand went inside her shirt. Zain didn't know what she was doing, but didn't expect to see a silver necklace dangling between her fingers. He'd never noticed her wearing it before. Asa grabbed the flat round medallion and held it up for him to read.

"Medic Alert," he whispered slowly, softly eyeing the snake entwined around the caduceus as he fingered the piece of metal.

"Zain, I'm a diabetic. I do take drugs. Prescribed drugs. I'm—"

"Insulin dependent!" he almost shouted as he read those two words aloud. "Thank you, thank you, thank you!" Thunderous relief flooded Zain's body. He didn't know how to act. He hugged her tight, then released her just enough to look into her eyes. "I knew it couldn't be true. I didn't want to believe that it was true."

"It's not. I am not a drug addict, Zain."

They were quiet for a while, Zain holding her against him, resting his chin on top of her curly head. "Asa," he called, not moving an inch, loving her exactly where she was. "Don't be mad at me for thinking you were a junkie."

She leaned back to peer into his face, a hand resting on each of his shoulders. Asa grabbed him with all her might. His shoulders barely moved under the force she exerted, but Zain felt the emotion beneath it. "Of course I'm angry. How could you think I would be so stupid? Drugs are for people who don't have enough sense to take control over their lives!"

"And that's not you."

"No way. I know who I am and where I'm going."

"And you're too smart and beautiful to ruin your life that way."

"Right. If you knew all this, how could you accuse me of being a junkie?"

"I didn't know how else to explain it. I didn't know you were a diabetic. Please don't stay mad at me."

Asa stared into his eyes and released a deep sigh. "How could I when you were so adamant about saving me?"

"I would have if that was the problem. I'm relieved that it isn't, but I don't understand something. Why was your diabetes such a secret?"

"It wasn't. I thought you knew. I even gave a copy of my schedule and medical files to Mr. Handle."

"To Lance? I didn't have a clue. There wasn't a thing in your file."

"I wonder what happened."

"We'd have to ask Lance."

"Yeah, ask Lance," she repeated with a contented purr, relaxing against him again. She suddenly sprang back up.

"Wait a minute! If you didn't know about my diabetes what was all that mess about my disease?"

"Alcoholism is a disease."

"You thought I was an alcoholic too."

Zain actually gulped. "The way you walked, no, swayed sometimes. The peppermints—"

"Peppermints!"

"To cover the alcohol."

"To put some sugar back into my body! Whenever I was around you I seemed to have a low."

"The Dry Dock," Zain listed as evidence. "Those drinks with Ernie the enabler."

Asa burst out laughing. "Oh, no. I wondered why you didn't like Ernie. I thought you were just jealous."

"I was, but I wanted to kill him for constantly refilling your glass."

"With water."

"Water?"

"Water and an olive. It made me feel as if I was doing something bad."

"So you're not an alcoholic either."

"No."

"I guess I went to all those Al-Anon meetings for nothing."

"You didn't."

"I did. All for you Asa. I fell in love with you and wanted to do what I could to help you."

"Oh, you helped me, Zain Darby," Asa told him softly. "You helped me fall in love. I love you."

"I was hoping you would say that."

"I do, so much, but I was unsure of so many things. I was beginning to see you as a wonderful man. Then I started to think that you were just another Mr. Stewart—."

"The dead Mr. Stewart of Stewart Enterprises?"

"Yes. He couldn't tolerate my disease, my schedule and my episodes of low blood sugar, though they were few."

"No wonder you were able to decode those files so fast. Mr. Stewart was an idiot. What I couldn't tolerate, wouldn't possibly tolerate, is being without you, my sweet angel Asa."

"I understand the feeling completely, even though I was going to try to—"

"Leave me. It wouldn't have been for long. I would have come after you and pulled every hidden piece of information from you."

"Shared secrets. We hadn't shared enough of the important stuff. We didn't share any last night."

"I missed that, but we made up for it tonight."

"You're right."

"Asa, there's something else I miss."

"What?"

"That sleepy look in your eyes that tells me you want me to kiss you."

"Is it there now?"

"It's been there."

"For how long?"

"Much too long."

Zain pulled her back to him and their breaths mingled creating an invisible wave of longing. Their eyes met, transmitting deep emotions words alone could never say. They slowly melted together, a sense of freedom surrounding them. Freedom that erupted from shared secrets and the shattering of false illusions. He reveled in the soft texture of her mouth inside and out, the gentle feel of her tongue grazing, touching, rolling against his own, all which were simply the beginning of satisfying his greatest craving: to have Asa in his arms willing and ready, allowing him the freedom to express the love he felt for her. This was all he needed. To be inside her— that was a dream he had visited night after night as he waited for her to take this step with him.

Zain deepened the kiss, seeking more from her, finding it and connecting at a level that went beyond physical satisfaction. He pulled back. He wanted more. His body urged him to take her, guide her toward that dream experience. But that moment of respite allowed another thought to creep into his head.

Asa stood, slowly pulling him toward the bed, silently answering the question he had asked before with his eyes, with that first kiss. Are you sure? his expression, his stance had asked. Asa said not a word as she sat on the bed, both hands tugging him down until her head rested against his.

"Yes," she said, lying back on the soft bed, taking him with her.

Zain was overwhelmed with the gift she was giving to him. With love, she offered her virginity. The excitement of finally having Asa had easily tripled. A layer of perspiration popped out on his forehead, his breathing came in quick heavy gasps. The idea of making love to her flooded through him, along with a growing sense of honor. That little thought that had crept to the back of his head had grown, overpowering every other thought or action. He was honored to be the man to receive such a gift in this day and age.

Zain rested his elbows on either side of her, lying above his sweet angel Asa, so beautiful and giving. He wanted her. His body ached with wanting. He wasn't afraid to accept her gift. As he'd said once before, he was more than ready when she was. Except now...

Asa's fingers glided to his neck, trailing feather-light touches down his throat to the buttons of his shirt. "Zain?" she asked, a touch of confusion in her voice.

She was his, right now, just like this. But he couldn't take what she freely offered. He knew Asa better than any woman alive. He was willing to do for her more than he thought he ever would for any woman. His sweet angel deserved more. She deserved his respect, his promise and his ring before he made her truly his.

"What are we waiting for?" Asa whispered. "I'm ready." She raised her hips to meet his pressing her softness to his hardness. "You're ready."

Zain hissed as the brief touch sent hot pulsating waves through him. "What we're waiting for is a marriage ceremony."

Asa stared at him, stunned, for so long Zain's heart raced with fear. Did she want to marry him?

"We are?" she finally asked.

"I hope."

"Was that a marriage proposal?"

"No." Zain leaned in just far enough to lay a moist kiss on her forehead, next her soft lips, moving down to the her neck, the cleft between her breasts exposed by a button that had come undone. "No, not yet."

He moved down, using his body to caress her, unable to stop himself from tasting her navel and placing a quick hard kiss on the vee between her thighs as he knelt there before her.

Asa sat up, a gasp on her lips when he touched her so intimately. Her breath was coming fast, her eyes were sleepy, heavy, and sexy all at once.

"No, my sweet angel Asa, this is a marriage proposal. Share your life with me, secrets and all. Make love with me, only me, forever."

"Yes," she breathed.

Zain stood. "When?"

"Soon."

"This weekend."

"Why this weekend?"

"Why not?"

"Where?"

"Here, at the resort," Zain suggested, already knowing the perfect place.

"Yes," she told him again, then took him by surprise by asking, "but what if *I* don't want to wait? What if *I* wanted to make love to you now."

Zain had wanted to hear her say yes. He was happy with the yes, but those other words were not what he expected. His sweet virginal Asa had shattered another illusion. He couldn't believe it, but Zain heard his voice asking, "Can you wait?" His hand traveled sensuously up her thighs and down to her knees once, twice, three times, his touch a contradiction to his words. "It's only a few days. Wait with me." His eyes asked for understanding as his hands continued stroking, caressing her inner thighs. "Please."

"I'll try," Asa promised, staring down at his hands. "But you're making this hard."

"For me, maybe, not for you."

"What do you—Za-a-a-ain!"

Asa's question was cut short. Zain's roaming hands had found the perfect place to land. Pushing the wide leg shorts she wore as far up as possible, they landed in the spot where her hips and thighs met. Both thumbs stretched across her pelvis, meeting, stoking the warm essence that was Asa.

She moaned low and long. If this was waiting, she wanted more. Each stroke of his thumb brought alive a tension that grew, raising her to a higher level in seconds. Asa grabbed Zain to her, afraid that she was falling.

Zain pressed his face under her blouse, against her belly, creating a current of warm air that heated her bare skin. The steady stokes he pressed against her pushed a powerful wave of excitement higher and higher until excitement burst with speed and force and spread far and wide to every inch of her body. A sound flew out of her mouth. A moan, a squeal, it was hard to tell, but it didn't matter. The entire experience threw Asa. She fell back onto the bed, pulling Zain right along with her.

He lay on top of her, his breathing harsh. "Are you okay?" she asked when she herself could breath again.

Zain leaned up on his elbows. "I was going to ask you that."

"I'm fine, I just didn't expect you to—"

"—make you scream."

"So that's what I did."

"Don't tell me you don't remember."

"Not quite. I was occupied, much too busy feeling. For someone who just asked me to wait that was something."

"It was something all right. Something I needed to give to you."

"Not that I didn't appreciate, or goodness knows, enjoy the magic you did with your hands, but what about you?"

"All I need to sustain me until our wedding night is to be with you, my sweet angel Asa. Nothing else. Is a night in your arms too much to ask?"

Asa traced her fingers across his lips before kissing him. "You'll get nothing less."

Zain pushed away from her slowly standing. Asa watched as he removed the lightweight shirt he wore, exposing his solid chest, stirring the waves inside her. His pants slid down quick and easy, the briefs he wore in no way hiding his arousal.

"Your turn." Zain pulled her up. He began unbuttoning her blouse until she stopped staring at him enough to finish the job. She stood before him in her matching bra and panties. Zain went to the bed and pulled back the covers.

"Join me," he invited.

Before slipping inside Asa removed the medical necklace she had shown him earlier, and snuggled next to Zain. The contrast of the cool sheets to his warm body urged her to press into him even further. She was nearly on top of him before she knew it, her head resting on his firm, smooth chest, one leg across both of his. As she moved to snuggle even deeper into him, her thigh brushed against his hardness. Asa felt him inhale sharply before releasing a slow, steady breath.

"Are you sure about this, Zain?"

"It's pure heaven to have you in my arms, Asa."

Those words sent a shower of warmth to her heart reaching every cell of her body. She felt cherished and loved as Zain held her in his arms.

Heavenly torture, Zain repeated five hundred times before he finally felt that heaviness in his eyes that led to sleep. "Lance, man," he whispered to the dark room, "I'm a man in love."

CHAPTER 19

A few hours later Zain found himself wide awake. As he gazed at a sleeping Asa in his arms, Zain felt like the luckiest man alive. He now understood his partner's strange behavior and desire to get married. Suddenly Zain wanted her awake. He wanted to see her eyes. He wanted to kiss her and watch them turn sleepy with desire. Then he would make her scream and moan again despite the torture he would feel afterwards.

Not knowing if she was a sound or light sleeper, Zain blew a soft current of air toward her ear. She didn't budge. He tried again, but still didn't get a response. So, his sweet angel was a sound sleeper, he thought, happily tucking that piece of information into the back of his mind as he thought of ways to rouse her from such a deep sleep. She was ticklish, he remembered. With a feather-light touch, Zain ran his fingers along her rib cage. Nothing. That surprised him. When she was awake the barest touch threw her into fits of laughter. Maybe she was even more ticklish someplace else.

Zain carefully removed himself from under her and crept to the edge of the bed. He trailed one long finger down the bottom of first one foot, then the other. Absolutely nothing. Zain moved to the other side of the bed just as her feet jerked upward barely missing his head. She had turned on her back and lay spread-eagle. The covers were now on the floor. She was beautiful, every brown inch of her. He studied the curves of her body and the perfect fit of the rose-colored matching bra and panties.

She seemed unaware that he was there but could be fooling him, playing possum, pretending to be asleep?

As a little boy Zain had played a game of possum with Grammy Dee on many occasions. He wasn't going to let Asa get away with it. She couldn't out-possum the king of possums. He had other ways of making it impossible to hide her reaction.

Zain paused at the edge of the bed, once again admiring the lacy underwear that barely covered the parts of her body he planned to awaken. For a split second he wondered if he should go any further with this game. Asa's chest rose high, in her supposed sleep as she took a deep breath, stretching the limits of what the small piece of material could hold. That decided it for him.

Zain crawled back up to the head of the bed. He lay down beside her and rested his head on the palm of his hand. The other, led by his thumb, traced a path from her collar bone down to the vee between her full, waiting breasts. His thumb eased under the edge of the lacy mate-rial. His eyebrows rose in question at what he discovered. Small beads of moisture lay there. His entire hand covered her breast. The material was damp. Zain leaned over her. Asa's forehead was moist. He touched her neck, her arms, her stomach. There was a fine layer of perspiration over her entire body. The room wasn't hot. The air conditioning unit was providing cool air. He could feel it. This wasn't normal.

Zain shook her gently. "Asa."

She moaned, but not like before. This sound held no pleasure. There was a painful edge to the noise that came from her lips. Zain shook her harder. "Asa, come on, wake up, angel. Tell me what you need."

She moaned again, this time swatting at him. Zain, a man who knew very few moments of fear, felt it rising in his throat. Think, man. What's logical? She's sweating so turn up the air, was his first thought. He jumped off the bed and went to the unit by the window to turn it up full blast. He then went to the bathroom, his mind firing logical solutions inside his head. He got a cool damp towel and began wiping her body down. He used soft, slow strokes, trying to control the fear that was gnawing at his insides. The towel wasn't doing any good. Asa was shaking, small jerky movements, as if she were restless.

Zain threw the towel away from him in frustration, knocking the necklace from the night stand. It was the one she'd showed him. Didn't he see an 800 number on it? He grabbed it and the covers from the floor wrapping the blankets around her as he begged her to wake up. She moaned again, and he could almost feel the perspiration pouring out of her. Zain's hands shook as he turned the medallion over. If he didn't know what to do, and Asa couldn't tell him, then he would call someone who could.

Zain reached for the phone just as Asa let out a painful scream, "He-e-e-l-l-l-l-p m-e-e-e!"

Terror froze him for a second. The phone rang while his hand was still on the receiver. "Damn it! What do you want?" he yelled into the phone.

"To speak with Asa," Thomas' voice came through the line.

"You can't! Something's wrong. Get off the line so I can call for some help!"

"Aah-h-h-h-h!" Asa moaned loud and long.

"I'm all the help you need."

Those words calmed Zain immediately. That last moan had sounded so gut-wrenchingly painful it had nearly pulled him apart. Asa was asking for help and he didn't know what to do. Thomas was offering help. He'd take it. "Tell me what to do."

"It sounds like she's having a severe low. She may have already passed out. Give her some sugar—."

"Sugar, right." Zain threw down the receiver. He found a packet of sugar near the coffee machine and opened it as he moved across the room. He poured some onto her lips. Her tongue hungrily passed across her sugared lips, taking in the needed sugar. He watched as she ate every last grain.

"I gave her some sugar, what else?" Zain shouted into the phone.

"What kind?"

"What kind? What do you mean, what kind? Sugar. The kind you get from sugar cane. It was one of those little white packets."

"That's not enough, but wait, don't go anywhere."

Zain stopped himself from throwing the phone on the bed. If she needed more then he was going to get more. There were at least three other packets there.

"Juice is better. It's liquid, gets into her system faster and is more nutritious."

"Where am I going to find juice this time of night? I can't wait on room service. She's in pain, Thomas."

"I realize that. Do yourself a favor and calm down. Look around. Asa has some in the room somewhere, I'm sure. She doesn't go anywhere without some kind of juice."

Zain looked at her. She didn't seem as restless as before, but there were still beads of perspiration all over her. At the same moment Thomas suggested, "Look in the fridge or something," he remembered the juice she had dumped out of her purse.

That made sense. The fridge was easier to find than her purse. Zain once again threw the receiver onto the bed and opened the door to the small refrigerator. There were a half dozen miniature juice boxes exactly like the kinds he had seen at her house. He grabbed one, tore the straw from the box and jabbed it into the foil-covered hole. Then he wondered how he was going to get her to drink the juice. He grabbed the phone to ask Thomas. "What am I suppose to do? Squirt it into her mouth?"

"No, just put the straw to her lips. She'll drink. It's almost as a reflex."

Throwing the phone aside once again Zain laid her across his lap and watched as Asa drained the box, going as far as pulling all of the air out along with the juice. Holding Asa against him with one hand, he tossed the box across the room and retrieved the phone. "All right, Thomas, it's all gone. What else do I do? She's all sweaty, she looks a little bit shaky, and she hasn't talked to me yet."

"Those are just symptoms of low-blood sugar. They'll go away when her sugar's regulated."

"How long will that take?"

"Not long. She'll be talking to you soon. In the meantime, find some crackers or something for her to eat. She's going to be starving."

"Brent," Asa mumbled.

"She *is* talking. Don't go away."

Zain was both thankful and irritated with the fact Thomas was his only help. He gently laid Asa on the pillows and went to the fridge once again. He found a small pack of cheese crackers resting on top. He opened it before reaching the bed. Asa was pulling herself into a sitting position. "Here, eat this." he softly told her.

Her eyes weren't quite focused, but she took the cracker sandwich, eating it as if it she hadn't had food in days. "That was soooo good. Can I have another one?"

Zain gave her another and another until she had eaten all four sandwich crackers. Thomas' voice calling from the receiver drew his attention away from the decadent enjoyment Asa was getting from cheese cracker sandwiches.

"Yeah, I'm here."

"How's she doing?"

"She ate an entire pack of cheese on cheese crackers."

"And loved every bit of it, right?"

"She acted like she was eating some sinful dessert."

"I know what you mean. Can I talk to her?"

"Yeah, hold on. Asa." Zain touched her shoulder. She suddenly seemed to be herself again.

"Zain, I didn't—! No, don't tell me—! I couldn't have!"

"You passed out, but you're all right. Thomas is on the phone. Talk to him."

Now that his fear for her had been eased, jealousy rose up high and free. She had called for Thomas when she was out of it, not him. A deep, almost crippling pain stabbed his heart. Asa wasn't all his. She would never be all his with Thomas somewhere in the picture.

Zain went into the bathroom, wanting to hear but not able to stand the sound of Asa's soft voice as she spoke to the man who was obviously more important to her than him.

Zain splashed some cold water on his face and stared at himself in the mirror. Did this situation need to be that way? No, he was Zain Darby and this obstacle needed to be destroyed now! Zain marched into the room and froze.

"Okay, cuz, thanks for everything," he heard her say. "Especially your blessings." She paused. "I know, I didn't need them, but I wanted them anyway. Good night, Brent."

Asa absently put the receiver back in its place. The pain in Zain's heart slowly lessened until it didn't exist anymore. Zain studied her face. She was lost in thought. But he wasn't. He wasn't lost to anything. He had found out tons of information. Most importantly, he had found no reason to be jealous of Thomas ever again. He would never be able to express how happy this news made him. Zain almost ran to the foot of the bed. "Your cousin? Thomas is your cousin?" he yelled and laughed at the same time.

As if she hadn't heard a word he had just said Asa was off the bed and in his arms. "I'm so sorry you had to deal with me passing out. It was all my fault."

"Your cousin!" he yelled, spinning once and landing with her in the big chair he had spent so much time in earlier.

"That's why he knows so much about you and your diabetes. He's your cousin!" Zain repeated.

"Yes, he is," Asa said, her hands against his chest, carefully pushing herself away from him.

He grabbed both hands, kissing each one.

"But you knew that. We didn't want it known when I first started working at Execute, but I thought you were on to us. Weren't you?"

Zain grinned wide as he shook his head no.

"I thought you knew we were related."

"I never knew!" He grinned even wider.

"And you're not upset about it."

"Upset? Absolutely not. This explains everything. The moment I saw you with Thomas I knew there was something between you. I am so relieved that it's just blood."

He kissed her on the lips, on the nose, on her chin and on each finger he held in his hands.

"I'm so sorry you didn't know. There's so much you didn't know."

Zain stopped kissing her. He thoughtfully gazed into her eyes for a long minute. "I'm not."

"Why not? All these misunderstandings, they seem to have caused you a lot of trouble."

"Trouble I was more than happy to deal with. Trouble I was looking forward to tackling because it was all for you, my sweet angel Asa."

A tear ran down her face, then another.

"What's all this for?"

"Oh, Zain, you were fighting for a woman with an imperfect body."

"*You* are perfect."

"My pancreas is dead."

"But you're still alive. You're beautiful. You're wonderful, and I want you exactly the way you are."

"But we haven't talked about so many things. Like tonight, you didn't even know what to do if I passed out. I'll understand if you change your mind and don't want to marry me. You proposed before you knew exactly what life with a diabetic might be like."

"Oh, so this happens every night?"

"No, of course not."

"Once a week, a month?"

"No, this is the second time I can remember passing out in my sleep. But it can happen anytime."

"Which is why you take precautions and keep juice, peppermints and snacks on you at all times."

"Yes," she told him slowly.

"I don't see a problem here. I was ready and willing to deal with an alcoholic and a drug addict. You think I'm not man enough to help you live with diabetes?"

"I didn't want you to have to deal with me passing out like I did tonight." Asa hopped off his lap and walked across the room. "It was all my fault."

"Now, I don't know a lot about diabetes, but how could passing out be your fault?"

"I didn't have my bedtime snack. I didn't check my sugar before I went to bed. That was my responsibility," she almost shouted, pointing to herself before softly saying, "I let other things get in the way."

Zain went to her. Wrapping his hands around his sweet angel he told her, "It seems to me that *we* let other things get in the way. More specifically, my preoccupation with making you moan and scream."

"But I knew better. I knew what had to be done and you didn't."

"Now I do." Zain turned her to face him. "That was one mistake, Asa. Are you going to allow a mistake to get in the way of the wonderful life we can have together?"

"It might not be so wonderful, Zain."

"How can that possibly be true?"

"Children."

"What about them?"

"Do you want them?"

"Of course. With you. Only with you."

"What if complications with my diabetes make that impossible?"

"I'm not into what if's, but I'll tell you this. We would still have each other."

"Would that be enough? Could you live with that?"

"What I couldn't live without is you."

"Are you sure?"

"I love you, my sweet angel Asa. Need I say more?" Zain knew he had her when the worry melted away, replaced by her sweet smile.

"Not a thing more, Zain Darby. I love you and I take back the option for you to back out of that beautiful marriage proposal."

CHAPTER 20

The next morning Asa woke to the buzzing sound of an alarm to find the bed empty and a note on the pillow next to her.

This was so romantic. Asa hadn't known Zain had it in him to be so romantic, and so precise. He had even timed the morning meal perfectly. She was still within her scheduled mealtime.

Asa hopped off the bed searching for something appropriate for an engagement breakfast for two. She took from the closet a skirt she had bought recently and packed for the trip. It wasn't her standard office wear. This skirt, a cool mint color with sprigs of green and yellow flowers all over, shouted springtime. It stopped mid-thigh and was easily half as long as what she was used to wearing. She found the matching blouse she had bought at the same time as the skirt.

Asa showered quickly, checked her sugar, drew up her insulin and dressed. She slipped the skirt on easily. It seemed to be even shorter than when she'd tried it on in the store. The matching blouse was almost sleeveless and tapered to fit her curves. It ended where her skirt began. Nothing to tuck in. Nothing to cover the bit of skin that showed when she moved a certain way.

Asa took care of her hair next. When she was done, she admired herself in the full length mirror that was her closet door. She loved the look. The phone rang as she sat on the edge of the bed to strap on white sandals.

"Hello."

"Morning, cuz."

"Brent."

"I wanted to catch you before you left for breakfast."

"How did you know I was leaving for breakfast?"

"Oh-oh, I mean, you have to eat before seven-thirty, right?"

"As we both know."

"Then that's what I meant."

"Are you in cahoots with Zain?"

Brent laughed. "Cahoots, Asa girl, please."

"I like that idea."

"You do?"

"It's a whole lot better then standing in the middle trying to stop you two from tearing into each other."

"I can safely say those days are over. Just this morning—"

"Ah-ha, you are in cahoots."

"Guilty. Zain called to ask a few question about this special breakfast he's arranged for you. What you can eat, what time. Stuff like that."

"That's very thoughtful of him."

"That's a man in love. If I wasn't sure before, his reaction to your low last night and his plans this morning proved it to me. Besides, I'm a man in love myself. I was finally able to look beyond these strange, overprotective tendencies and see the signs. "

"Lucky me."

"Lucky Zain."

"So it's Zain now, is it?"

"What else should I call my future cousin-in-law?"

"Don't breathe a word to anyone. I'd like to give the family the news myself."

"My lips are sealed."

There was a knock on her door. "I gotta go. Love you, cuz." Asa didn't wait for a reply. She grabbed her purse and the syringe of insulin. She'd wanted to take her shot before walking out to meet Zain. There was another discreet knock. Asa decided to take the syringe with her. They were getting married, he would have to witness her taking her shot some-time in their life together, what better time to start than now? She went to the door just as the knock sounded once again. One of the uniformed doormen she had seen on her first day at the resort greeted her.

"Good morning ma'am. I've come to escort you to break-fast."

"Thank you," she said, closing the door behind her and following the polite young man down the path toward the entrance of the resort. Asa wondered what spot Zain had in mind for this engagement breakfast. It could be as beautiful but not as meaningful as the one she had in mind. Maybe he'd chosen that bridge crossing the huge duck pond. But no, it wasn't she realized, when they went past it without slowing down.

Asa stretched her neck, searching left and right for any sign of Zain, a possible location to get married or have break-fast paraphernalia. They were almost at the spot she had been thinking of as a marriage place when she spotted Zain next to a white-covered table set for two. He was standing in front of 'The Leaning Oak.' Asa stopped where she stood. If she needed a sign to tell her they were meant to be, this was it. Without either of them knowing, they had chosen the perfect place together.

"Breakfast is waiting, ma'am." The young man, stretched his arm to direct her to the spot where Zain stood waiting. Then he was gone.

She couldn't move. She was so full of joy, she couldn't move. Zain walked toward her. He gave her a tender kiss on the lips before pulling her to his side and asking, "What do you think?"

"I think it's beautiful. I think I have a secret to share."

"You do?"

"Oh yes."

"Then out with it, angel."

"This is the spot where I wanted us to get married. I chose it yesterday."

"I found it the day before."

"Then it was you the old man told the story to. He said he had never told it two days in a row."

"Asa, this is amazing."

"Isn't it."

"My beautiful angel." He took her face in his hands and pressed a deep kiss upon her lips. "This was meant to be. We were meant to be. This oak reminds me so much of you."

"That's exactly what I thought. It reminds me of you. You're strong, majestic, powerful and persistent. You won't let anything get in your way. You strive to do the impossible. Exactly like this tree."

"Oh, but, Asa, it's more like you. Strong yes, but determined. Even when I assumed you were an alcoholic, I thought of your determination to work hard to battle that disease. I had no idea then that it was diabetes you were tackling on an everyday basis. But it doesn't matter because you push your way forward to do what you need to do without whining, without making excuses. You just do what needs to be done. Like this tree, you grow and thrive despite the obstacles life has thrown at you."

"Then it's settled, we get married here?"

"This Sunday, at 'The Leaning Oak.' We'll invite Grammy Dee, Lance and Katrina, your family."

"Even Brent?"

"Even Thomas. We finally understand each other. The problem has always been that we both love you. In two different ways, of course."

"Thank goodness."

"And now we're on the same side. He even helped me set this all up."

"Nice of him. Very sweet of you."

"Thank you. Now, will the future Mrs. Zain Darby join me for breakfast before it turns to ice?"

"I'd love to."

Zain pulled a chair out for her. He sat and quietly waited while she unobtrusively gave herself a shot in the thigh. She placed the syringe in her purse until she could dispose of it properly.

"Does it hurt? Does it bother you to do that two times a day?"

"No, it's a part of life my now. Has been since I was eight. I look at it as simply something I have to do before I eat. Like washing my hands."

"See what I mean? No whining, no excuses."

"It's not a big deal." But he looked at her as if it was.

Despite being out in the open where people and cars passed frequently, Asa didn't notice any of it. She had eyes only for Zain and he for her. They ate a leisurely breakfast Asa choosing small portions of fruit, biscuits, grits, ham, and country potatoes. As Zain refilled her mug of coffee from a carafe the same young man who escorted her to this beautiful clearing returned with a cart. No, her eyes had to be deceiving her. But they weren't. The top rack of the cart was full of jewelry boxes, ring-sized jewelry boxes. The young man parked the cart next to Zain, a woman came to clear away the dishes and Zain proceeded to lay the black, gray, and navy blue cases on the newly cleared table. Asa noise-lessly counted as Zain laid them on the table before him. There were twenty-five in all.

"I didn't want to pick just anything for you. I thought we would start this off right. We can't have an engagement breakfast without an engagement ring. Choose the one you like best, and if you don't see any you like here, we'll keep looking until we find the right one."

Asa didn't know what to say. "I—there are so many to choose from."

"It's easier to choose if you open the cases."

"That would be a good start, but should I open them all at once?"

Zain lifted a black case. "Why don't *I* open them for you, one by one. I'll pop the question and the one that touches your heart when you first lay eyes on it is the one for you."

"You're going to ask me to marry you twenty-five times?"

"I'd ask a million if need be."

Holding the case in the palm of his hand, Zain slowly lifted the lid. "My sweet angel Asa, will you marry me?"

"Yes," she answered, her eyes taking in the white and yellow gold diamond ring with its twisted band and huge oval diamond. The sunlight reflected off the diamond. Leaving the case open Zain placed it before her.

Asa answered in the affirmative each time Zain lifted the lid of a soft velvet case. Every time a case was opened, a soft creak preceded the same question, Will you marry me? Each time he uttered those words, Asa felt as if he was asking for the first time.

Zain laid in front of her engagement rings with white, yellow, and rose gold. There were wide, raised and split bands, and princess, emerald, tear drop, oval and marquis cut diamonds to choose from. There were also engagement rings with sapphires, rubies, and emeralds.

Every case was opened. Each ring winked at her in the bright sunlight, reminding Asa that she had been proposed to twenty-five times. There were so many to choose from, but Asa knew which one was hers. The very first case had Zain held out to her. The oval cut diamond with the twisted white and gold band.

"You've decided."

"How did you know?"

"Because your eyes landed on my favorite and haven't moved for the last two minutes."

"You know which one I chose?"

Zain left his seat, coming to stand behind her. "I could tell that rubies, sapphires and emeralds, though beautiful, aren't exactly your thing." Zain snapped closed the lid of seven of the cases. "Solitaires are traditional, but not unique enough for you." Ten more cases were snapped shut. "No marquis, tear drop or princess cut for you." Zain closed each lid one by one, open only leaving the very one she had decided on. "Tell me why," he whispered, kneeling beside her.

"The twisted band makes me think of us, two different people coming together to share a life. The oval diamond, clear and bright, a hope that our future is just as bright."

"I couldn't have said it better myself." Zain lifted the ring from the velvet box and placed it on her finger.

"Yes, I'll marry you. Should I say it twenty-four times more?"

"'I do,' is what I want to hear next, angel." Zain laid his forehead against her own in a silent show of contentment.

The next three days Zain and Asa skipped the conference sessions to make plans for their wedding. They visited the small town of Fairhope to get a license and explored the quaint streets and businesses of the small city. Asa even found a wedding dress in one of the town's boutiques.

They spent time lounging on the beach and at the pool. They took long walks along the path beside the bay enjoying the breeze. And every night they would sit on the swing under the canopy of oak leaves before strolling to the spot they had chosen for their wedding.

At the end of the week, the evening that would have been their last if they had stayed only for the convention, Asa sat on the swing with her fiancé. A breathy laugh escaping her lips as he set the swing in motion.

"What was that for?" Zain rested his arm on her shoulder as she snuggled closer.

"I was remembering how surprised everyone was when I called them with the news that I was getting married."

"Grammy Dee wasn't."

"Grammy Dee knew who I was before she met me. Don't you remember what she said that first day we met?"

"I do. She called you Sweet Angel as if she knew exactly who you were."

"Your future wife."

"My future wife. Grammy Dee's a wise woman."

"What time are we expecting them?"

"Miss Rose says they'll be here by eleven tomorrow."

"That's about the same time I expect everyone. Be warned, they'll probably ask a dozen questions and give you a hard time."

"I couldn't expect anything less after the bomb we dropped on them. Just wait until Lance and Katrina get here. My buddy and partner thinks I'm playing some kind of joke. I'm just scared I'm going to wake up, find you gone and that somebody's pulled one on me."

"Not a chance."

Footsteps sounded on the path as the swing rocked. Asa vaguely recognized the sound but ignored it since it had nothing to do with them.

"Ah, there's the newly engaged couple," Zain's friend James called out to them.

Asa lifted her head and smiled. Zain asked, "Convention over?"

"As if you cared, but yes. The resort has nearly cleared out. Did you get those reservations you wanted for your families?"

"I was lucky enough to get three more cottages. That should be enough. You are staying for the wedding, right?"

"I wouldn't miss it for the world. First Lance and now you. Two of my good friends married. It's scary."

"If you're lucky, you could be next."

"I could do without being lucky for a while."

"You don't know what you're missing," Zain laughed. "I didn't."

"Neither did I," Asa added.

"What do they say? Can't miss what you don't have. I'll leave you two to the business of being in love. Goodnight."

Goodnights trailed after James. Asa and Zain lingered on the swing until it was completely dark, then strolled to 'The Leaning Oak' hand in hand. Zain rested against its strong wide trunk and pulled Asa against him, her back to his front, her bottom resting against his hardness. Zain savored the sexual between them. The anticipation had been building since the moment he laid eyes on her. Zain was looking forward to having his sweet angel Asa completely naked and totally his through the vows they would share in less than forty-eight hours.

Asa shifted before him. He stiffened in response then suggested, "We better head back. We've got a long day ahead of us with everyone coming in tomorrow."

Asa agreed, dragging her feet, not wanting the night to end. As soon as they reached the cottage Zain would head straight to his room as he had the past two nights, not even suggesting that they at least sleep in each other's arms. Heavenly torture, he said it was. Asa knew he was right because she was dying for his deep kisses and soft touches longing to love him completely. She shivered at the thought sending waves of wanting through her.

"Are you cold?" Zain asked.

"No, just wanting."

"Me, I hope."

"You of course."

"It won't be long now."

"No, it won't." If he could wait, then so could she.

They were at the cottage. Zain unlocked and pushed the door open. Asa stepped in behind him. Zain lips skimmed across her own, he whispered an almost silent goodnight and was gone before she opened her eyes. This waiting had to build character because it offered no satisfaction. Asa went into her room, checked her sugar, had a small snack and was in bed before ten o'clock.

Zain closed the door to his room, stripped completely and stood over the air conditioning unit until his body gradually relaxed. He took a shower and was also in bed before ten o'clock. Zain was thankful that their families would be in tomorrow. Nothing like family to help keep his mind on track. He sat in the middle of the bed wondering if Asa had checked her sugar, if she'd had her snack, and if so, did she have enough? If she passed out again, would he hear her?

Zain went to the door and opened it so that he would hear if she cried out. That didn't ease his mind enough. He sat on the edge of the bed and dialed the number to her room. Hearing her voice would be enough to bring him to back to the state he was in when they came into the cottage.

"Hello," she answered on the second ring.

"Can't sleep either, can you?"

"No."

"Good, I don't like to suffer alone. Don't worry. This will all be worth it."

"You'll have to prove that to me, Zain Darby."

"Not a problem. I have been imagining dozens of ways of showing you the value of waiting. Did you have your snack?"

"Done. I'm safe for tonight." Asa appreciated his concern. He was probably still shaken from the experience of her passing out. She didn't remember a thing beyond falling asleep in his arms and then eating cheese crackers in the bed.

"Good. I'm right here if you need me."

"I know."

"I've got a secret."

"I'm listening."

"If I had stood next to you a moment longer. If your lips would have lingered a second more tonight, you would not be on this phone right now."

"I've got one for you."

"Go on."

"I knew that."

Zain chuckled. "Good night, angel."

"Good night."

CHAPTER 21

"There's my sweet angel," Grammy Dee greeted Asa in the lobby. "Grammy, Miss Rose, I'm so glad you made it."

"Made it? A category five hurricane wouldn't have kept me away."

"It's not hurricane season, Grammy, and don't I get a hello or is sweet angel the only person you see?" Zain asked. He had been standing beside Asa when Grammy walked in.

"Since you finally got the good sense to ask this angel to marry you, I guess I can recognize you. Come give your old Grammy a hug, boy."

"You're not old, Grammy Dee." Zain kissed her on her wrinkled cheek and gave Miss Rose a hug as well.

"Hear that, Rose? I'm not old. These young people…"

"Asa! I'm so excited for you!" Lisa came rushing toward her. "This is so romantic! Getting married to the boss man."

"Thanks, Lisa. Everybody's here?"

"Brent, your parents, and his are outside."

Zain introduced Lisa to Grammy Dee and Miss Rose. The introductions continued as Brent, her parents, and aunt and uncle joined the small crowd in the lobby. With the help of the desk clerk and the polite young doormen, everyone was settled in their cottages in less than fifteen minutes. Miss Rose and Grammy shared one. Asa's parents and Brent's another. Lisa and Brent settled in one they would share with Lance and Katrina, who hadn't arrived yet.

They all gathered for a private lunch in a corner of the hotel restaurant. The group of ten sounded more like twenty as congratulations and well wishes were expressed. Zain noticed the cautious looks and quiet salutations Asa's parents issued. Her father, especially wore a stiff, stoic expression. Brent's folks were a little more relaxed. Champagne, ginger ale, and diet Seven-up for Asa were poured into narrow flutes. Brent stood ready to toast the couple when James walked in with a couple.

"Look who I found wandering around the lobby."

"Lance! Katrina!" Zain looked up. Everyone turned to the threesome.

"Something special going on here?" The partners grabbed each other by the right hand for a vigorous shake. Lance pulled him close and they pounded each other on the back, evidence of a longtime friendship. "I heard a rumor."

"An impossible one," Katrina chimed in.

"Not impossible," Zain declared turning around to pull Asa to his side. "I'm going to be a married man. You've met my fiancée. I don't think I thanked you for bringing her into my life."

"My pleasure."

"How much work has he brought to this celebration?" Katrina asked.

"Not a bit," Asa confirmed. "As a matter of fact, he hasn't mentioned work in the last three days."

"It worked," Katrina told her husband. "I cursed him with a love spell."

"Not a curse, 'Trina, a blessing. I found myself an angel." Zain looked at his watch once again. "Where's the food? They're late. I told them that the food had to be on the table no later than eleven forty-five. They're already five minutes late." Zain frowned. "Excuse me," he said before storming off.

"That's right, that schedule of yours, how did things work out with that?"

"You don't want to know," Asa said to the man who'd hired her, remembering how attractive she had thought he was at her interview. He was still good-looking, Asa admitted to herself, but nowhere near as handsome and fine as Zain.

"Try me."

"It all started with me assuming Zain knew about my diabetes."

"He should have. I left a note and the information in your file."

"Lunch is coming," Zain interupted. "Let's get some food into you and save the conversation for later."

Before everyone got back to their places a small army was placing plates of hot food before them. Asa received hers first, by Zain's orders, she was sure. Brent suggested that they save the toasts for the wedding reception and everyone enjoyed the food. Her mom and dad seemed more relaxed than she'd noticed before. Asa didn't know if it was the champagne, Grammy Dee, who sat beside them most likely extolling her and Zain's virtues, or that they were simply getting used to the idea that she was getting married. Her aunt's and uncle's concerns had been appeased by Brent's glowing report, she knew, not having had the chance to privately speak with any of them yet.

After lunch Zain rented a sailboat large enough to contain them all. They spent the afternoon skimming across the bay. At one time Asa spotted Zain at the bow of the boat speaking quietly to her parents. She moved toward them, sure that she was the topic of conversation.

"I love your daughter, Mr. Taylor, and I intend to make her happy." Asa heard Zain declare.

Asa was suprised when her stern-faced father clamped a hand on Zain's shoulder, "That's all I wanted to know, son."

Both her father and mother walked away before Asa could maneuver herself around Brent and Lisa who were standing directly in her path. "Hello, there," she told Zain. "Did I miss something important?"

"I was just establishing a relationship with my future in-laws."

"Then we're in the same boat. I'm still trying to establish a relationship with my parents."

"Have you talked with them yet?"

"Not alone."

"You need to."

"I will. Tonight."

Zain glanced down at his watch. "Ready for a snack?"

"It is about that time, isn't it? I was enjoying myself so much I didn't realize how late it was."

Zain signaled a break from sailing a half an hour into her mid-afternoon snack time. Asa was impressed with how quickly and easily he had learned her schedule and adapted every activity to it. They anchored, bobbing quietly on the bay. Zain had ordered some food from the restaurant that included a variety of fruit, crackers, cheeses and sparkling water. Zain served her drink in a martini glass with an olive. They laughed hysterically as everyone looked on.

"That's what love does to you, huh?" James commented.

"Yes, indeed," Lance answered, an arm around his wife.

"I can amen that!" Brent placed a kiss on top of Lisa's head.

"It's sweet," Auntie Reenie laid her head on her husband's shoulder.

"It's real," Asa's mother whispered to her father.

"It's about time, is what it is!" Grammy Dee shouted, throwing everyone into fits of laughter.

That evening Asa and Zain had planned a dinner with Asa's parents, her aunt and uncle and Grammy Dee, but she had taken a nap after the sail and Miss Rose refused to wake her since they would later attend a buffet and dinner with a live jazz band. Asa realized it wasn't exactly the right place to talk so she asked her parents to meet her at the cottage she and Zain shared while Zain met her aunt and uncle in the lobby.

"Remember, things between you and your parents are better," Zain reminded her. "Be open. Don't let hurt block communication."

"I've got it, now leave," she demanded, opening the door to find her parents on the other side.

"Asa, is that any way to talk to your fiancé?" her mother asked. A sense of deja vu overwhelmed Asa as she remembered her mother saying similar words to her at Execute's offices.

"Don't worry about it. I don't take it personally," Zain said as he left. "See you in the lobby?"

"We'll be there." Asa closed the door behind him. "Mom, Dad."

"Oh, Melvin. Did you hear that? Did you hear what she said?"

"Yes, I heard her."

"What? Did I say something wrong?" Tears were freely falling from her mom's eyes. Her dad looked choked up. Asa paused, trying to remember the words that had come out of her mouth a second ago. She hadn't said anything that would offend them. "You have to help me here, Mom. What did I do?"

Her mother took out a white handkerchief and attempted to dry her eyes. "You called me Mom."

"I didn't, did I?"

"You haven't called me Mom since I sent you away to live with your aunt and uncle. You hated me. You wouldn't talk to me or your dad on the phone. Reenie would tell you that your mother and father were on the phone, but you wouldn't come. Months later when you finally did, you wouldn't call us Mom and Dad. It's always been Mother and Father since you were five."

Asa looked up at her dad. He nodded his head in confirmation. "I don't remember. I'm sorry to have caused you so much pain. I didn't realize how much until recently. The only explanation I have is that I was hurt and didn't know how to handle it."

"Which made things worse because I wanted to fix it for you, but I made my choices and I don't blame you. Your father and I talked about it. We understand if you want Reenie and Boyd to stand in as your parents. We were horrible parents."

"That might be true when talking about me, but Ann Marie, how dare you say that about yourself!" Melvin Taylor demanded.

"He's right. You shouldn't say that about yourself, Mom, and neither should you, Dad. I discovered something a few days ago."

"What was it, Asa?" Ann Marie asked.

"Memories. I can't explain why I blocked them out or why they came back to me."

"What kind of memories?"

"Memories of both of you painting flowers in every room I ever slept in so that it would look like the one I left. I hated moving."

"You did," her dad agreed.

"I remembered other things. Stories you read to me, coloring on the floor, my fifth birthday party."

"It was a good-bye party for me. I didn't want to lose my little girl."

"I never knew."

"Now that you do, do you still hate us?" Asa's dad asked.

"I never hated you, I was always hurt. But that was because I loved you. If I didn't care, you could never hurt me again."

"Then you still love us?" her mom asked. "Because we've never stopped loving you."

"I do. I would like to get to know you again. You created me, you nurtured me for the first five years of my life. Aunt Reenie and Uncle Boyd took over where you left off. Mom, I want you at my wedding as the mother of the bride right alongside Auntie Reenie. Dad, I want you on one side of me and Uncle Boyd on the other and both of you to give me away."

"We would be honored," her dad answered.

"Shall we join the other half of this group for a lovely jazz dinner?"

"We'd love that. And, Asa, your dad and I wish you a world of happiness. When you called to say you were getting married—"

. "We didn't know what to think," her normally quiet dad finished for his wife.

"We were worried, thinking you were getting married to kept us pacified, to keep us off of your back. I just wanted to get to know my baby girl again."

"What do you think now?"

"That you and Zain are the two luckiest people in the world to find love so quickly and so strong. That man loves you, Asa."

"He had better," her dad said.

Asa hugged them both, a spontaneous, sincere response to all that had been said. The three of them started down the path, a new understanding freeing them to chat with each other and smile.

CHAPTER 22

"You're getting married by a tree?" Lance asked with the same amazement his voice held when he first learned that Zain was getting married.

"It's a special tree." Zain paced up and down in Lance's room. "What's taking Thomas so long? I can't believe I forgot the ring."

"Neither can I. You've gone sentimental and forgetful, my friend. If the signs weren't there I'd say you were faking it. Zain Darby, in love."

"You're my best man, Lance, you're supposed to be supportive."

"I am. I'm all for love and marriage. I'm here right now, remember. I'm just having problems connecting you with the same man I left a month ago.

"I'm the same man, just better. Loving Asa made me better."

The door to the cottage opened before Lance could comment on that. "Got the ring. You better be glad I got out of there alive with it. Those woman are too much." Brent tossed the black velvet box to him.

"Thanks, Thomas. Did Asa get the morning snack I sent?"

"The fresh pineapples shaped like keys? Yes, she did. That's what they were ooohing and ahhhing about. You're making this hard for the rest of us, Zain."

"Another sentiment?" Lance asked.

Zain ignored his friend, who laughed. "Did she eat any? She had her snack, right?"

"Relax, you're acting like me," Brent warned. "Asa's going to do what she needs to do."

"But this is her wedding day, she's going to be nervous and she might forget."

"*She's* nervous?" Lance guffawed, but swallowed it at the look Zain threw his way.

"It's almost time. Did she look like she was ready? What if she changes her mind? I can't stay in here another minute." Zain rattled on as he had never done before.

"Calm down, man. You've been here less than an hour, long enough to shower, change and worry." Lance, finally acting as a best man should, laid a hand on his shoulder in understanding.

Zain looked down at himself. He had rented a tux. It was formal and elegant and he couldn't go traipsing all over the resort to end up dirty and sweaty at his own wedding. Last night he had slept in the cottage he shared with Asa but left when the women, mainly Grammy Dee, woke him, kicking him and his tux out of his own suite of rooms. He didn't get a glimpse of Asa. Bad luck, Grammy had told him.

"Let's walk to that tree where you plan on getting married. You could tell us the sentiment behind it."

"It's 'The Leaning Oak,'…" Zain told Lance and Thomas as they exited the room. Zain repeated the story the old man had told him and explained how he and Asa had chosen the same spot.

"Sounds like you were meant to be," Lance said when the story was told.

"I did pretty much everything I could to interfere with that," Thomas regretfully turned to Zain to say.

"True enough."

"Couldn't have been too much. You and Brent are talking to each other. And you still have a job at Execute, don't you Brent?"

"I do, but it was pretty rough for a while. We had this huge misunderstanding—" Thomas began.

"Talking about misunderstandings, why didn't I know Asa was a diabetic? That information would have saved me a lot of heartache."

"The information was in her file. I put it there myself."

"There was nothing there when I looked through it."

"All she had to do was tell you."

"She didn't," Zain grimanced. "I made some assumptions."

"What kind of assumptions?"

"I thought she was an alcoholic."

Thomas, who had been quietly listening, almost yelled, "You didn't!"

"I found her syringes and thought she was a drug addict, too," Zain sheepishly admitted.

"And she still wanted you after that?" Lance asked.

"Yeah."

"She's in love," Lance declared while Thomas laughed so hard it looked as if his curls were going to bounce right off his head. "You won't have to worry about her not showing up."

When they got to 'The Leaning Oak' Zain was relieved to see that the decorators had shown up. The beautiful old oak was dressed in white lace draped from its branches to form an arbor over the spot where he and Asa would be married. A perfect line of white orchids formed part of a semicircle in the small clearing before the tree. A path outlined by more orchids was formed in the center for Asa to walk toward him, so that the ceremony could begin.

The preacher had shown up. He was waiting under the arbor with the old gardener who had told him the story behind the oak. Zain had invited the gardener but he would have to sit behind the orchids where a line of chairs waited for guests so that the ceremony could begin.

Grammy Dee and Miss Rose had just shown up. Grammy was straightening his clothes, talking non-stop and trying to rearrange the chairs so that they were lined up to follow the path of the orchids. Zain respectfully insisted that she sit down next to James, leaving the chairs where they were so the ceremony could begin.

Zain waited under the arbor with his best man, as a trio of jazz musicians, sax, trumpet and clarinet, stood to the side. A soft serenade of love songs from the live band and its accompanying vocalist filled the air with the sweet sound of music as the guests gathered before the ceremony began.

The preacher cleared his throat. Zain shifted nervously and Lance gave Zain an encouraging pat on the shoulder. Lisa, as Asa's maid of honor walked down the aisle as the vocalist sang a song of love that lasted forever. And most importantly, his sweet angel Asa showed up and the ceremony began.

In a white gown with touches of glittering points reflecting the sunlight, Asa came to him. She glided on the arms of her father and uncle to a jazzy version of the wedding march. No veil covered her beautiful face but a circle of tiny white flowers and thin shiny ribbons sat like a crown on her head. Her arms were bare, and she held only a single white orchid. Her father and uncle kissed a respective cheek before presenting Asa to him. The preacher united them, and Zain kissed his bride with pride, signaling that the ceremony had ended.

Married and happy Zain kept Asa at his side as everyone came up to congratulate them. Pictures were taken as a small army unobtrusively set up tables for the small buffet they had planned. Zain wanted their marriage to be as strong as the tree they sat under. They would build a wonderful life together, no matter what came their way.

❋

Asa fell backwards on the king sized bed in her room. *Happy* wasn't the word to describe the feelings flowing through her. *Content, delighted, ecstasy* was more like it. It was four o'clock in the afternoon and she'd just left her wedding reception, encouraged by her new husband to meet him at their cottage. He had a surprise for her, Asa had been told.

Asa waved her arms up and down in a parody of making a snow angel where no snow could possibly fall. She felt happy enough to be the actual angel Grammy Dee and Zain claimed her to be.

Asa stood and looked at herself in the full length mirror. Her wedding dress was a simple creation that made her feel elegant. Glittering thread had been woven into the soft material. The sleeveless shift clung to her, the vee in the bodice dipping just far enough so that she felt comfortable wearing it in public while still displaying an enticing view for Zain. Asa had never before dressed to please anyone but herself. She was enjoying the appreciation she found in his eyes each time she put forth the effort to change that.

Asa didn't have a train but a long stretch of material hung past her shoulders down to her waist. She removed the circle of flowers and ribbons from her hair. Her hands were on the zipper at the back of her gown when she heard the cottage door open. There was a knock on the bedroom door before she could get to it.

"Mrs. Zain Darby?" her husband's voice called from behind the door.

"The one and only."

He opened it, pushing before him a cart similar to the one the doorman had brought holding the wide selection of engagement rings Zain had presented to her just two days before. A quick glance told her that this time there were only three cases, all black velvet and in various sizes. Her eyes didn't linger on them for long. They were glued to her handsome husband as he stood before her. He had taken off the tuxedo jacket but still wore the formal shirt, cravat and cummerbund, emphasizing the class and style that would always be Zain.

"Are you ready for your surprise?"

"Do I get to choose my favorite again?" Asa asked with a touch of coyness tinting her voice.

"No, they are all yours. The only decision you have to make is which one to open first."

"Then I want the big one standing behind the cart."

He didn't hesitate a second, declaring, "If that's what you want, my sweet angel Asa, that's what you get." With a slight push the cart was no longer standing between them. Zain removed the cravat, the cummerbund, and cuff links, slowly advancing toward her. "And how would you like the big one?"

"Completely naked," she was bold enough to say, "so that I can fully appreciate what he has to offer and what he's promised me."

"Marriage vows have changed you, Mrs. Darby. I think I'm going to like this."

Asa watched as Zain pulled the white formal shirt out of his pants, unbuttoning it and leaving it hanging open. If she'd thought he was sexy a minute ago, Asa couldn't imagine what she should call him now. His eyes were trained on her steadily as he moved to slip off his shoes, coming a step closer with each item he disposed of. Another shoe, another step. The black pants that had fit him so perfectly slid down firm brown legs, bringing him two steps closer. Navy blue briefs were gone in a flick of an eye, revealing his maleness pointing straight and stiff, close enough to brush against her wedding gown-clad belly as he stood before her.

"Is this naked enough for you?"

"Not quite." Asa reached up with shaky hands to his smooth, broad shoulders. Her hands did not shake from fear or nervousness. Asa knew what she wanted. She simply didn't know entirely what to expect. The sensations he created in her were always intense. Even now when he had barely touched her yet. How much more of him could she take? All of him, she assured herself, because they were meant to be, because they had been through so much, because Zain was hers now.

Asa's hands slid down his arms, removing the white shirt with ease, enjoying the feel of firm muscles. The tactile sensation produced a building wave of desire from the tips of her fingers to every inch of her palms. Asa needed to touch. Zain gave her free rein as his lower body pressed against her. She explored the muscles in his back, sliding her hands down to his buttocks, which she spent some time getting to know before moving forward to the part of him that refused to be ignored. With both hands she held him, the pulsating waves in her hand increasing, beating inside her veins as she held him, caressing his hardness, reveling in the heat of him.

"Asa," he said in a strained whisper as he gently removed her hands. "I am going to have to remove this dress and be inside of you in the next minute. I have married not an angel, but a devil in disguise."

His words sent a huge wave of longing surging through her. He cupped her bottom, pulling her even closer. Asa savored the feel of his hardness against her as he reached for the zipper at the back of her dress. The soft material rubbing against her, the heat of his naked body so close caused a pounding in her head that echoed one word, *hurry.*

True to his word, Asa's dress was gone before she knew what had happened. They were on the bed, bodies connected in every possible way except for the ultimate connection Zain had promised her. But that too wasn't long in coming. Zain laid wet, hot kisses on her neck, her breasts, her stomach, and the pulsating source of her, everything she wanted. The kisses were intimate and not at all shocking, a simple prelude to what they would share. Her panties were gone, her bra a barrier Zain had already whisked away.

Zain coaxed her to the edge of the bed. He lifted her legs one by one resting each on a broad shoulder. With knowing fingers he caressed each leg from knee to thigh, his fingers finding her moistness, getting lost in her folds just as Asa became lost in the waves of sensations that had risen to hurricane proportions. Intense pleasure rolled over her, not too much to bear, rather bordering on the edge of all that is wonderful. Before she could come down from that wave, Zain was there inside her, inching, slowing, pausing at the barrier, then bursting through it.

He stopped. The feel of Zain inside of her was everything. She felt no pain, no discomfort, merely everything else. She was near the crest of a huge wave and Zain, the wind pushing her forward had stalled. Asa pushed her body forward, wanting him to give her more, to take her farther. And he did, moving in and out, slowly at first until Asa increased the pace, showing Zain that his angel did not want him to hold anything back. The rhythm they established had them rising beyond the crest of that wave of pleasure that raged between them, a shared storm that held them, both attaining a level that few ever reached together.

The mattress moved. In her sleepy, dazed state Asa turned over, seeking the warm body of her husband. He wasn't there. Strange, three times before she had done that to be rewarded with another lesson in lovemaking.

Asa heard voices. Zain's and another she didn't know. She turned over again, this time fully awake and curious as to why Zain had left her all alone. Asa, without a stitch on, crawled on her hands and knees to the edge of the bed, to investigate. That's how Zain found her when he came back into the room. His milk chocolate eyes told her exactly what was on his mind.

"We haven't tried that yet, sweet Asa, but we've got time."

"What's wrong with now?"

"Dinner time. The food's here "

Asa glanced at the bedside clock. So it was. "When did you have time to order dinner?"

"What a question! Don't you know me as a man who gets things done? Why don't you check your sugar and take your shot before the food gets cold. Come dressed any way you please, I'll be waiting for you."

Asa reluctantly got out of bed, going to the small table where the glucose monitor, her insulin and all her supplies lay waiting for her use. Zain had done that too. Asa sighed. She would have preferred another lesson in love rather than the meal she knew she had to eat. Then she immediately felt guilty because Zain had been more conscious of her schedule than she had been. Far from being the intolerant tyrant, Zain had been nothing other than helpful and considerate since he had realized his mistake about her disease.

And that wasn't the only way he had been helpful and considerate. So far, Asa's entire experience with Zain as a lover had been amazing. She barely remembered loading the sharp lancet she used to prick her finger, let alone actually pricking her finger when the machine beeped, flashing a reading and interrupting her thoughts. Nothing Zain had done to her had been too intimate. Every touch, every caress her husband gave wrapped her in a blanket of love so that she felt treasured and cherished. Her own explorative touches had been encouraged and guided with a gentle ease. Every meeting of skin, any contact, shouted I love you.

Pleased with the reading, Asa took her shot in the left arm, using the door jamb to help her pinch a spot to inject. Her arm was a more difficult area in which to take her shot but she needed to alternate injection sites. Disposing of the syringe in the diet Coke bottle brought a flash of memory into her head. Asa had no doubt that Zain loved her. For a man who was willing to do so much for her when he thought she had so many problems, how could she doubt it?

"Come dressed any way you please," replayed in her mind. Asa toyed with the idea of joining Zain without a stitch on but decided against it. After the shot she had just taken Asa needed food. Leaving the bedroom as she was might distract them from that important fact.

Asa dug the baby blue nightgown she had brought along from the bottom of her suitcase.

The gown wasn't much of a gown. It was sheer and frilly with thin spaghetti straps and a deep vee that reached as far as her navel when she put it on. It was the most intimate and revealing piece of clothing she had ever worn. But Asa felt not a bit of shyness about wearing it for Zain. She threw on the jacket that was just as sheer and didn't cover much more, its length the only modest quality about it.

As soon as Asa opened the door, Zain turned to her as if he had been waiting. "I was starting to get…" His voice trailed off as his eyes both lingered and caressed her from head to foot. Standing where she was and letting him have his fill was enough for the waves of sensations to begin once again. Not only to begin but to build. Asa hadn't noticed what Zain had been wearing before, but she did now. He stood next to a laden table of food that Asa completely ignored because she had eyes only for her husband. He wore one piece of clothing. How could pajamas bottoms be so sexy? A wave of longing traveled up her spine. It wasn't necessarily the black silk pajama bottoms that sent a thrill through her, rather the fine man inside them. They were perfect for Zain. Asa wondered how long she could keep him inside the cottage wearing nothing more than what he had on now, until she wanted him to take it off, of course.

"I don't know where that outfit came from, but be warned, wearing it will insure that we will spend lots of time in this cottage finding ways to remove it." He was there before her, a hand at her collar bone, a long brown finger tracing the deep vee of the gown.

"We're having the same thoughts."

"About that outfit?" He laid a hand on her breast, caressed it and traced a swirling path around her nipple before studying the way the hardened tip rose under his touch.

"About your choice of clothes." Asa's hands were on his hips, easing under the elastic of the silk pajama bottoms when a wave of dizziness hit her. "Before we do anything about it, I think we had better eat first."

"You're having a low?"

Asa nodded sitting in a chair at the beautifully decorated table. Zain's focus quickly changed. "My sugar was eighty when I took the shot. It's just the fast-acting insulin working already."

"Here," Zain sat across from her, "drink some milk."

There was a glass jug of milk surrounded by ice. Zain poured some into a wine glass and handed it to her. Looking at the glass, Asa estimated that he had poured about a cup full. She was good at eyeballing just about any amount of food to identify the carb count. She drained the glass. Zain had dished out a plate of food and set it down in front of her before she had swallowed the last of the milk. He proceeded to watch her eat.

"I'm fine, now. Join me."

"Good." Zain appeared to relax. That relaxed state evolved into heated glances that made her forget what she was eating, making carb counting a bit more difficult.

"Are you done?" Zain asked.

"Yes," she whispered.

"Then let me remove that fluff you call a nightgown."

He did, but slowly, using the sheer fabric to enhance the sensations, adding a new touch to this lovemaking session.

The alarm on Zain's watch woke him a few hours later. He had finally let Asa rest. From the time he had first admitted his attraction to Asa, Zain knew that he had never wanted anyone the way he wanted his sweet angel. He hadn't thought that once he made love to her, he would want her to the point of exhaustion. But he did. He wanted her now. But he wouldn't do anything about it. Asa had been a virgin, a sweet, giving, wanting virgin. Zain had been worried about hurting her, but he'd had no reason. Asa was Asa, amazing. Zain looked down at the sleeping woman in his arms, marveling at the fact that she loved him and had married him. He would do anything for her. She looked like a sleeping angel, and was actually his. She had saved him from a life of nothing. The alarm beside the bed rang. Asa snuggled deeper into him. Zain shut off the clock's annoying buzzer. Asa must have set it. It was her snack time, which was the reason he had set his watch. He was worried that in the excitement of their wedding and lovemaking they would forget. Zain did not want a repeat of the other night. If it was up to him Asa would never pass out again in her life.

Zain blew gently into her ear. "Asa, angel, wake up." She opened her eyes immediately, so different from the other night. "So, you're a light sleeper."

"Always have been. How about you?" she asked, stretching a hand to skim his bristly cheek.

"Somewhere between a feather and a rock." Zain grabbed her hand to kiss the sensitive skin of her palm.

"Did the alarm go off?"

"Mm-mmmm."

"Would you care to join me for a snack, Mr. Darby?"

"I would love to, Mrs. Darby. But only after you open your surprise."

"I thought I had." She smiled up at him. "I chose the big one."

"The small ones. You can have the big one anytime you wish, angel." Zain kissed her lips, forcing himself not to linger. He went to the cart that he had rolled to the corner of the room.

Asa was sitting in the middle of the bed cross-legged in that blue thing that was supposed to be sleep-wear. It was making him think about anything but sleep. He laid all three boxes before her and positioned the nightgown so that it actually covered her delicious breasts. Which only made things worse because she gazed at him with that sleepy-eyed look that invited him to do what he pleased. The hard tips of her nipples were visible through the gown and even more enticing than if he had left the piece of blue torture alone. Zain took the sheet from the bed and draped it over her shoulder.

"Why did you do that?" she asked in a slow, sleepy voice that matched the look in her eyes.

"Because I want you to open your presents before we do anything else."

"I'd rather do what you were thinking instead."

"Not any more tonight."

"You would do that to me? You would deny me?"

"My sweet virgin angel—."

"Not anymore."

"My recent virgin angel then?"

"Much better."

Zain shook his head at her antics. "I am not an animal. I don't intend to make love to you until it hurts."

"But it didn't. I don't. I'm fine."

"Right now, wait till morning." Asa stared at him as if she didn't believe him. "I'm looking out for you. We've got a lifetime together, remember?"

"We do."

"Now open the gifts before I think you don't want them."

Asa looked down at her gifts once again. The only sound in the room was the snap of the lid on each case as Asa opened them. She said not a word but stared at the contents of all three. A pair of matching diamond oval earrings, a necklace with an oval diamond pendant, and a bracelet with tiny oval diamonds surrounding it. They all matched her engagement and wedding rings. Zain had made sure of that.

"You don't like them?"

"How can I not like them? I love them."

"That's hard to tell. Most women smile, say thank you, hug their husbands till they can't breathe." A short laugh escaped her lips. "You're not doing any of those things."

"Thank you." Her teary eyes lifted to his. "I don't know what else to say."

"Say you'll wear them without crying."

"I'll wear them, but I still might cry."

"Why?" he asked, one palm caressing her face.

"Because," she paused to take a breath, "I found in you a love I never thought I could have and I've just realized that you love me exactly the same."

"Did the diamonds make you realize all that?"

"No, they're beautiful, but they could never tell me that. Everything you do and have done since you asked me to marry you has shown me that. Even before that. Zain, you went to Al-Anon meetings for me. That's love."

"You'll always have my love, angel."

"And you have mine, but that doesn't mean you have to dress me in diamonds to keep it."

"I want to." He had taken the bracelet from its case and placed it on her wrist. The necklace was next, then the earrings. "They're yours. When you wear them, remember that I love you."

"I'll always know that whether I'm wearing a bank vault of diamonds or not." Asa gave him a loving kiss, the diamonds sparkling just as the glittering highlights in her wedding dress had shone in the sunlight earlier today.

"How about that snack?" Zain left the bed to go to the fridge. "White grapes? I believe it's my turn to feed you," Zain said as he lifted the bag of fruit.

"Then await me at the head of the bed, my slave husband. I will check my sugar and be right with you."

Zain lay on the bed and watched his angel wife, adorned in diamonds, as she pricked her finger to apply a drop of blood on the test strip in the monitor. The jewelry accented the sexy piece of blue she still wore but the casual ease in which she took care of herself amazed him more.

She pricked herself four times a day, sometimes more, and then had to give herself two injections a day, one in the morning and one at night. She did it all as if it were nothing. The monitor beeped, interrupting his thoughts.

"One thirty-six. That's good." She put away all the equipment and came to the edge of the bed. "You know, there's this new activity I'm interested in and my husband is trying to limit my involvement. It's even helped to keep my sugar at a decent level. What do you think about that?"

"If it's beneficial to your health, maybe some similar activities can be arranged," Zain teased. Asa clad in diamonds and that gown sent him over the edge. "But first you are going to have to be more specific. Tell me exactly what these activities are; that way I can be sure to provide them on a constant basis."

Asa whispered some things an angel would never say before reclining on the bed, her head in his lap. Zain counted the grapes, feeding her the fifteen she needed for her bedtime snack. He then put into action her suggestions, adding them to the many he already had for continuing their night of pleasure while still keeping his promise to himself.

Hours later, exhausted from the constant waves of sensation, they spent the rest of the night sleeping in each other's arms as all newlyweds do.

Zain and Asa waved good-bye to their entire wedding party and guests late the next day. They spent the rest of the week at the resort making love in the king-sized bed Asa had claimed when they first arrived, the double bed he had been stuck with, and the sofa bed out in the living area. Not to mention such interesting places as the shower, a quiet corner of the beach late one night, even out in the middle of the Mobile Bay on a sailboat they had rented. They couldn't get enough of each other.

Every morning they had eaten a picnic breakfast under 'The Leaning Oak.' It was here they talked about their future together. Where they would live; in Zain's condo for now until they found a house in Algiers Point, they had agreed. Children, later but not too much later.

Work. They argued about that, Zain insisting that she quit. Asa refusing to, demanding that he fire her if he was dissatisfied with her work, saying that she could get a job somewhere else. Both their wills on this issue were as strong as the oak they argued under, but they compromised. Asa would continue to work at Execute. When they began a family she would take a leave. Not quit, she had emphasized, merely take a leave. Afterwards they went back to the cottage to seal the deal.

This morning they sat on a wide blanket in front of 'The Leaning Oak.' It was the last they would spend at the resort. Zain hadn't taken a month-long vacation as Lance had, but they had all next week to themselves. Asa would get settled in Zain's condo and they would even start looking for a house. She was ready to start her life with her husband but wasn't looking forward to the end of their honeymoon.

"Are you going to eat that yogurt or just play with it?" Zain asked.

"I'm not really hungry anymore. I'll have some milk for the rest of my carbs." Zain poured more into the glass she had emptied earlier. She sipped it slowly, not in the mood for milk either.

"I know how you're feeling, angel. The end of our honeymoon is not something I'm looking forward to," Zain told her. He leaned against the tree and patted his thighs.

Asa rested between them. "We'll come back one day. I'll even give you a month-long honeymoon on our first anniversary."

"A whole month? What has marriage done to Zain Darby the workaholic?"

"Taught me how to live and love something besides work."

The rattle of a cart on the path announced the waiter who had come to take away the remains of their meal.

"I hope you enjoyed your last breakfast at the resort," said the same young man who had been serving them every morning.

"It's been wonderful and so has the service."

"We aim to please," the young man said as he wheeled away the dirty dishes.

Asa scooted back, then turned to face Zain. "I have something for you."

"You do?" Surprise etched his face.

"Nothing as expensive as the gifts you gave me."

"Asa, that doesn't matter."

"I knew you would say that."

"See how well you've gotten to know me."

"So well that I know you'll take good care of this."

Asa reached for the purse she took everywhere with her because it held all her medical essentials. She pulled out a box. It was small and flat, not the same shape as any of the ones he had shown her.

Zain took it from her, an excitement she had never seen before on his face. "I can't remember the last time I got a gift that made me nervous."

"Open it."

Zain lifted the lid. Then the gift. "A key chain?"

"The one you gave me took some time, but it fits perfectly into my life now."

"A to Z," he read from the base of the key chain forming the first initials of their name. He looked up at her puzzled. "Isn't something missing?"

Asa nodded. She reached inside her shirt to pull out the medical necklace she normally wore with the exception of her wedding night. Zain watched as not only the medallion he had gotten used to seeing emerged but also a golden key similar to the one he'd given her, but much larger than a standard key. She removed it from the necklace but held it in her hand. "Our love is as essential to me as the insulin I take everyday of my life."

Asa kissed him and softly laid the key in the palm of his hand. *My heart, forever, Asa,* he read.

"Thank you."

Those two words, said in a deep sincere voice, thrilled Asa.

"Now we're stuck with each other forever."

"Happily," she added, turning around to rest once more between the thighs of the man who held her heart and she his.

CHAPTER 23

Asa woke up from a fitful sleep. She raced to the bathroom, barely making it in time because she had forgotten where it was. They had arrived at Zain's condo only a few hours before, immediately christening it with a session of intense lovemaking. But now Asa stood over the toilet retching and gagging as she lost every bit of her dinner and bedtime snack.

Zain stood in the doorway behind her waiting for her to finish being sick. She could feel his concern. The heaving stopped, the spasms in her stomach ended. Asa sat before the toilet feeling weak and clammy.

Zain pulled her up and took her to the bed. "Are you okay, angel? What can I get for you?"

"Water," was all she could say. Asa wanted to tell Zain not to worry, but her stomach was cramping and she was doing all she could not to double over in front of him, sure that would cause him to call an ambulance immediately. She ran back to the bathroom before Zain could return with the water.

There wasn't much left in her stomach by the time Zain found her. He was in the doorway again. The intensity of his worry filled the room. He hesitated before bringing her back to the bed. "Would you rather stay in here awhile?"

"No, I don't think there's anything left in my stomach."

"Come to bed then. I've got your water," he said as solemn as a undertaker.

"Zain, I'm not dying. I think it was something I ate."

"We both had chicken, and I'm not throwing up."

Asa didn't waste her breath arguing. She let Zain tuck her into bed and took the water he offered. He left the room but was at her side again almost immediately.

"You've got nothing left in your stomach!"

"Yeah. I hope I can keep this water down."

"I'll be back. You just lie there and rest."

"I don't plan on doing anything else." Asa felt drained but knew she would have to rouse herself to do something about the carbs she had to replace in her system to avoid a low. Zain had realized it too. Asa wished he didn't look so upset. She reached for her purse and found a peppermint and popped it into her mouth. It wasn't much, but it was a start.

A few minutes later a more relaxed Zain came into the bedroom. "I talked to your doctor—"

"You did what?" Asa lifted herself and rested against the headboard.

"I called your doctor and he said that you have to replenish your body with more carbohydrates since the insulin is already in your system."

"I know. Why did you do that?"

"Do what?"

Asa didn't have the strength right now to deal with this strong-willed man. "Call—my—doctor," she stated slowly.

"Because I had to."

"I knew what to do."

"You did? Are you sure?"

Knowing he had her best interest at heart, Asa held back the smart reply that lay on the edge of her tongue. Instead she repeated the advice her doctor had given her on more than occasion. "Drink lots of fluids, making sure to have at least fifteen carbohydrates every hour."

"Okay, so you knew. But why are you throwing up?"

"I don't know. It could be a virus."

"Maybe. I don't like this, Asa."

"It's not a picnic for me either."

"I know, angel." Zain sat on the edge of the bed and brushed a stray curl out of her face. "What do you want to drink?"

"A half cup of apple juice. You can add it to this water."

Zain took the glass from her hand and was back before she could open and close her eyes. "We don't have much juice left in the house. I'll have to go to the store. Drink this before I leave."

He watched her take a sip. Zain rushed around the bedroom. For the first time she realized that he was naked. Asa peeked under the covers, she was naked too. The thought caused a giggle to push past her misery. Zain slipped on a pair of jeans and a t-shirt. Now why had he covered that delicious body? Asa made a face. She couldn't do anything with it right now anyway.

"What's wrong?" Zain was at the bed. "Do you have to throw up again?"

"No. I was missing the view."

"The view?"

"The one you just covered with clothes."

"What am I going to do with you, Asa?"

"Get me some juice? Make love to me when I'm better."

"Deal." He was at the bedroom door when he turned back to her. "Are you going to be all right?"

"Of course." Asa waved him off. Zain sped out of the condo, down the stairs and across the street to the nearby grocery store. He grabbed bottles and boxes of juice, sports drinks and a six-pack of regular lemon-lime soda. In his hurry, he didn't get a basket or a cart but somehow managed to hold everything without dropping a single life-saving item. That's what they were. Taking insulin might be what had saved Asa's life since she was eight, but it also put it in danger. She couldn't even get sick without taking precautions.

Zain made it back to the condo in record time. Passing the living room, he dumped the plastic grocery bags onto the huge navy recliner without missing a step. He skidded to a halt at the foot of the king-sized bed where he normally slept. Asa lay in a semi-reclining position, her back against the headboard. She was still holding the glass she had been drinking from. It was empty, the bottom flat against her chest. She lay so quiet Zain stood frozen in fear before noticing the glass moving up and down with each breath she took. Zain moved to sit beside her. He had been gone no more than ten minutes he was sure. Sleep would be good for her. He ran his hand down her arm, the side of her face and neck to be sure that she wasn't perspiring. There wasn't a bit of moisture on her smooth brown skin, just beauty. Beauty sitting in the middle of his bed, in the middle of his life.

Zain took the glass out of her hand and crawled into the bed, pulling the covers around them. He set the alarm on his watch to go off within the next hour, just in case he fell asleep. Then he held her, hoping that all she had was a virus. Whatever it was, he was her husband. He would look after her.

Every hour on the hour Zain woke Asa to give her fifteen carbs worth of liquid, diluting it with water. Asa would drink it and fall back asleep. She didn't throw up again and by the next evening was her old self. But still Zain worried. He would do whatever he could for her, always. He was her husband and he was determined to look after her.

"Do you have everything that you need?" Zain pulled his arms into his suit coat. He hadn't worn his office gear in over a week. Neither he nor Asa had worn much of anything in the past few days, spending most of the time in the condo enjoying each other, except when Asa was sick. Zain let out a breath, still relieved that it had only been one of those twenty-four hour things. The experience still worried him, but it also had taught him how a diabetic dealt with sickness. A visit to the doctor for her regular appointment was a second, though informative, interruption of their time together.

Asa peeked her head out of the kitchen. "Did you say something?"

"Just asking if you have everything you need?"

Asa walked toward him and gently pulled the lapels of his coat to bring him closer. "I have absolutely *everything* I need." She kissed him deeply.

Zain kissed her right back. The double meaning was clear. Even clearer his reason for asking the question in the first place. He wanted to keep Asa healthy and safe. That visit with the doctor had filled in the blanks of everything he didn't know about diabetes. Possible problems in the future with vision, her kidneys, her heart. There were too many concerns to even think about without him getting concerned again. Not to mention the more immediate problem of low blood sugar, even to the point where she would become completely unresponsive and would need to take a special shot that would release sugar from her liver. Asa didn't know it, but he had gotten an extra prescription for the glucagon, a medicine given as an injection if she ever passed out to the point where she couldn't be revived by juice or sugar. He would always be prepared. He wanted his beautiful wife with him for a very long time.

"Good answer, but that's not what I meant."

"I know, but that's all I'm going to say. I do realize that I have been away from work for two weeks, but I can still remember what I need to take with me to survive the day."

"In other words, 'Shut up Zain.'"

"In other words, 'Trust me Zain.'"

He nodded, giving her a deep, long kiss. "I love you." He didn't say all the other words clamoring to be heard. Zain knew he had to back off. He would watch her in his own way, without her knowing it.

Getting back into the office routine was smooth and easy. Work had always been how Zain channeled his energy. He enjoyed pushing himself to create new ideas and meet self-appointed deadlines geared toward making a success of Execute.

They arrived at the office at seven-thirty sharp as usual. It was quiet; no one else came in so early. Even Lance usually arrived an hour later. Zain stopped with Asa at her desk. He wanted to convince her to join him in his office but settled for one last kiss before tackling the mound of paper work he knew awaited him while Asa went through the messages Lance must have left on her desk. It took some time but Zain's concentration shifted to work, remaining there because he knew he had Asa to go home with and a satisfying night of love making to look forward to.

More than an hour later Asa's voice reached him before the knock sounded and the door opened. "Got a minute?" She was holding a message in her hand.

"Depends on what you have in mind."

"Work."

"You're no fun, Asa Darby, female assistant." He rose from his desk to see what she was holding. Zain meant only to read the note in her hand but the sweet scent of her drew him closer and he found that nuzzling her neck was a much better idea.

"And I thought this was a place of business," Lance's voice rang out, interrupting Zain's exploration.

"I never said it wasn't, now did I, Asa?"

"No, but when has a type of place stopped you from doing what you wanted?" She laughed up at him and Zain forgot Lance was standing behind them in his open office.

"Ahhh," Lance dragged out loud and long, "to work and love in the same place…"

"Speaking of work, don't you have some to do?" Zain narrowed his eyes at his partner.

"I'm right where I'm supposed to be. We've got a meeting in half an hour. I need to fill you in on some details."

"Aw, that's right. Asa," he looked down at her, "whatever that is, can you handle it yourself?"

"No problem, give me the keys to your car."

"What for? Where are you going?" he asked aloud, thinking, *Nowhere without me.*

"Mr. Vallet is in the hospital."

"Nothing serious, is it?"

"Knee surgery, but he needs to sign the revised copy of the contract. In the shuffle of preparing for the surgery he says he misplaced the copy we mailed him before the conference."

"So, why do you need the keys?"

"To drive to the hospital to get this signed so that our guys can go in to install and train his people."

"Mmmmm." Zain didn't like the sound of that. He couldn't go with her. Lance had set up this appointment and the client wanted to meet both of them.

"The keys. I can drive, Zain."

"I'll go with you at lunch."

"Can't. The surgery's today and he wants this done before he goes in. Besides, our people are supposed to go in today."

What to do? Zain didn't like the idea of her going anywhere alone. What if she passed out while she was crossing the street and a bus ran over her?

"Do you get the feeling he doesn't trust me?" Asa asked Lance.

"I'm not sure. I have to think on that."

Zain ignored the comment, instead asking, "Who's going in to load the system and train the staff?"

"Thomas and Collins," Lance answered.

"Take Thomas with you. Collins can handle getting together whatever they'll need and meet Thomas at Vallet's offices."

"If that will make you feel better."

It would. It did. "Give me five minutes, Lance." Zain shut the door to his office and kissed his wife, nuzzling her neck once again before handing over the keys. "Be safe."

"I promise to come back alive."

"I'm holding you to it," he whispered before opening the door.

Asa humored Zain and took Brent with her to get the papers signed. Mr. Vallet was very appreciative and promised Asa a dinner at The Dry Dock when his knee was better. Asa knew that Zain was worried about her. He had shown concern and was conscious of her needs as soon as he knew what they were. But what had at first been sweet concern was rapidly turning into obsessive protection.

At the condo every morning he laid out everything she needed to take her shot and check her sugar. He had the fridge and the pantry overflowing with a wide variety of juices. At work he called her in for dictation every morning at her snack time, to make sure she ate, Asa figured. To suggest that she go anywhere by herself was met with great resistance. She had not fought for independence from Brent to be smothered with concern by her husband.

Asa had put up with a week of it now. She'd tried using subtle hints and reason, but they simply did not seem to be working. She loved him, she didn't want to hurt his feelings, but he was driving her crazy with this over-protective attitude. Coming out of Zain's office after a another dictation session, Asa landed in her chair and released a deep sigh.

"Can't be that bad, cuz."

Asa looked up to see her cousin standing at her desk. "You would think no one could beat you in the over-protective category, but Mr. Zain Darby wins, no contest."

"He's been stifling your independence?"

"Choking it is more like it."

"It's because he loves you, Asa girl."

"Well, Brent, I think I'm going to be loved to death."

"With wills as strong as the both of you have, you might do each other in."

"Not before your wedding, I hope. I can't wait to see you and Lisa get married."

"It won't be long. In a couple of months I'll be a married man."

"In a couple of months I'll be a crazy person."

"Want me to talk to him?"

"I doubt if that'll help. Thanks anyway. Did you need something?"

"We ran out of stamps. Lisa doesn't have any either. How about you? We've got to mail these follow-up packets today."

"Stamps. I was—correction, Zain and I were supposed to pick up stamps for out-going mail yesterday. He wouldn't even let me go to the post office by myself." A plan began forming in her mind and Asa suggested, "Give me what you need to mail. I'll take care of it myself."

"Without your husband's approval?"

"I don't need that." What she needed was a husband who not only loved her but one who understood her needs and could trust her enough to let her go. Asa had been hoping he would ease away from the over-protectiveness but that stomach virus and her doctor's explanation of diabetes and its risks had tripled his concern. Subtle hints weren't doing it. Asa needed to take action. "Would you ask Lisa if I could use her car?"

"Will do."

Asa was out the building and driving down Canal Street toward the post office in less than ten minutes. She would eat lunch and return safe and sound, hopefully demonstrating to Mr. Zain Darby that she did not need a constant protector.

"Asa, how about some Mexican…" Zain's voice trailed off when he didn't see Asa at her desk. He went to the office across from his and knocked on the door. "Hey Lance, seen Asa?"

"She's not outside, I guess."

"No, but I didn't look anywhere else. She might be in the lunchroom, or she might have had a low and had to get a juice from the fridge because she ran out of juices in her purse. That means she could be lying on the floor in the hall unconscious and in need of a glucagon shot."

Zain ran out of Lance's office. Relieved at not finding her on the floor, he searched every inch of Execute's domain, including the restrooms. She was nowhere to be found. The few employees who were not at lunch had no idea where she was either. But Thomas was gone; maybe she was with him.

"Have you seen Mrs. Darby?" Zain asked the girl covering at the receptionist's desk. She shook her head no. The fearful expression on her face told him that he looked as upset as he felt.

"Did you at least see Thomas leave?"

"Yes, sir," the girl gulped. "He left with Lisa."

Dead end. Zain went back to his office. "Where could she have gone?" he mumbled to himself.

"She's gone to teach you a lesson."

Zain turned. Lance stood across from him in the doorway of his own office. "What's that supposed to mean?"

"That you need to be taught a lesson, partner."

"A lesson? What kind of lesson?"

"A lesson on trust."

"I trust Asa."

"Enough to take care of herself?"

"She'll never be able to completely take care of herself. I need to be there for her."

"I understand all that. But it seems to me that you're there too much for her. You don't want to start your marriage by driving her away from you."

"That's experience talking, right?"

"You bet. I've been married a whole month and a half longer than you."

"What you're saying is ridiculous."

"But true. Think about it."

Zain didn't want to think about it.

"I'm going to lunch," Lance announced. "Wanna keep me company?"

"No, I'm waiting for Asa."

Zain went back into his office. He didn't have long to wait. Through the open door he could hear Asa laughing and talking to someone.

"Brent, buy this woman a new car."

"Sheba has been good to me," Lisa protested, "I don't need another car."

"Take the keys. I'd rather drive my Beetle any day."

"Asa."

All three heads turned to him.

"I'd like to see you in my office."

"Of course." Asa waved to Brent and Lisa as they went back down the hall.

"Where were you?" he asked before she had even crossed the threshold. "I don't remember giving you permission to leave."

"Before I answer that question, are you Mr. Darby, my employer, or am I talking to Zain, my husband?"

Zain thought a second, wanting to pick the title that would have more leverage. "Your employer." He hoped he'd chosen right.

"Well then, Mr. Darby, I wasn't aware that I had to get approval to go to the post office and have lunch."

"You went to the post office? When? Before or after you ate?"

"Before, but don't worry, all of Execute's important letters and packages were mailed."

"I don't care about that. Why did you go to the post office so close to your lunch time?"

"I don't believe that's Execute's business."

"It's your husband's business."

"In that case be assured, my husband, that I can take care of myself. I've returned safe and sound."

Zain cringed inside. Asa had done something she hadn't done since he proposed to her. The sound of that cool office voice vibrated inside of him. "Is that all you have to say to me?"

"I've said more many times, but I guess I'll have to say it again. You do not have to protect me every minute of the day. I can and will take care of myself."

"But what if—"

"I don't live by ifs." One of her hands landed on his shoulder, the other lay across her chest as she said this. Zain was listening to what she had to say, but he didn't want to hear it. All he wanted to do was take care of her. All he wanted to do was take the other hand that lay against her heart and place it on his shoulder, and kiss this protest right out of her. But something stopped him. Instead, Zain listened.

"How about love?" he asked.

"Love doesn't mean suffocation."

"That's how you feel? We've been married for three weeks and you think I've been suffocating you!" Zain's voice rose. He couldn't believe this. When Lance had gotten married Zain had seen marriage as a suffocating trial. It hadn't been, not with Asa, and he doubted if it ever would. But she felt that way.

"That's how you make me feel sometimes. You've told me before that you admire the way I take care of myself. Let me do it!"

"I don't understand this. Love and protection go hand and hand. What if you need something? Am I supposed to ignore it?"

"No, because I *do* need you. Not as my protector but as my husband." Asa's other hand moved to land on his shoulder. She was in the perfect position for him to kiss this nonsense out of her, but he didn't.

"I can't help it. I'm both rolled up into one."

"Zain, you can be supportive without taking over my life. When you realize that, I'll be ready to talk."

"So what are you doing, refusing to talk to me?"

"Until you're ready to treat me like an adult."

"An adult? How can I when what you're doing is childish?"

"Childish?" she asked him cooly. "No, I'd call it a silent protest."

So the protest began. Asa nodded and smiled and followed Zain's orders in regard to work. She took her afternoon break and ate in the lunchroom. Zain just happened to be there while she ate. She would answer him in regard to anything she had to do at work. Anything else fell on deaf ears, it seemed. Zain figured that she would get tired of this by the time they got home. She couldn't spend the entire weekend not talking to him. Especially since he had a surprise planned for her.

At the end of the work day Zain sat on the edge of her desk. "Ready to go home?" She nodded. Zain didn't move. He wanted to hear his sweet angel Asa's voice. Not that of the cool office lady who worked for him.

They drove home in silence. Asa cooked pasta and chicken for dinner. He wanted to remind her of that night she'd made this and how he almost choked to death. But he didn't. How could a desire to protect someone you love change things this much? And they had changed. For the first time since they got married Asa went to bed without him. Zain sat on the huge recliner and played with the remote.

"I guess we're an old married couple tonight," he mumbled to the television. Zain sat flipping channels for the next few minutes, not satisfied with anything on television. He rarely watched it anyway. He roamed around the room, then decided to take a shower. Walking into the bedroom they shared, Zain leaned silently over Asa as he waited. He heard only her even breathing.

He took a shower, but it didn't make him feel any better. Zain wanted to be near her, but now he was angry.

Why was she doing this to them? He wasn't ready to crawl into bed yet. Instead of waking her up and starting a fight just to get her to talk to him, Zain went back to the den and flicked on the televison again. Before he could begin channel surfing the picture on the screen caught his attention. A huge bird, a sea gull, he thought, was soaring through the air high above a beautiful body of water. The only sounds were the wind, the waves, and the calls of the sea gull. The sun was setting and the bird was flying toward the horizon. It gracefully circled back, heading to the shore. The picture froze. A deep voice from the television filled the quiet room. "If you love something, let it go. If it's truly yours it will come back to you."

That was it. That's what Lance was trying to tell him. Zain was going to lose her by holding on too tight. That's what Asa was trying to tell him. She wanted to spread her wings and he wouldn't let her. It made sense. But could he do it? Knowing everything that could possibly happen to Asa could Zain let her go, trusting that she would always come back to him safe and healthy. More importantly, could he risk not even trying to let her soar?

Zain went to bed and pulled his wife close, her warm body pressed against his. "I'm going to try, angel. I'm going to try to love you and let you fly." Sleep was easier to come than he'd anticipated.

Asa woke up the next morning. She was immediately saddened by the fact that she was the only person in the bed. She lay there for a second. Well, she knew from experience that independence was won the hard way. Asa went to the bathroom. There wasn't a sound in the house. They had already developed a habit of making breakfast together on the weekend. Asa went back to make the bed. Her heart jumped. There on the pillow was a note she'd overlooked. A note from her husband. Asa was scared to read it. Her thumbs went to the corners of her eyes and her fingers raised in a prayerful pose. "Please," she prayed, "let it be something good." Asa opened it and read:

Meet me at The Dry Dock for lunch. Twelve noon.
I love you,
Zain

That was it. For the first time since they had been married he had left her alone. Asa danced around the bedroom, then the entire condo. Zain trusted her, he had given her the independence she craved, and the first thing she wanted to do was find him and kiss him. She would have to wait till noon. Now she was going to do what she needed to do without anyone looking over her shoulder. Asa loved her husband even more for being able to let go. She knew this was hard for him.

Asa checked her sugar, took her shot and ate a breakfast of bagels, milk and fruit, then found that she had nothing to do. She wanted to be with her husband. To pass the time she flipped through the real estate section of the newspaper. They had been browsing through it on a regular basis hoping to find a house in Algiers Point. She couldn't concentrate. Zain was home to her and she couldn't look for a new home without him.

Asa grabbed an apple for a morning snack and went for a walk along the lake to kill time. The walk was refreshing and burned some of her nervous energy off. When she got back it was only eleven. "Close enough," she murmured and hopped into her blue bug to meet Zain.

Asa walked into The Dry Dock. The whole place was different.

"Hey, Asa, you're early," Ernie called out to her.

"Hi, Ernie, how do you know that?"

"Zain just left here."

"He did? Did you just say Zain?"

"Yeah, you've married yourself a nice guy. He's been here since ten. We got to talking. He apologized."

"And now you two are buddies?"

"Pretty much." Ernie nodded his head in agreement.

"That's great." Asa spun around in a circle. "This place is great. You expanded the bar, got a big screen TV, and the wooden floors are beautiful."

"Thanks, but it wasn't my doing. Tell the boss lady."

"I will when I see her. I'm kind of excited about meeting Zain here. Did he say if he was coming right back?"

"No, but I'm supposed to give you this." Ernie handed her an envelope.

"Another note?"

It wasn't a note. It was a map. Asa was intrigued. "See you later, Ernie," she waved walking out the door and heading in the direction the map indicated. There was a weird drawing of little feet next to each set of directions. *Walk down one block, turn left.* She was heading in the direction of the house she had shared with Brent. Could that be where she was going? Had the two of them cooked up something together? *Walk past the house where you used to live and to the next corner.* Asa followed the directions. One left turn, one right and two blocks later she was standing in front of a beautiful two-story Victorian with a corner turret. The address was listed and the words *Come In* next to the "X" on the map.

Asa went up the walk to the beautifully carved door and did as the note said. Zain turned toward her as the door squeaked, announcing her presence.

"You're early." Had he gotten more handsome since last night?

"I couldn't wait to see you." They were talking across the room. Why? Asa wasn't sure.

"The whole morning without you was torture. I was hoping you would come."

"I'm here, safe and sound." Asa wanted to say more but ended with, "Thank you."

"For what?"

"For trusting me."

"I had to let you go so that I could have you."

"That's going to be forever."

He eliminated the space between them. His arms wrapped themselves around her, and he simply held her. Asa held him just as tight, savoring the feel of his strong hard body against her own.

"I've got something to show you." He pulled away just far enough to say that, then grabbed her hand and began a whirlwind tour of the house. They were back in the place they'd started from in less than ten minutes.

"What was that all about?"

"This house, do you like it?"

"Of course, who wouldn't? It's beautiful."

"The backyard. You haven't seen the backyard." Zain pulled her to the back of the house. "Isn't it great? The kids can play in the yard."

"Whose kids?"

"Ours."

"The imaginary ones we have now?"

"Our future kids."

"This house…are you telling me it's for us?"

"If you like it. I saw it in the paper. The agent is showing it to some people at two who are really interested in buying it. She showed it to me this morning. All I need to know is if you want to live here."

"Mmmm." Asa spun on her heels. "Beautiful Victorian, historic neighborhood, a wonderful man to share my life with. Yes!"

"I knew you'd say that. I love you, my sweet angel Asa."

"And I love you more then ever before."

He kissed her this time, taking her breath away, not ending until a knock sounded on the door. "I think that's lunch. I ordered something from The Dry Dock. I hope you don't mind."

"Not at all. I am under no illusions that you would completely let go of your take-charge personality."

"And I have no doubt that we will live our life loving each other, raising a bunch of kids, and growing old in this house together."

Asa reached up to pull his head toward her delivering a kiss that confirmed how very much she agreed.

"Zain, you don't understand."

"I do." His head leaned down toward her neck. Then he did the strangest thing. He took a deep breath, then released it, letting the warm air caress her neck before kissing his way under her jaw, her chin and then finding her lips. Lips that were ready this time.

Asa experienced a wave of passion that would not allow her to deny that Zain was what she wanted. He was hers for the moment. She kissed him, really kissed him, with her entire being. Her lips pulled his inside where her tongue claimed possession of him.

It was Zain who pulled back a breathtaking, disappointing moment later.

"Breathe, Asa, breathe," he whispered into her ear.

Asa released a pent-up breath she hadn't realized she had been holding.

2007 Publication Schedule

January

Rooms of the Heart
Donna Hill
ISBN-13: 978-1-58571-219-9
ISBN-10: 1-58571-219-1
$6.99

A Dangerous Love
J. M. Jeffries
ISBN-13: 978-1-58571-217-5
ISBN-10: 1-58571-217-5
$6.99

February

Bound By Love
Beverly Clark
ISBN-13: 978-1-58571-232-8
ISBN-10: 1-58571-232-9
$6.99

A Love to Cherish
Beverly Clark
ISBN-13: 978-1-58571-233-5
ISBN-10: 1-58571-233-7
$6.99

March

Best of Friends
Natalie Dunbar
ISBN-13: 978-1-58571-220-5
ISBN-10: 1-58571-220-5
$6.99

Midnight Magic
Gwynne Forster
ISBN-13: 978-1-58571-225-0
ISBN-10: 1-58571-225-6
$6.99

April

Cherish the Flame
Beverly Clark
ISBN-13: 978-1-58571-221-2
ISBN-10: 1-58571-221-3
$6.99

Quiet Storm
Donna Hill
ISBN-13: 978-1-58571-226-7
ISBN-10: 1-58571-226-4
$6.99

May

Sweet Tomorrows
Kimberley White
ISBN-13: 978-1-58571-234-2
ISBN-10: 1-58571-234-5
$6.99

No Commitment Required
Seressia Glass
ISBN-13: 978-1-58571-222-9
ISBN-10: 1-58571-222-1
$6.99

June

A Dangerous Deception
J. M. Jeffries
ISBN-13: 978-1-58571-228-1
ISBN-10: 1-58571-228-0
$6.99

Illusions
Pamela Leigh Starr
ISBN-13: 978-1-58571-229-8
ISBN-10: 1-58571-229-9
$6.99

2007 Publication Schedule (continued)

July

Indiscretions
Donna Hill
ISBN-13: 978-1-58571-230-4
ISBN-10: 1-58571-230-2
$6.99

Whispers in the Night
Dorothy Elizabeth Love
ISBN-13: 978-1-58571-231-1
ISBN-10: 1-58571-231-1
$6.99

August

Bodyguard
Andrea Jackson
ISBN-13: 978-1-58571-235-9
ISBN-10: 1-58571-235-3
$6.99

Crossing Paths, Tempting Memories
Dorothy Elizabeth Love
ISBN-13: 978-1-58571-236-6
ISBN-10: 1-58571-236-1
$6.99

September

Fate
Pamela Leigh Starr
ISBN-13: 978-1-58571-258-8
ISBN-10: 1-58571-258-2
$6.99

Mae's Promise
Melody Walcott
ISBN-13: 978-1-58571-259-5
ISBN-10: 1-58571-259-0
$6.99

October

Magnolia Sunset
Giselle Carmichael
ISBN-13: 978-1-58571-260-1
ISBN-10: 1-58571-260-4
$6.99

Broken
Dar Tomlinson
ISBN-13: 978-1-58571-261-8
ISBN-10: 1-58571-261-2
$6.99

November

Truly Inseparable
Wanda Y. Thomas
ISBN-13: 978-1-58571-262-5
ISBN-10: 1-58571-262-0
$6.99

The Color Line
Lizzette G. Carter
ISBN-13: 978-1-58571-263-2
ISBN-10: 1-58571-263-9
$6.99

December

Love Always
Mildred Riley
ISBN-13: 978-1-58571-264-9
ISBN-10: 1-58571-264-7
$6.99

Pride and Joi
Gay Gunn
ISBN-13: 978-1-58571-265-6
ISBN-10: 1-58571-265-5
$6.99

Other Genesis Press, Inc. Titles

A Dangerous Deception	J.M. Jeffries	$8.95
A Dangerous Love	J.M. Jeffries	$8.95
A Dangerous Obsession	J.M. Jeffries	$8.95
A Drummer's Beat to Mend	Kei Swanson	$9.95
A Happy Life	Charlotte Harris	$9.95
A Heart's Awakening	Veronica Parker	$9.95
A Lark on the Wing	Phyliss Hamilton	$9.95
A Love of Her Own	Cheris F. Hodges	$9.95
A Love to Cherish	Beverly Clark	$8.95
A Risk of Rain	Dar Tomlinson	$8.95
A Twist of Fate	Beverly Clark	$8.95
A Will to Love	Angie Daniels	$9.95
Acquisitions	Kimberley White	$8.95
Across	Carol Payne	$12.95
After the Vows	Leslie Esdaile	$10.95
(Summer Anthology)	T.T. Henderson	
	Jacqueline Thomas	
Again My Love	Kayla Perrin	$10.95
Against the Wind	Gwynne Forster	$8.95
All I Ask	Barbara Keaton	$8.95
Ambrosia	T.T. Henderson	$8.95
An Unfinished Love Affair	Barbara Keaton	$8.95
And Then Came You	Dorothy Elizabeth Love	$8.95
Angel's Paradise	Janice Angelique	$9.95
At Last	Lisa G. Riley	$8.95
Best of Friends	Natalie Dunbar	$8.95
Beyond the Rapture	Beverly Clark	$9.95
Blaze	Barbara Keaton	$9.95
Blood Lust	J. M. Jeffries	$9.95
Bodyguard	Andrea Jackson	$9.95
Boss of Me	Diana Nyad	$8.95
Bound by Love	Beverly Clark	$8.95

Other Genesis Press, Inc. Titles (continued)

Breeze	Robin Hampton Allen	$10.95
Broken	Dar Tomlinson	$24.95
By Design	Barbara Keaton	$8.95
Cajun Heat	Charlene Berry	$8.95
Careless Whispers	Rochelle Alers	$8.95
Cats & Other Tales	Marilyn Wagner	$8.95
Caught in a Trap	Andre Michelle	$8.95
Caught Up In the Rapture	Lisa G. Riley	$9.95
Cautious Heart	Cheris F Hodges	$8.95
Chances	Pamela Leigh Starr	$8.95
Cherish the Flame	Beverly Clark	$8.95
Class Reunion	Irma Jenkins/	
	John Brown	$12.95
Code Name: Diva	J.M. Jeffries	$9.95
Conquering Dr. Wexler's Heart	Kimberley White	$9.95
Crossing Paths,	Dorothy Elizabeth Love	$9.95
Tempting Memories		
Cypress Whisperings	Phyllis Hamilton	$8.95
Dark Embrace	Crystal Wilson Harris	$8.95
Dark Storm Rising	Chinelu Moore	$10.95
Daughter of the Wind	Joan Xian	$8.95
Deadly Sacrifice	Jack Kean	$22.95
Designer Passion	Dar Tomlinson	$8.95
Dreamtective	Liz Swados	$5.95
Ebony Butterfly II	Delilah Dawson	$14.95
Echoes of Yesterday	Beverly Clark	$9.95
Eden's Garden	Elizabeth Rose	$8.95
Everlastin' Love	Gay G. Gunn	$8.95
Everlasting Moments	Dorothy Elizabeth Love	$8.95
Everything and More	Sinclair Lebeau	$8.95
Everything but Love	Natalie Dunbar	$8.95
Eve's Prescription	Edwina Martin Arnold	$8.95

Other Genesis Press, Inc. Titles (continued)

Falling	Natalie Dunbar	$9.95
Fate	Pamela Leigh Starr	$8.95
Finding Isabella	A.J. Garrotto	$8.95
Forbidden Quest	Dar Tomlinson	$10.95
Forever Love	Wanda Y. Thomas	$8.95
From the Ashes	Kathleen Suzanne	$8.95
	Jeanne Sumerix	
Gentle Yearning	Rochelle Alers	$10.95
Glory of Love	Sinclair LeBeau	$10.95
Go Gentle into that Good Night	Malcom Boyd	$12.95
Goldengroove	Mary Beth Craft	$16.95
Groove, Bang, and Jive	Steve Cannon	$8.99
Hand in Glove	Andrea Jackson	$9.95
Hard to Love	Kimberley White	$9.95
Hart & Soul	Angie Daniels	$8.95
Heartbeat	Stephanie Bedwell-Grime	$8.95
Hearts Remember	M. Loui Quezada	$8.95
Hidden Memories	Robin Allen	$10.95
Higher Ground	Leah Latimer	$19.95
Hitler, the War, and the Pope	Ronald Rychiak	$26.95
How to Write a Romance	Kathryn Falk	$18.95
I Married a Reclining Chair	Lisa M. Fuhs	$8.95
Indigo After Dark Vol. I	Nia Dixon/Angelique	$10.95
Indigo After Dark Vol. II	Dolores Bundy/	$10.95
	Cole Riley	
Indigo After Dark Vol. III	Montana Blue/	$10.95
	Coco Morena	
Indigo After Dark Vol. IV	Cassandra Colt/	$14.95
	Diana Richeaux	
Indigo After Dark Vol. V	Delilah Dawson	$14.95
Icie	Pamela Leigh Starr	$8.95
I'll Be Your Shelter	Giselle Carmichael	$8.95

Other Genesis Press, Inc. Titles (continued)

I'll Paint a Sun	A.J. Garrotto	$9.95
Illusions	Pamela Leigh Starr	$8.95
Indiscretions	Donna Hill	$8.95
Intentional Mistakes	Michele Sudler	$9.95
Interlude	Donna Hill	$8.95
Intimate Intentions	Angie Daniels	$8.95
Jolie's Surrender	Edwina Martin-Arnold	$8.95
Kiss or Keep	Debra Phillips	$8.95
Lace	Giselle Carmichael	$9.95
Last Train to Memphis	Elsa Cook	$12.95
Lasting Valor	Ken Olsen	$24.95
Let Us Prey	Hunter Lundy	$25.95
Life Is Never As It Seems	J.J. Michael	$12.95
Lighter Shade of Brown	Vicki Andrews	$8.95
Love Always	Mildred E. Riley	$10.95
Love Doesn't Come Easy	Charlyne Dickerson	$8.95
Love Unveiled	Gloria Greene	$10.95
Love's Deception	Charlene Berry	$10.95
Love's Destiny	M. Loui Quezada	$8.95
Mae's Promise	Melody Walcott	$8.95
Magnolia Sunset	Giselle Carmichael	$8.95
Matters of Life and Death	Lesego Malepe, Ph.D.	$15.95
Meant to Be	Jeanne Sumerix	$8.95
Midnight Clear	Leslie Esdaile	$10.95
(Anthology)	Gwynne Forster	
	Carmen Green	
	Monica Jackson	
Midnight Magic	Gwynne Forster	$8.95
Midnight Peril	Vicki Andrews	$10.95
Misconceptions	Pamela Leigh Starr	$9.95
Montgomery's Children	Richard Perry	$14.95
My Buffalo Soldier	Barbara B. K. Reeves	$8.95

Other Genesis Press, Inc. Titles (continued)

Naked Soul	Gwynne Forster	$8.95
Next to Last Chance	Louisa Dixon	$24.95
No Apologies	Seressia Glass	$8.95
No Commitment Required	Seressia Glass	$8.95
No Regrets	Mildred E. Riley	$8.95
Nowhere to Run	Gay G. Gunn	$10.95
O Bed! O Breakfast!	Rob Kuehnle	$14.95
Object of His Desire	A. C. Arthur	$8.95
Office Policy	A. C. Arthur	$9.95
Once in a Blue Moon	Dorianne Cole	$9.95
One Day at a Time	Bella McFarland	$8.95
Outside Chance	Louisa Dixon	$24.95
Passion	T.T. Henderson	$10.95
Passion's Blood	Cherif Fortin	$22.95
Passion's Journey	Wanda Y. Thomas	$8.95
Past Promises	Jahmel West	$8.95
Path of Fire	T.T. Henderson	$8.95
Path of Thorns	Annetta P. Lee	$9.95
Peace Be Still	Colette Haywood	$12.95
Picture Perfect	Reon Carter	$8.95
Playing for Keeps	Stephanie Salinas	$8.95
Pride & Joi	Gay G. Gunn	$15.95
Pride & Joi	Gay G. Gunn	$8.95
Promises to Keep	Alicia Wiggins	$8.95
Quiet Storm	Donna Hill	$10.95
Reckless Surrender	Rochelle Alers	$6.95
Red Polka Dot in a World of Plaid	Varian Johnson	$12.95
Reluctant Captive	Joyce Jackson	$8.95
Rendezvous with Fate	Jeanne Sumerix	$8.95
Revelations	Cheris F. Hodges	$8.95
Rivers of the Soul	Leslie Esdaile	$8.95

Other Genesis Press, Inc. Titles (continued)

Rocky Mountain Romance	Kathleen Suzanne	$8.95
Rooms of the Heart	Donna Hill	$8.95
Rough on Rats and Tough on Cats	Chris Parker	$12.95
Secret Library Vol. 1	Nina Sheridan	$18.95
Secret Library Vol. 2	Cassandra Colt	$8.95
Shades of Brown	Denise Becker	$8.95
Shades of Desire	Monica White	$8.95
Shadows in the Moonlight	Jeanne Sumerix	$8.95
Sin	Crystal Rhodes	$8.95
So Amazing	Sinclair LeBeau	$8.95
Somebody's Someone	Sinclair LeBeau	$8.95
Someone to Love	Alicia Wiggins	$8.95
Song in the Park	Martin Brant	$15.95
Soul Eyes	Wayne L. Wilson	$12.95
Soul to Soul	Donna Hill	$8.95
Southern Comfort	J.M. Jeffries	$8.95
Still the Storm	Sharon Robinson	$8.95
Still Waters Run Deep	Leslie Esdaile	$8.95
Stories to Excite You	Anna Forrest/Divine	$14.95
Subtle Secrets	Wanda Y. Thomas	$8.95
Suddenly You	Crystal Hubbard	$9.95
Sweet Repercussions	Kimberley White	$9.95
Sweet Tomorrows	Kimberly White	$8.95
Taken by You	Dorothy Elizabeth Love	$9.95
Tattooed Tears	T. T. Henderson	$8.95
The Color Line	Lizzette Grayson Carter	$9.95
The Color of Trouble	Dyanne Davis	$8.95
The Disappearance of Allison Jones	Kayla Perrin	$5.95
The Honey Dipper's Legacy	Pannell-Allen	$14.95
The Joker's Love Tune	Sidney Rickman	$15.95

Other Genesis Press, Inc. Titles (continued)

The Little Pretender	Barbara Cartland	$10.95
The Love We Had	Natalie Dunbar	$8.95
The Man Who Could Fly	Bob & Milana Beamon	$18.95
The Missing Link	Charlyne Dickerson	$8.95
The Price of Love	Sinclair LeBeau	$8.95
The Smoking Life	Ilene Barth	$29.95
The Words of the Pitcher	Kei Swanson	$8.95
Three Wishes	Seressia Glass	$8.95
Ties That Bind	Kathleen Suzanne	$8.95
Tiger Woods	Libby Hughes	$5.95
Time is of the Essence	Angie Daniels	$9.95
Timeless Devotion	Bella McFarland	$9.95
Tomorrow's Promise	Leslie Esdaile	$8.95
Truly Inseparable	Wanda Y. Thomas	$8.95
Unbreak My Heart	Dar Tomlinson	$8.95
Uncommon Prayer	Kenneth Swanson	$9.95
Unconditional	A.C. Arthur	$9.95
Unconditional Love	Alicia Wiggins	$8.95
Until Death Do Us Part	Susan Paul	$8.95
Vows of Passion	Bella McFarland	$9.95
Wedding Gown	Dyanne Davis	$8.95
What's Under Benjamin's Bed	Sandra Schaffer	$8.95
When Dreams Float	Dorothy Elizabeth Love	$8.95
Whispers in the Night	Dorothy Elizabeth Love	$8.95
Whispers in the Sand	LaFlorya Gauthier	$10.95
Wild Ravens	Altonya Washington	$9.95
Yesterday Is Gone	Beverly Clark	$10.95
Yesterday's Dreams, Tomorrow's Promises	Reon Laudat	$8.95
Your Precious Love	Sinclair LeBeau	$8.95

ESCAPE WITH INDIGO !!!!

Join Indigo Book Club©
It's simple, easy and secure.

Sign up and receive the new
releases
every month + Free shipping
and
20% off the cover price.

Go online to www.genesis-
press.com and click on Bookclub
or
call 1-888-INDIGO-1

Order Form

Mail to: Genesis Press, Inc.
P.O. Box 101
Columbus, MS 39703

Name _____
Address _____
City/State _____ Zip _____
Telephone _____

Ship to (if different from above)
Name _____
Address _____
City/State _____ Zip _____
Telephone _____

Credit Card Information
Credit Card # _____ ☐Visa ☐Mastercard
Expiration Date (mm/yy) _____ ☐AmEx ☐Discover

Qty.	Author	Title	Price	Total

Use this order

form, or call

1-888-INDIGO-1

Total for books _____
Shipping and handling:
  $5 first two books,
  $1 each additional book _____
Total S & H _____
Total amount enclosed _____
Mississippi residents add 7% sales tax

visit www.genesis-press.com for latest releases and excerpts.